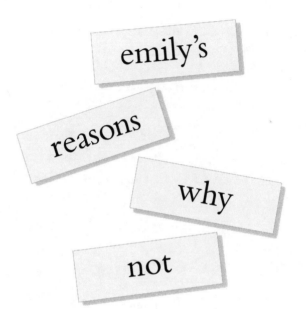

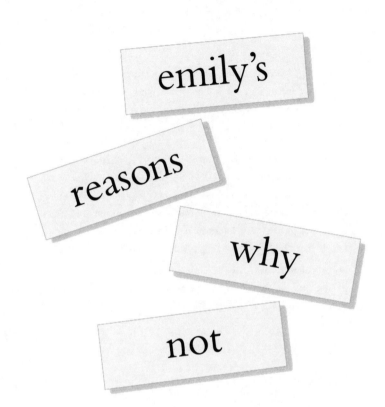

emily's reasons why not

carrie gerlach

wm William Morrow *An Imprint of* HarperCollins*Publishers*

HarperCollins books may be purchased for educational, business, or sales promotional use. For information please write: Special Markets Department, HarperCollins Publishers Inc., 10 East 53rd Street, New York, NY 10022.

FIRST EDITION

Designed by Chris Welch

Printed on acid-free paper

Library of Congress Cataloging-in-Publication Data

Gerlach, Carrie.

    Emily's reasons why not / Carrie Gerlach.—1st ed.

      p.   cm.

    ISBN 0-06-059424-1 (alk. paper)

    1. Women public relations personnel—Fiction. 2. Dating (Social customs)—Fiction. 3. Los Angeles (Calif.)—Fiction. 4. Mate selection—Fiction. 5. Single Women—Fiction. 6. Lists—Fiction. I. Title.

PS3603.E28E46 2004

813'.6—dc22
                                        2003068875

04 05 06 07 08 WBC/RRD 10 9 8 7 6 5 4 3 2 1

This novel is dedicated to Christian Van Gregg, who gave me the courage, inspiration, and skill to find my voice. His talent as a writer touched many people, but more important, his heart and friendship shined light on whatever and whomever he touched. If not for him, this book would not exist.

He was a friend of the right hand who lived for the perfect wave and the perfect fastball. A son, brother, and uncle. A love, a friend, a kid, and a man all wrapped in one. He was introspective, funny, intellectual, sexy, kind, and a true gift from above. His life will live on in his family, friends, work, and the work of the people he guided.

I miss him every day.

chapter one

Dr. D.
The Coach's Office

I wouldn't be here if I weren't alone. I haven't lost touch with reality and I don't hear voices. I'm just having trouble concentrating on anything except the chiming of my ovaries. They're a ticking clock, telling me the game is almost over. Time is running out. Ten . . . nine . . . eight . . .

Two men and a baseball player ago I was confident. Now I am feeling the pressure. I may be behind, but I'm not ready to settle for some random anyone, not ready for a life of loveless, overwhelming compromise. What I need is some good advice, the kind you don't take chances on with friends or family. If they had the answer I would have heard it already.

I am a professional woman. I need pro counsel. Well, *need* seems strong. I don't *need* anyone. I am part of the generation who *got this far*. But now, as if stripped of all defense and pretense, I find no comfort in this hollow independence. And these chiming ovaries are so loud that I can't ignore them anymore. I'm terrified that someday soon the chiming will STOP! The buzzer will sound. The players will leave the field. And I will be forced to watch from the sidelines.

I'll miss the chiming that drove me nuts and be forevermore reminded by the silence that I missed the life I *once upon a time . . . wished upon a star . . .* I'd have. I will be neverendingly tortured by the longings of a little girl inside who doesn't understand why taxes, mortgages, and car payments won.

And that's why I'm here, in this coach's office, waiting for a man I've never met. I look from the framed Doctorate of Psychology across from me to the dog-eared *House & Garden* on the table and what do I see? A bridal magazine. I hear the blood rushing in my ears like the roar of the crowd. Why is a bridal magazine out here in full view? To torture me? Some twisted sense of irony? A warped form of inspiration? Ugh! This isn't a party planning office. What the hell?

Oh, jeez. I'm picking it up. I can't help it. Like a binge masochist, I am out of control, operating on pure chemical instinct here. Who is doing this? I scream from the cheap seats of my brain at the obviousness of this bad call. I'm flipping the pages. I'm lost in the perfection of the platinum-wrapped diamond ring sparkling at me on the page, the fairy tale incarnate. I am sliding my finger next to it. Mustering courage, I flip the page, only to sigh at the bride and groom kissing on a tropical beach. She looks so . . . so . . .

I hold the magazine closer, blinking rapidly . . . so much like me. Holy shit! What the hell am I doing in the magazine?

I smile back at myself, a smile of the past, a firm and busty twenty-one-year-old fantasy version of me. I shake my head and look again at the photo, now of a perfect model type.

I guess I need therapy worse than I thought. I toss the magazine back on the table and quickly cover it up again. Am I kidding myself? Has the clock already expired? Is the game over and I'm the last to know?

I need a distraction. Something! A gentler, kinder Emily picks up the *Los Angeles Times*. I thumb through the pages and stop on the Calendar section, finding the horoscope. *Libra: If today is your birthday, you are passionate, loving, and kind. Wear bright colors.*

I pick at a loose piece of fuzz on my gray cashmere sweater. *Your day will be filled with unexpected fortune, some good and some bad. Don't tell intimate secrets to strangers.*

Well, that would be great, except that I am waiting in the lobby to see a damned therapist. How am I not supposed to tell him my intimate secrets? That's why I'm here. Or . . .

Is this a sign, my cue to flee? It is. Isn't it? My pulse quickens. I grab my bag, take two steps toward the door, and hear the knob turning behind me.

I quickly backtrack, sit, and act natural as the inner door swings open and an attractive man in his early forties looks down at me. "Emily Sanders?" he says with a voice that sounds like warm T-shirt sheets, fresh from the dryer. I nod. "I'm Dr. Deperno. Come on in."

I note the hardback books filling the shelves, the framed Seurat's *Sunday Afternoon on the Island of La Grande Jatte* on the wall above his large mahogany desk in the corner. No personal photos of framed family outings. He waits for me to sit on the plush burgundy sofa before he sinks into a black leather chair with his legs crossed, yellow pad resting on his lap.

I force a smile. He smiles back without saying a word. I smile again, picking the pale pink polish off of my newly manicured nails. The silence is consumed by a car alarm going off in the distance. I laugh nervously and wonder, *When was the last time I did that?* I can't remember laughing lately. As a little girl I laughed all the time. Now, maybe, on my best day, three times, and usually just a chuckle at a joke e-mail sent from a friend.

"Tell me about yourself." He pulls his glasses off his head and puts them on. I'm surprised I didn't notice those. They're small with tortoiseshell frames that complement his olive skin. I can tell that somewhere in his background a grandfather was Portuguese, Italian, or Greek.

"Like what? I mean, where should I start? Childhood? Adolescence? My twenties? What do you want to know?"

"Wherever you want is fine."

Where to start? Where to start? I think as I blow my dried nail polish off the arm of the sofa, wondering if I should tell him that I feel as if my life is not complete, not a full circle, until I find *the* man to love me. How can that be? I mean, I am a perfectly self-sufficient woman, working hard to be all that I can be. Maybe I should join the army. Now there's a decent place to meet men. The ratio has got to be better than L.A. But then, anything has to be better than here, where every beauty pageant winner is an eight in a sea of nines all wishing they were Julia Roberts, whom I saw the other day at Fred Segal wearing rose-colored sunglasses.

A cuckoo clock ticks. A damn cuckoo clock in a therapist's office. Is that another sign of his sense of humor? If it is, it is not funny. Has it been five minutes already? Five minutes of silence. I want to say something. I want to tell him that my generation of women was raised to take care of themselves and that I have, for the most part, done just that—the best way I could in my twenties. Yet here I am, still single and searching.

I wonder if the search will ever be called off and I will pronounce myself complete. Just Emily. All alone. Oh God. That word. I want to claw it from the English language, ALONE, as in, adrift, without companionship, incomplete, a lone traveler, a donkeyless Don Quixote.

I want the married-with-2.3-children-tucked-away-in-a-beach-city-with-a-picket-fence kind of life. This is what the oyster of my heart has been protecting, nurturing, and growing all these years. This is my dream, the sand at the center of the pearl of my life. In a panic, I am discovering what I must have known all along . . . The dream has an expiration date, and mine may be close to expiring and I can't bear it.

I smile at Dr. D. and he smiles back, waiting, observing me like Pavlov studying a dog.

Dr. Deperno is one of the best therapists in the greater Los Angeles area. I've done my research. At least three people I know have gotten married after seeing him.

Although I've never been to therapy, I have read a ton of books on the subject, always it seems during the postmortem on some breakup to figure out where I went wrong. Books like *If It's Love You Want, Why Settle for Sex?* or *Men Who Can't Commit* line my shelves with more multicolored highlights than I ever put in my college communications books. I have perused every *Cosmopolitan* quiz for a decade, reading into them like a monk with a revered religious text. Is that all I'm here for? Another senseless autopsy of the soul, like Madonna studying the Kabala.

What have I learned from all of it? Only that I would rather have a career and be in a single relationship with a battery-operated device than in a coupled relationship with an asshole.

It isn't that I have trouble landing a guy. I just can't get them past the ninety-day trial period and into my real life, and I want to know: Is it me or them?

"How about telling me why you're here," he nods. "Then we can work our way around."

I sit silently, staring at his face, trying not to feel awkward for $130 an hour.

Should I tell him the truth, that we are conditioned to believe there are men out there who will take care of us, love us, make us feel beautiful, safe, and sexy? Is the conditioning the problem, or the men? Is the problem finding them, holding them, or do they only exist in the realm of unicorn posters and straight Ken dolls?

"Is there such a thing as a stable guy who actually calls when he says he will?" I finally blurt. "Because too many years of the other kind has left me questioning the dream."

He jots a note and looks up, waiting for more.

If you really want to dissect my inner workings, let's slice into the men around me. Shall we? My father, who, "Mr.-busy-with-his-other-family," I only remember through fragments, like the sight of a green golf shirt or the smell of Aqua Velva.

"Cuckoo!" The little yellow canary pops out and chimes in before disappearing behind the ticking clock.

"My father," the hurt little girl tone rises in my voice, "left when I was six. I don't hate him for leaving. If anything I am guilty of overloving and overwanting him. He was never abusive or unloving or anything. He just wasn't there. One day it seemed he just decided he didn't want to be my dad anymore."

Dr. D. stares with these eyes that say he understands, maybe even cares.

It gives me a faux sense of comfort. The ice is melting. My thoughts begin to flow. "I was really young when I started searching for a man to love me. What this does to the female inner workings is incomprehensible."

"Yes, but fortunately not irreparable," he counters.

"I spent my twenties in relationships—overcompensating, forgiving, and basically trying to figure out how to make . . ."

I drift into silence. "Please, I want to hear," he says.

Does he really? His eyes say he might.

". . . trying to figure out how to make that one man . . . who left me in Mary Janes and white knee socks . . . come back home to love me."

Dr. D. nods, peering from behind his frames. Somehow he keeps me talking.

"The funny thing is that at thirty, I am now friends with my father, closer than we ever were. But the six-year-old, the ten-year-old, the eighteen-year-old girl inside is still waiting for her father's love, for her 'Dad and Daughter' day freshman year. It's as if I have some weird, empty space in here," I touch my chest, "that I filled with Styrofoam memories learned from episodes of *The Brady Bunch* instead of real life. Sometimes I feel that if I could somehow fix those missing years I could figure out how to be lovable."

He scribbles something on his pad, and I suddenly realize that I am uncomfortable.

Maybe I should have saved all of that for my second session, a little too much self-disclosure. Breathe. I take some emotional velocity off my backstory.

"I guess I'm dissatisfied with my personal life, my love life really." I laugh nervously. "That's really why I'm here. I mean what single woman in her thirties, isn't? Right?"

"You're dissatisfied?"

"*Dissatisfied.* Dissatisfied with dating."

"Can you give me an example of how you've been dissatisfied?" he asks in a tone of voice that has a lullaby quality.

"Yeah, um, well . . ." My internal censor knows what I'm about to say and is already trying to keep me from going there. I take a deep breath. "Three months ago I realized that my boyfriend, Reese," I look away from Dr. D., "who I fell in love with instantly, desperately, who I thought was the one . . . hmm, how do I put it?" I take a deep breath and look back at Dr. D., who is waiting for me to somehow sum up why I ran away from the one guy who I'm sure to this day was my soul mate because . . . because . . . I was *dissatisfied.*

"He had two cell phones. One of which I didn't know the number to. It kept ringing and he never answered it when I was around. Do you see the problem?"

Who wouldn't see the problem?

I can feel my throat starting to fill, the lump growing, my eyes tearing. I must change the subject away from Reese. Wow, I really need to save some of this for future sessions.

"I don't know. Basically, I would just like to find a single guy who I like and who likes me back."

Dr. D. is scribbling again.

"I am not alone in this, just so you know. There are an estimated forty-three million single women in the United States today . . . and thirty-five percent of us are twenty-five to fifty-five years old. That's a lot of SSWs," I pause, "*single, successful, women,* looking for love. We're cute, funny, fairly successful, independent, yet love, normal guys, potential mates elude us."

I try to read Dr. D.'s upside-down chicken scratch.

"The SSW was a good positioning statement in my twenties, but now, well, lately it seems that all my friends are getting married or are, at least, in serious relationships. That means that they are finding love and I can't."

I pause, looking for some sort of understanding, but he obviously doesn't get a damn word I'm saying. Therapy, I can see, is going to be a joy. I should have gone to a woman. Although on the tactical side, a male might give me the missing edge, the insight into their psyche that's been lacking all these years.

"I've been a bridesmaid seven times."

"You have a lot of friends. That's good," he points out.

"Yeah, but they're all *married!* Well, except for Grace and Reilly, but Grace is engaged. In November my best friend in the world is getting married. I need to have a date to her wedding. Okay."

"Okay?" he questions.

"My friends are dropping like flies. My roommate from college has two kids and is leaving her husband. Kathy, Grace's sister and my other roommate in college, just had her first child and they're building a house on Gray Hawk Country Club in Scottsdale."

Mothers. Wives. Homeowners. At what point did we stop chugging beers in college at Cannery Row, stumbling home and barfing long after we thought we were done? Now we're supposed to be breast-feeding, going to Target and the PTA? Maybe it's me, but I am obviously way behind on the learning curve, like a novice swimmer in an 8K, open-ocean race through heavy surf. I am drowning here, people. Drowning!

Poof! You're a wife, a maid, a cook, a mother, a taxi. Your life, as you knew it, is over. No more sleeping in, shopping for Kate Spade bags, spa days, mashing with strangers. Before you know it, your breasts have gone from a 34C to a 34C LONG. Yet I yearn for it. For Tiffany baby rattles, an SUV stuffed with strollers, baby bags, offspring, and the comfort of a husband to spoon me at night.

Suddenly I notice the stuffed yellow canary pop out from the wooden clock. "Cuckoo!" Has it been fifteen minutes already? God, when was the last time I said anything?

"Tonight I would just like to sleep next to somebody I care about. Is that too much to ask?" I say, a little sadly.

"What *kind* of somebody do you want in your bed?" His pen perches above his pad as he waits to scratch something on it.

I look out the window at a palm tree blowing in the wind. "Someone over six foot. I have a six foot rule. With nice forearms and good teeth. Teeth are important. And maybe someone who likes to dance. Someone who stirs me inside, who gives me the 'flutter, flutter.' "

"Flutter, flutter?" he repeats.

"You know? The 'flutter, flutter.' I get it right here." I rub my belly. "Maybe it's a girl thing?"

He obviously doesn't know. This is a bad sign. He doesn't understand that we, women, know within the first thirty seconds if we are interested in kissing, courting or having sex with a man. If he doesn't know that about women, what the hell does he know?

I decide to level with him. "Anyone who thinks that women are somehow less driven than men by chemical instinct is deluding himself. We do *not* see past the potbellies and back hair, looking for nothing more than a seven series BMW, a three-bedroom house, and a 401(k). We want the guy that floats our boat. And what's true of most women is especially true of me. I mean, if I don't want to instantly press my lips onto that guy in the first, I mean first thirty seconds, forget about it. Call me shallow. Call me whatever. But if I don't want to throw him on the bed and get sweaty and naked, it's over. I don't want a lifetime of financial security if the trade off is passionless kisses while dreaming of George Clooney."

Is it possible to find a man who makes me hot, but who will still be a loving, loyal husband who makes me laugh? A provider and wonderful father to my children? Is this, too, a concoction of my preteens?

"Every time I meet my potential husband, or someone I think could be my potential husband, or at the very least someone I will have sex with, the men who will have an impact on my life, hit it like a meteor hitting a small village, disseminating its populace, I get the 'flutter, flutter.'"

"That's your internal warning system," Dr. D. states clinically. "It's good that you're in touch with it. But next time you get . . . the 'flutter, flutter' I would prescribe the following behavior: Run. It's your fight-or-flight instinct. A lot of women confuse it with fate, or destiny, or some other illusion clouding good judgment. Please continue about the potential boyfriend."

"Well, a guy who makes me laugh is important. And definitely a guy with a job." I scratch my head . . . "And has his own car." I pause for a minute. "A kind smile. I don't know, that's a good start . . . wait, and, and maybe," I look down, "someone who makes me feel pretty."

"You are pretty," Dr. D. states flatly.

"Thank you. I guess I'm just waiting for my prince to come," I add in hopes of taking the focus off my ridiculous list.

Dr. D. looks concerned. "Emily, I am going to tell you something now and I want you to brace yourself for it."

No wonder I am single. Jesus, why did I go into the "flutter, flutter" thing? Is my list unrealistic? Is that why I'm single? I'm shooting beyond my means. NO. NO. NO. A guy with a job, nice forearms, and straight teeth is not too much to ask. Stay focused. Stay on the path. He's coming. Right?

I sit back and take a deep breath, clearing my head for whatever Dr. D. has to say.

"Your prince is never coming." He takes off his glasses and looks me straight in the eye. "He doesn't exist. You need to stop looking for the right man and start looking out for the wrong men."

I hate therapy.

"Here's what I want you to do for our next session." Dr. D. sets down his pad and pen. "I want you to think back to the first adult relationship that you had with a man in your twenties. Teens are too early. Then I want you to make a list, a list of ten things that went wrong, not with the relationship, but with the man. The cell phone with what's his name . . ." he looks at his legal pad ". . . Reese, is a perfect example. Then, as we progress and you begin to date again, as, Emily, you will find love, you are going to write down ten potential problem areas, reasons you should not be with your new man *before* you give your heart away."

"Ten reasons?" I question, thinking to myself that Dr. D. is a mix between Tony Robbins and the professor from *Gilligan's Island*.

"It's an exercise that will help you learn from the past and protect yourself in the future. Because, Emily, if you can come up with ten reasons why you shouldn't be dating a person, you probably shouldn't date him. Writing it down will just help you figure it out a little sooner with less pain involved."

I PUT THE white top down on my navy '68 Mustang and start the engine. She dies. I pump the gas, turn the key, and she revs right up. Pulling out of the garage onto Sunset Boulevard, I turn up Tom Petty's "American Girl" and sing along.

At the end of the session, I committed to weed out the losers and become my own prince, which is fine, although, I don't really want to be the prince. I think that was my whole point for going to therapy. I am tired of being the prince. The she-wolf, SSW. The cor-pra-sexual. The woman working so hard to get ahead in corporate America, she bypassed love. I can check my own oil and take out the garbage, but it's still a man's job. I just do it by default.

I came up with my own secret vow. I will find love. I just need Dr. D.'s help to guide me though the clutter in the maze of dating.

Saturday night I am folding laundry. Sam, my six-year-old dog, a rescue pooch, part wolf, part German Shepherd, is lying with his tongue hanging out of the front of his mouth, as it's too long for his snout and gives the appearance that he's always sticking out his tongue at you, and refusing to get off. Every time he sees me folding clothes he thinks I am packing to go away. Thus he blocks the whole process even when it is just about having clean towels. I think the whole rescue thing has given him abandonment issues, made him codependent. I know the feeling. He gets a scratch behind both ears. "Come on, boy . . . get off."

We live in a one-bedroom fourplex in Brentwood. It's a cute forties bungalow-type apartment with hardwood floors, arched entries, and overstuffed shabby-chic furniture. I pull Sam out of the laundry basket and he goes for the forbidden sofa. His bad hips cause him to pause before jumping onto the end cushion. I can't really blame him for settling in, as it is one of those sofas that makes you want to cozy up in it for the night and watch bad movies. Overall the apartment is a spacious spot with a little yard where Sam can sun and howl at passing strangers. No dishwasher, no garbage disposal, no washer and dryer. But plenty of charm. It's home for Sam and me.

The doorbell rings and Sam begins to howl.

"Happy birthday to you. Happy birthday to you. Happy birthday . . . dear Emileeeeeeeee!" I hear the girls singing outside the front door. Sam howls and wags his tail, joining in the festivities. I open the door to Grace and Reilly holding a birthday cake with a huge "30" candle burning on top.

"Happy birthday, you whore," Reilly laughs, pushing in the door and patting Sam. "Helllloooo, Sammmmmy!"

"Lovely," I say, hugging Reilly.

Reilly Swanson and Grace Hunter are my best girlfriends. Grace and I met in college after the DGs, the sorority we wanted, didn't want us because our bangs weren't big enough . . . it was the late '80s. A cute blonde from Davenport, Iowa, Grace is the type of girl who will ruin a New Year's Eve to rescue a kitten. Reilly, an Asian with the biggest breasts I've ever seen, was adopted into the Swanson family of Manhattan Beach, California, the whitest, beachiest family in the area. Not only is she the youngest of all boys, she's also the only Asian of the bunch. We all met at Cannery Row, a dive bar within walking distance from our freshman dorm at Arizona State University.

Would-be frat boys in a beer chugging contest surrounded Reilly. She won and the boy she beat threw up all over me while I was waiting for a Coors Light at the bar. Eleven years ago we began our thicker-than-thieves bond. Wow, eleven years. The thought sends shivers.

Grace kisses me on the cheek as she steps in the door. "Happy birthday, Em. You didn't think we were going out tonight without us wishing your twenties good-bye with cake and vodka, did you?" Reilly holds up a bottle of Absolut Citron. We all head into the kitchen.

Reilly starts to mix cocktails as we sit at the breakfast nook to eat strawberry birthday cake and drink Citron martinis. "What'd you think of Dr. D.?" Grace asks.

"Why do you need to pay some stranger a hundred-plus dollars an hour when we have a licensed therapist among the ranks?" Reilly volleys at me, referring to Grace.

Grace adds in her therapist voice, "Friends aren't supposed to counsel other friends. We're too personally attached. Besides, she stopped listening to me somewhere between Jeff and Dennis."

"We do it all day," Reilly counters.

"Repressive male-bashing is not necessarily healthy counseling," I retort.

"Stick together we must!" Reilly laughs.

We raise our glasses and Grace toasts, "To our girl. May she find a man to love her as much as we do."

Our glasses clink at the rim.

"Happy birthday, Em," they say in unison.

We pat Sammy good-bye, filling him with enough love so he knows we're coming back. At least love between people and their dogs is still intact. Sammy wags his tail as if satisfied, at least for the moment, that the laundry is still unfolded and inside.

Reilly crawls into the back of my car and I notice a hickey on the back of her neck.

"I see you're dating Denny again," I say as I shut the door behind her and lower the top.

"I wouldn't call it dating," Reilly rebuts. "More like exercise with a hint of heartache."

"And you now understand why we shouldn't take relationship advice from our friends." Grace looks back at Reilly.

I am always the driver. Call it control, call it love for the Mustang, but mainly call it the security that I can leave wherever we are whenever I want.

I turn on the ignition. It dies. I pump the gas, turn the key again, and rev once as we embark on the unlikely adventure of a Hollywood fund-raiser on girls' night out.

"Lemme know if Dr. D. tells you anything we don't know already," Reilly says as she puts on her seat belt.

Grace pipes in, "As a licensed therapist I will tell you one thing for sure. Deep down we already know what therapy is trying to teach us way before we ever go in. We know when to leave a shitty relationship. We know when men are bad for us. We know what it means when they don't call. We just need to pay someone to tell us before we believe it." She smiles, satisfied, as if she has just changed the lightbulb in a dark room.

Grace is the friend that I know is my ticket to heaven. She saves everyone from homeless crack addicts to her perpetually single girlfriends. She is the one who comes over when I am PMSing and drowning in a single, bottle of pinot, self-pity party. She reminds me that indeed there is love out there for me, and on a good day she can be pretty convincing.

"Go ahead and smile," Reilly shoots back in at Grace. "But if you're so smart, why'd you take on one hundred thousand dollars in student loans to get 'Doctor' before your name so you could make forty thousand dollars a year counseling junkies and freeloaders? Where's the fucking sense in that?" Reilly blows smoke from her Marlboro Light into the night air.

"They're homeless, and I am trying to make them be productive citizens." Grace shakes her head.

"Save it for the pearly gates," Reilly says as she finishes her smoke.

"Em, is Josh coming out with us?" Grace changes the subject.

"Hot, rich, loving, great taste . . . ," Reilly says. "Such a waste of a perfectly good penis."

"No, he has some new boyfriend. They're going to some new club in Boy's Town. Although he did say, for my birthday, that he would be my donor if I needed to breed in the next decade."

"You could do worse," Reilly smiles at me.

"I think I actually want the penetration."

In reality, I don't think having a donor backup plan is such a bad idea. I mean, with Josh, at least I know he's going to be my friend forever. He's going to love me when my boobs are saggy, when I am PMSing and the baby is crying. I know that he'll take the kids to soccer practice and cheerleading tryouts and he'll help our daughter pick out the perfect prom dress. I mean, it seems a lot more reliable than believing that love, passion, and monogamy are going to last forever.

"Red or pink?" I hold up two lip liners as we wait in 10:00 P.M. gridlock.

"Definitely red. Red says take me, I need it, and I need it bad on my birthday," Reilly laughs.

"For God's sake, we're heading out into the wilderness of Los Angeles on a Saturday night, wear the red," Grace backs Reilly up.

I check the red lipstick in the rearview mirror as the Mustang waits on little Santa Monica Boulevard behind a convertible BMW full of twentysomething-backless-shirt-wearing model types and an oversized black SUV with a P. Diddy look-alike bumping to rap music behind us. We finally reach the valet stand outside the Beverly Hills YMCA.

Who knew they even had YMCAs in Beverly Hills?

We enter the Y and the doorman directs us to the gymnasium. We walk through the metal doors of the gym and immediately notice that it is decorated like a high school prom in the eighties. I start to itch.

I hated all the insecurity that came along with being a sixteen-year-old in braces whose breasts had yet to develop. I had hives all through my sophomore year and now I remember why. This gym has thrust me into the past and suddenly I am feeling like an awkward, knock-kneed geek. I am wishing I was home watching reruns of *Magnum, P.I.* in my pajamas with Sam.

Scanning the room, I make out all the familiar faces, and it dawns on me that Hollywood is exactly like high school. There are the popular kids. The jocks. The freaks. And the annoying student council types trying to get ahead—only now they are agents, studio executives, managers, publicists, and lawyers.

They are all crammed together in Armani trousers, Hugo Boss sweaters, and backless shirts. They are the same two hundred people that I witnessed four nights ago pouring out of a premiere at the Director's Guild theater as I sat in the Mustang at a stoplight watching them all smoke cigarettes and discuss the pros and cons of film noir.

Two hundred of exactly the same people, only now they are crouched together smoking cigarettes and trying to figure out who is more important than whom, which isn't Reilly, Grace, or me.

We make a beeline for the bar. Reilly fires up her second Marlboro Light and blows her smoke into the chest of George Clooney.

Wow. George Clooney is a babe. Keep moving. I look over my shoulder at him and he smiles.

"Actors," Reilly says with disdain.

"I don't know, he has the sexiest eyes," I defend him.

"He is the epitome of the American bachelor and makes no bones about it. He never wants to get married. Never wants kids." Grace lays it out like it is.

"George is another example of perfectly good genes going to waste," Reilly realizes.

George . . . I could love George, with his perfect hair, sly smile, and strong forearms, a perpetual prankster. I could fall madly in love with a man who professes to find marriage the ultimate death for men. George, a man whose longest caretaking relationship is with a potbellied pig. George, who would rather spend Sundays shooting hoops with his buddies or riding his Harley than lie naked with me watching *The Way We Were*. But I could change him. Teach him about the benefits of intimacy, nurturing, and commitment. JESUS! George is the exact type of man that I am attracted to for all of the wrong reasons. George easily has ten reasons why NOT to date him. How much clearer does a man need to be to me? He printed his disdain for monogamy in *People* magazine!

"But he's so utterly, completely beautiful," I say. We all nod in agreement as we watch his tight butt sashay away in 501s.

After downing my entire drink in one gulp I ask the girls, "One lap, you ready?"

Reilly unbuttons the top of her sweater, revealing her very large cleavage, smiles at us, and mimics in a lusty, bar-wench tone, "Oh, I'm ready."

We go on the move, cutting in and out of the groups of

popular kids, hoping to find one trinket of possibility that love exists in L.A. and is just waiting for me to stumble into it.

I pass by Patrick Whitman, a super-hottie superagent to stars like Matt and Ben. He flirts a little with me while eyeing Reilly's cleavage. Grace looks bored. Patrick's flirting quickly ends when he spies an actress who is firmer, younger, and much richer than any of us.

"We should get together," I murmur under my breath.

Still eyeballing the actress over my shoulder, he says, "Yeah, sure, have your assistant call mine. We'll put something on the books." And he walks away.

I turn and look at Grace. "Can you get right on that?" I say with disbelief.

"Yeah, right after I book the church for your wedding to Clooney." She shakes her head.

What is wrong with these people? The phenomenon of not being able to have a conversation while looking you directly in the eye never ceases to blow me away. The constant need to look around for someone better is worse than deplorable. Over your head, shoulder, arm, back, while you are trying to have a meaningful or not-so-meaningful chat with them, is a special form of crazy-making L.A. torture. I wonder if this neck-craning disorder is entertainment-industry specific or if it happens everywhere. Maybe it's me. Maybe it's my conversation skills. Whatever it is, I am reminded why I didn't want to go out tonight.

I take Grace's hand. "Is it me, or are all of these guys complete dickheads?"

She hands me another cocktail. "It's not you. Here, have a vodka crème soda."

Thank God for the girls.

We make our way under a heat lamp and I see George Clooney again. He is talking to a group of guys, one of whom is his equally hot friend, Waldo.

SHIT. I get nailed staring right at him. Jesus, how long have I been looking at him with these horny thoughts running through my head? To George, I now appear to be a party stalker. Instead of smiling at me he gives me a quick, puzzled look that may be fear-based.

I look for a diversion and notice two random guys standing off in the corner behind George. I smile and wave at the taller of the two. George looks from me to the guys and his face fills with relief.

I head toward the two guys, dragging Reilly and Grace behind and telling them, "Trust me." We saddle up to the strangers. Please let them be normal. Let them be nice. Let them be single. Let them not be a couple.

"Hi, I'm Emily, and this is Reilly and Grace."

My boondoggle seems to have relaxed George and now my immediate thought is how the hell do I get out of here, although the taller guy, up close, is really cute. He's got short dark hair, gray-blue eyes, and one of those shirts Vince Vaughn wore in *Swingers*. His lips part in slow motion, and he has the most perfect teeth I have ever seen, straight, white, and large, which amounts to a great big dangerous smile. He sticks out his hand. "Stan, and this is my friend, Adam." Reilly instantly hates them both.

"Drink?" Reilly asks Grace as she grabs her arm and drags her away, leaving me standing there.

Tons of thoughts continue to flood my brain like a flash flood in the Arizona desert. *Shoooosh!* Thoughts like, *Please don't let this guy be in the entertainment business. Please let him look me directly in the eye.* Who is he? Where did he come from? Why is my heart racing?

Flitter, flutter.

Huh, not quite a "flutter, flutter." But a "*flitter,* flutter." Oh, shit! I have a damaged flutter.

Wow, in five minutes or less, my internal warning system, or my internal sex meter, has gone off.

Two A.M. and I have been sitting on the patio talking to Laguna Beach stockbroker Stan for over two hours.

"I have to find my friends." I run my finger over the rim of my empty vodka crème soda glass.

"They left about an hour ago, waved and gestured that they were leaving. The blonde gave me a big thumbs-up," he says.

"Really?" I raise my eyebrow.

"Would I lie?" he says, raising his eyebrow, comically matching mine.

Hmmmmm, would a man lie? Silly, silly question. Of course he'd lie. Men will lie about anything to avoid anger or confrontation with a woman.

I set my drink down. "I don't know, would you?"

"No, not to you."

I like him already.

chapter two

Keep It Out of the Office

People who are late annoy me. Aren't we all in a hurry? Isn't all of our time valuable? So I try to be on time. Call it respect . . . for myself, for who I'm meeting. Just be on time. Living in Los Angeles, you leave an extra forty-five minutes to get anywhere, knowing that you will inevitably be stuck in traffic.

I am never late. Yet I'm late for Dr. D.'s office, as I'd rather lose twenty dollars of therapy than sit in the lobby, waiting, running the risk of being subjected to inappropriate "bridal" reading materials. I know it's silly and a waste, but I'm willing to pay it.

Rushing into the inner lobby, I push the button outside his door to let him know I'm here and pace around because I don't want to sit. I can see that . . . that . . . bridal magazine, but I shake it off. Shake it off. The door opens. "Sorry I'm late."

"It's your time," he says, opening the door to his office. In my spot on the burgundy sofa I already feel more relaxed this visit. The cuckoo clock actually brings a grin to my face.

"I met someone."

"Did you get the flutter, flutter?"

"No, I got a *flitter,* flutter . . . but, yeah, I guess I got the flutter."

Dr. D. sighs. "Did you sleep with him?"

"No, I am a self-respecting woman."

I leave out the fact that I really, really wanted to, as it has been too long since I have even been kissed.

"Did you do your reasons for him yet?"

"No, but I did notice his eyebrows are waxed. Not really a reason, but it was weird, he has these really groomed eyebrows. They come to a perfect point at the end. It's a little off. I mean, for a guy. At what point did men go from being the Marlboro Man to arching their brows like Ru Paul? It's not really a reason, more a question."

"I want to hear about the new flitter guy, but more importantly, did you bring your list?" Referring to my homework assignment from last week.

"I did," I say, reaching into my Kate Spade bag. "The list of ten reasons that I guess I should have known or at least thought about before dating David."

"That's good." Dr. D. gestures for the list and I hand it over like a teacher's pet. He glances at it, places it on his yellow legal pad, and takes his place across from me. "Tell me about him."

As I start to remember David, it seems like I've already been through it in my head a thousand times. Within a few sentences I am back in that place and time, reliving it.

Four and a half years ago, Asheville, North Carolina, day one of our entertainment company retreat. Josh, my gay friend, and I are late for our first meeting of the morning. I spent the last hour lying on the double bed in Josh's hotel room while he e-mailed his boyfriend, Ronald.

I am reduced to vicariously living through my gay male relationship for testosterone intake. Frankly, I think Ronald is a jerk who doesn't deserve Josh, but then again, I don't know who would be good enough for Josh. We've been friends since I moved to L.A. in the early nineties. He's from Nebraska and always says he's the only gay Jew from the state. We're both single, both in PR, both looking for men. He's my date to any social function where a girlfriend is unacceptable, unless of course you are Melissa Etheridge, Ellen, or Rosie.

I look at Josh as we run down the hotel corridor holding hands. He is the perfect specimen for me, if only he weren't gay. But maybe that is why we are so close. There is no pretense, no hiding who we really are in hopes of getting the other naked. Just two people with similar morals, ethics, and senses of humor.

I would probably have an easier time getting him to say 10 Hail Marys and take Jesus as his favorite savior than I ever would getting him to visit my little man in the canoe, my flower, my whoo-whoo.

We're late for a presentation on corporate collaboration by our new CEO and president. I tug on Josh's hand. "Come on!"

He barks back at me as we hurry down the hall holding hands, "Five minutes is fashionable, not late! Always the company do-gooder."

"If I didn't have to wait for you to instant-message Ronald, the sausage king, we wouldn't be late," I say, out of breath.

"We broke up," Josh says nonchalantly.

I stop dead in my tracks as we hit the lobby area. "You wait until now, not on the four-hour flight to Atlanta, two-hour bus ride to Asheville, and thirty minutes on the treadmill to tell me that you broke up? What's up with that?"

Why is it that Josh's breakups are never as dramatic as mine? As if by being gay he holds some secret knowledge that there will always be another. Apparently there is a plethora of gay men looking for love and no straight men looking for anything more than a beer and a nice set of hammers.

Josh tugs at my hand as we search for the Azuma conference room. "It was never going to last with someone named Ronald," Josh says as we find the conference room. He opens the door to the huge ballroom where Avery, the head of PR, my boss, is addressing a hundred happy Warner employees. The audience claps as Josh and I duck into the back and sit on hard wooden chairs.

Then, I see him . . . He saunters onto the stage clad in a dark gray Hugo Boss suit and wonderfully bright yellow tie. "Good morning, everyone. For those of you I haven't met, I am David Jenkins, your new president."

I grab Josh's hand and we both mouth "babe."

Oh, my dreamy president. Now I know what happened to Monica Lewinsky. Except I don't think I could ever roll in the hay with Clinton. He 100 percent does not give me the "flutter, flutter." But I understand how the power can do it for some women. Must be like good teeth for me.

I pause my story about David and look at Dr. D. "Looking back on it, David's allure, standing at the podium in his leadership position larger than life, got me bothered and a little hot."

The reality that he was a great-looking man in a tailored suit making seven figures a year somehow dazzled me. Wow, does that make me shallow?

Plus he had one of those voices that can make your toes tingle. Voices are important. I don't think I could date a guy with a whiny, high-pitched voice. Match David's power with his low raspy tones and translucent green-yellow eyes and I was pretty much willing to be thrown up against any desk or nearby file cabinet by him.

I stop my train of thought on the track and smile at Dr. D. "I am starting to realize why I am single." He smiles back and writes a note on his yellow legal pad.

Reason #1: *If your boss is bigger than life in your company, that doesn't necessarily mean he is bigger than life in real life.*

"Please continue," Dr. D. says.

Josh leans over and whispers in my ear, "I wouldn't mind being collaborative with David."

"Shhhhhhh . . . ," I say, trying to analyze what it is about that man up there that is making my palms sweaty. His mouth moves . . . his upper lip is slightly smaller than the bottom. He has gray at the temples. His eyes are slightly creased at the corners from too many tennis games in the sun or too many smiles at pretty girls. He shaved this morning, but he has slight stubble already peaking out of his tan skin. OH MY!

He is giving his rousing, inspirational, motivational speech about . . . Shit, I have no idea what he's talking about.

I look around the room and everyone seems as riveted as I am. I realize that I have been lost in the hundred different ways to kiss him and have not been listening at all. He's probably rambling on about demographics or programming. It could be about a sewer treatment plant in Uganda and I'd gladly watch those lips move all day long. He's a six-foot-one-salt-and-pepper Alpha fox through and through. Making my six-foot rule. Nice teeth, good voice, has a job. No ring. Things are looking good in Asheville!

We break for coffee and Josh calls Ronald, but before it rings he stops me, delicately touching my arm. "Let me pose a few words of wisdom to you, Kitten," Josh says, leaning out of his phone booth, waiting for Ronald to answer. "Don't shit where you eat. Don't fish off the company pier. There is a reason that so many sayings exist about relationships gone badly in the workplace. Not that I don't see why you want him. Hell, I want him. But sweetie, Em, throw this one back. He's exactly the wrong guy."

I jump back to reality, sit up, and twist my back from side to side, subtly eyeballing Dr. D. "You look like you want to say something," he says.

"Well, this is where I came up with my second reason."

Reason #2: *If there are kitschy little sayings about the guy you're dating, there is probably a universal reason why it is a bad idea.*

"Your friend, Josh, sounds like a smart guy. And your reason is a solid one. Too bad you didn't see it then."

Josh closes the door to the phone booth as I scrunch my face at him and mouth through the door, "I am going for coffee."

Why does there always have to be an obstacle in the way of love? Perhaps this workplace obstacle is like any other. It simply must be conquered. There are mental, physical, and spiritual hoops that one must jump through to really feel satisfied that we deserve our ideal relationship. It makes perfect sense.

I try my best to seductively grin at David while he waits for me to finish pouring my coffee. "Emily, right?" I swear to God he low-growled at me.

Tingling. Toes, knees, thighs, tingling. "Good guess."

"Not really." He points at my laminated name tag.

SHIT! I am such a looosssssseeerrr. I am wearing a name tag. No one looks at all remotely sexy in a laminated name tag that says, "Hello, my name is Emily Sanders, I am in the PR department."

David and I stand around a nicely decorated table with silver serving trays overflowing with bagels, cream cheese, lox, croissants, and glazed pastries.

He takes a bagel and walks away. I stare at the back of his head as he stops to talk to Avery.

Flutter. Flutter.

"I knew right then with David." I smile at Dr. D. He jots a note and shakes his head, understanding.

I must have been drooling when Josh snuck up next to me and rolled his eyes. "Coffee, cream, Sweet'n Low, doggy-style?"

Proceed or retreat? That is the question. Is it nobler in the mind's eye to move forward with the hope of finding the "right" love, or to go back to my room and watch an old movie while I stuff my face with French onion soup and a club sandwich from room service?

I say, CONQUER! Conquer him. Conquer them all. Make them give you their balls so you can keep them safely tucked in a Tiffany satchel around your neck.

I think at that point in my life, at only twenty-six years of age, a one-night whoop in the hay-ho with my boss's-boss's-boss didn't seem like such a bad idea.

There he sits, at the top rung of the success ladder, just waiting to let down the rope so I can climb up.

Day three of the retreat I wear a tight, gray, above-the-knee, linen skirt with strappy red heels and a stunning black sleeveless V-neck sweater that maxed out my Visa. I make my way to the lobby bar, sit down on the stool, order a Kettle One and cranberry, and wait patiently for Josh to curl up next to me.

"Kitten, learn from what I am about to tell you. No good comes from drinking at company functions." Josh looks at the bartender. "I'll have a Crown and soda." Then back at me. "Great shoes."

"Gucci outlet," I say, holding out my foot. We spot hotty-president-boyfriend-to-be sauntering across the lobby in black trousers and a black cashmere sweater.

Josh turns and watches him. "He's trouble. Big, yummy trouble." David spies us looking at him as I pretend to laugh and look away . . . I sort of spin around on my barstool, frolicking and carefree, but I lose my balance and bash my elbow into the brass railing. "Shit! Why do they call it a funny bone? That's not fucking funny." I wince, rubbing my elbow.

"Subtle, flirty turn, nicely done with a hint of I-don't-give-a-shit-about-Mr. Beautiful-late-thirtysomething-God." Josh gives me a little golf clap.

He rubs my elbow for me. "Em, I don't want to see you get hurt, or fired."

Two martinis, two glasses of wine, and one tequila shot later, Josh and I are singing to Frank Sinatra's "My Way" on the dance floor.

We tango across the floor. "I did it mmmmmmmyyyyyy wwwaaay." Josh dips me. "Thirsty, Kitten?"

"I thought you'd never ask," I say, rolling out of his arm.

Do you see why Josh is the perfect date? Sexy dancer, singer, friend, and cohort, and he even knows when I need a drink. He is practically the perfect man.

However . . . this is where anyone in his or her right mind would have said no to more alcohol. But instead I stand waiting at the bar for our beers.

The DJ spins the Village People's "Y.M.C.A." and Josh hurries back to the dance floor, drawn by the irresistibility of a flashback to summers in the Hamptons in the heyday of the eighties. He spins in a circle and claps above his head. I hold my arms in the air at Josh making a Y, M, C, AAAAAA. The bartender sets down two Bud Lights and two tequila shots. I hand him a twenty.

"Want to dance?" David says from behind me in his low-sex growl as he lightly brushes up to me and sets every hair on my body aflame. I am dizzy with him. Maybe it's the tequila. No, it's him. Yep, definitely him, David, wow, front and center, Mr. President, Mr. Sexpot, Mr. Perfect, Mr. Power Boyfriend candidate.

Then I look around the room and see a few people watching me out of the corners of their dirty little minds. Wondering what I was wondering. Why was this man of great importance paying attention to this lowly director of PR?

Or I guess maybe it was obvious with the Gucci stilettos.

"I'll be right back," I say, "and yes, I one hundred percent want to dance with you. Just, can you wait one, maybe two minutes?"

He does this sexy little shoulder shrug and agrees.

I look at Dr. D. "That's when the whispering officially started."

Reason #3: *That which is considered scandal in a relationship is bad, really, really, bad.*

"I guess I knew then, really. Well, at least Grace told me," I explain.

"What do mean?"

"Well, after David asked me to dance, I walked outside and called Grace from my cell phone . . ."

"I need a voice of reason, need you to stop me from tearing the president of my company's clothes off, which I know sounds terrible, but I haven't had the 'flutter, flutter' in a long, long time. I haven't found someone who actually likes me back in a long time. What exactly is wrong with seizing the moment?"

Grace takes a deep breath and puts on her would-be-therapist's voice. She was getting her master's in social work at this time. So every time she gave me advice, I got the calm-stern voice of reason. "Walk away from anyone in your company who has a bigger title than you. Walk away from anyone in your company who will cause jealousy, gossip, and notoriety from your peers. Even the mail guy. Don't *do it* at work. It's your bread and butter. It is the place that enables you to shop, eat, pay your rent, go on vacations, and buy overpriced Kate Spade bags, not to mention pay your cell phone bill. WALK AWAY!" Grace is now barking into the phone. "And stop drinking, you're borderline slurring."

"Walk away?" I repeat, not convinced. "Walk away?" I repeat to myself, shuffling back into the bar. I should walk away.

But my willpower defenses are dulled by what would be at least a 2.0 on the alcohol blow meter. I stop at the entrance of the bar and see him watching me with his confident, I-want-to-have-sex . . . wait, I-*will*-have-sex-with-you eyes. I look from him to the elevator outside the bar. It's an easy twenty steps to a scandal-free existence in the corporate jungle. And then, as if he is reading my mind, he winks at me and mouths, "You're okay" and gestures with his head for me to come back.

Cheek to cheek, sweaty, another drink, another dance, the smell of him, the way he guided me on the dance floor, held me close with his strong arms. At that moment, with our bodies pressed together, I knew that he was meant to be my boyfriend, and I didn't give a damn who knew.

There is safety swaying in the arms of a man you are really, really hot for.

I bury my head in his chest, right at his collarbone, run my hand over his forearm, melt and disappear into him.

It was a flawless moment that I wish I could have put in a pink box and saved for every time I was feeling lonely. Just that one song, Billy Joel's "The Piano Man," one dance, the moment when I felt the faux-man-woman-stranger connection. It made me feel wanted, sexy, alive.

As we left the bar to get some air outside, it played like a slow-motion instant replay on ESPN highlights. The entire room watched. It was like one of those big blindside hits a 320-pound defensive lineman lays on the quarterback, a meat-wagon shot that makes your stomach sink, a textbook corporate version of—YOU GOTTA SEE THIS!

Then, sensing my fear . . . Josh gave me a wink and waved. David smiled at him and waved good-bye. My heroes.

We walk along the outskirts of the resort. "I think those are the Blue Ridge Mountains," David says. "They're really magnificent."

He's magnificent. Powerful. Smart. Handsome. A great dancer. Take a deep breath. Slow down. In, out, in out. "Yes, they are," I slur.

Jesus, why am I all *Rain Man* inside?

Just be Emily. Be cool. Calm. Focus on the full moon and the stars that are clearer and brighter than they've ever been in L.A., the smell of fresh-cut grass fills my senses. We walk onto the golf course.

"Do you like working in the PR department?" David asks as we walk along the moonlit greens.

"Ah-huh. Sure, it's good," I say.

Stupid. Stupid. Stupid. I wish I wouldn't have had that last beer. Tequila shot. Martini. Where is my witty banter?

"We need good PR people. I hear that you're an up-and-comer. Avery speaks very highly of you. Being the new guy in school, I haven't really met that many people, but I think I would have remembered meeting you. We haven't met, have we?" He stops.

I shake my head, "No, we haven't."

I play with the flag on the ninth hole of the green.

"Do you play?" David asks, referring to my golf game.

"Yeah, actually I do a little."

"The perfect woman."

I put the flag back in the hole and coyly walk ahead of him when in reality I am at a loss for words. I remember what my Gram says: "It's better to say nothing than say something stupid and look like an ass." Good advice, particularly coming from a seventy-five-year-old woman from Indiana.

"I belong to the Bel-Air, maybe when we get back we can play. Would you like that?" David asks, catching up to me.

YES! I want to scream. I want to go to the club and play golf with my perfect power boyfriend.

He touches my hand. I mumble, "Sure, that would nice."

He leans down and studies my eyes . . . I am weak in the knees. He runs his finger over my bottom lip . . . then kisses me.

It's raining. Mist, really. The glow from the moon. My cheeks flush from the excitement. Alcohol. The cool drops from heaven washing between us. I'm walking above the ground. Floating next to him as he talks about living at the beach and loving the TV business, graduating from law school, starting in the mailroom at NBC. Recently single. Total bonus!

And ready. Did I mention he said he was ready? Ready for a relationship.

I am ready! Ready. Ready. Ready. He holds my hand and leads me back to his room. We rip off each other's clothes and cascade onto the bed.

I should have said no. No to the coffee. No to the bagels. No to the drinks. No to the dancing. No to the sex. But I didn't.

And God, was it all so aaaammmmaaaazzzzinnnggg!

I awake to the repercussions of one's actions. Lying naked next to the president of my company. Jesus! What have I done? I ease David's arm off of my hip and gently slip out of the bed and onto the floor with a thud. I make my way to the bathroom and turn on the light.

Headache. I have a headache. I pick up the phone on the wall next to the toilet and call Josh as I wipe the mascara from under my eyes. I pray that Josh will come and do a check of the perimeter to make sure that the coast is clear for a get-away back to my room. But he is already out.

My head is pounding!

I slip on my clothes, grab David's Dodgers baseball hat, and scurry out of the room. I pause at every corner, every turn, peeking around the hall, making sure that NO one catches me doing the sorority walk of shame.

Four Advil and one hydrating mask later I am dressed and showered, sitting in a breakfast meeting with an entire group of people who will not speak or look at me. Scandal. I am scandal. Where the hell is Josh?

"Congratulations, you and David have now become . . .

HBO's *REAL SEX 500,* the corporate episode, 'Fucking your Boss's-Boss's-Boss at the Company Retreat,'" Josh says, sitting in the chair next to me. "It's a good thing that I don't care what people say about me hanging out with you. Besides, they can't fire me for being friends with the company Scarlet Letter, as I am protected by the velvet curtain, thus untouchable." He looks around the room. They turn away from his gaze. One woman gives him a phony smile while squinting her eyes. "Oh, it's bad, Emmie, but more importantly, how was he?"

I give Josh a postglow smile, and he can't help but laugh.

"Worth it. It was so worth it. I hadn't been kissed like that in over three-hundred-and-two days. I needed a good kiss. I felt like the girl who got to kiss the quarterback at the prom. Only I never went to the prom, so kisses like that are that much better. We're both consenting adults." I whisper with resentment at this sudden alienation. "Don't these people have lives? Perhaps they should worry about their problems or better yet, get laid."

Josh cocks his head at me. "That behavior is going to make no friends. Shame. Shame. Play nice with the other boys and girls." He raises an orange juice glass at some marketing woman giving me the eye. She looks away.

"David missed his early-morning meeting, only adding more speculation that he was where you left him, naked and hungover in bed, cuddling a Pepto Bismol bottle." Josh finds amusement in his cleverness.

I punch him. "It's not funny. This is my life. My professional future. And he could be my potential power boyfriend."

"Emmie, Kitten, don't be so hetero. Every guy that goes down on you isn't meant to meet you at the end of the aisle. Besides, David just jumped on the corporate jet back to L.A., justifying it with problems on the set surrounding Meg Ryan. Huh, interesting sign for a soul mate. Wonder how he'll handle the screaming children?"

Postretreat: Back in the safety and autonomy of my apartment in Brentwood. The alarm clock goes off and I look over at Sam, who is lying on his back with his head on the pillow next to me. I can't help but laugh. I scratch his tummy, then bury myself under the covers in hopes I can hide and that the people at work will soon forget my bad judgment.

I can't get David out of my head. I hate the postsex days. I feel a little sad that the warmth washing over my whole body is now missing, replaced with anxiety. Will he call? Will he not call? What do I do if he does call? I can't possibly date my boss's boss's boss. It did, however, have some exciting quality to it. I close my eyes, take a deep breath, and the phone rings.

It's Grace and Reilly. They are three-way-calling me for a Monday-morning report on the weekend.

Shit, don't you hate that? When you want it so badly to be someone else and it is one of your loving friends calling to say hello, and you can't help but be disappointed, even annoyed?

"You didn't walk away, did you?" Grace shoots out before hello or good morning.

"No, and now I can't shake the endorphin shooters that are attacking my body following our enchanting sexual encounter," I say to the girls on the phone.

"It's a little early in the morning for your talk of moisture and endorphins," Reilly laughs.

Sam's head is resting on my arm. I pet his perfect bearlike muzzle. "I can't get him out of my head. I want to call."

"No calling!" Grace declares. "Try the battery-operated device in your top drawer and let it go. You need to keep it out of the office. There are no ifs, ands, or buts about it."

"I have to get in the shower and head to work. I'll call you guys later."

"NO CALLING," they both say in unison.

We all hang up.

I round the Mustang into the parking garage and pass David's black Mercedes S500. I sneak up the stairs to my office on the third floor, round the corner past the lobby, and shoot straight into my office, where I promptly shut the door.

"Nicely done." Josh opens my door, pops his head in my office.

"Piss off." I ease my jacket off.

"Good morning to you," he says, leaving.

I sit down at my desk, turn on my computer, open my e-mail, and see . . .

TO: Emily Sanders
FR: David Jenkins

Dear Emily,
I know it's not protocol, but then neither was the retreat. I would like to see you, in a per-

sonal way, not in the office. Why, you ask? Because I think that you are funny and sexy in a
quirky way. I like your style. And you're a
great kisser. How about dinner? Or golf?
David

I respond . . .

Dear David,

I am calling Human Resources as I will not be
sexually harassed by my boss's-boss's-boss.
Joking.

I prefer to be sexy and funny vs. sexy in a
quirky way. What exactly does that mean?

I am free for dinner tonight. But I cannot
guarantee any kissing. And the whole sex thing
was a fluke.

Emily

Wow! My body is on fire. And my witty banter is coming
back!

OUR INTERTWINED HANDS linger across the table.
Candlelight on the patio floods the darkness at The Ivy, a
trendy L.A. eatery formed out of an old red-brick house
tucked on Robertson Boulevard. The patio is laden with
green ivy, heat lamps, white wooden tables, flowery pillows,

and tablecloths. The food is comfort with a hint of hip and expensive. We sit nestled in the corner, out of sight, so I slip my feet into his chair. He gently strokes my ankles.

"You have the best smile," David low-growls. "It's honest, real. Your eyes sort of scrunch up and your dimples crease in when you laugh. You just have an incredible smile." Melting. I am melting. "See, there it goes again." He leans over the table and kisses the tops of my hands.

What is it about men when they give us compliments? There is something in me that goes to pieces. When David told me that my smile was incredible, all of sudden I thought that my smile must be one of the best things about me, and I never really thought that my smile was all that great. I did have braces, but I don't have one of those perfect, oversized, Miss Texas smiles, like singers. All singers must see the same orthodontist. Think about it. Whitney Houston and Madonna have the same teeth. My smile is more Meg Ryan with a hint of Patricia Arquette. Ducky with eyeteeth. It's cute, but by no means perfect. Now, at this moment, I wouldn't trade it for all of the white caps in the world.

Postdinner: He walked me to the door and met Sam. Sam just stood in the doorway unsure of what to do. Sam is usually a pretty good indicator of people. He either completely snubs strangers he doesn't like or if he likes you, you get the howl followed by rubbing between your legs in a silent plea for head scratches. Sam just stood there looking at him and then sat down in the doorway as if saying, The jury is still out.

I watch my dog and make a decision.

I want to let David in. I sooooo want to kiss him all night, have him on the floor, couch, bed, and kitchen table. But I am a woman trying to prove that I am not an easy corporate retreat hooker, that I am strong, with good moral fiber, that I will make a great vice president of PR, a good power girlfriend . . . not a one-nighter.

But then, here he was, and what if he never came back? What if he drives away in his Mercedes and crashes on the Pacific Coast Highway and I never get one last chance to lie in his arms? Death versus the ability to remain strong and hold onto my morality.

I am not sure who decided a woman's sexuality is the determining factor of our morality, but that MAN should be shot. Because I am a completely moral woman, but I like sex. Yet I will deny myself in order to prove that I am a nice girl. UGGH!

As much as I wanted it, I knew he had to go.

I sent him home, and of course my trickery theory of playing the coy and nonhorny, hard-to-get-girl worked. He called from his car on his way home . . . and again in the morning, just to wish me a good day.

It left me wondering, why is it that no sex equals calls? To me that is completely backward and irrational. If we give ourselves completely and get naked, revealing all possible body flaws, and release our pheromone of love, what happens? They don't call. If we send them packing without a hint of wanting, they in turn pay attention to us? So to understand the male perspective I must reevaluate all logical female thinking and reverse it. Completely turn the rational perspective inside out. Then possibly I might be in sync with men.

Week three . . . Lying on David's office floor after hours of listening to Madonna's *Bedtime Stories,* one of the all-time best makeout CDs.

"I may need some help with the press," David whispers between kisses.

"Of course. Anything I can do." I love that he needs me.

"But I don't want you to tell anybody. No one. Not Josh or Avery. This is something that I need to do under the radar of our corporate communications policy. Things are getting a little rough for me, as I am new, and now there's the merger, and well, frankly, I am not getting the recognition that I need to keep growing both here and in the industry. As you and I both know, perception and spin are everything." He adds, "I figure if I can't trust my girlfriend, who can I trust?"

I say to Dr. D., "Reason number four . . ."

Reason #4: *If helping your boyfriend makes you lie to your friends, boss, and mentor, don't help him.*

"You're spot on," Dr. D. replies. "He used the girlfriend word in the same sentence that he asked you to be deceptive to your boss. Subtle manipulation of your emotion to evoke action."

"I know. He said girlfriend, and it was all I heard. I was a girlfriend. And he needed me. It was nice to be needed."

Dr. D. looks me in the eye over the rim of his glasses. "Why is it that that you equate needing you to liking you?"

I look down, pondering Dr. D.'s question. "Because if he needs me, he can't leave me. I know I should let this misconception go, yet I can't explain the sort of security I feel when I'm needed. It's an issue."

He writes as I continue the recollection of David.

Now for the downside to helping David. Arriving at work every day is like walking the gangplank from a ship full of serial ax murderers only to fall off into a pool of hungry Great Whites.

"No one has forgotten your behavior at the retreat in Asheville," Josh says as we enter an empty conference room. People follow us in and sit as far away from me as possible. "Annnnddddd, they know you're still doing the pres."

"No they don't!"

"Yes, they do. What's the difference between a gossipy gay guy and a gossipy hetero woman in the entertainment business?" Josh asks.

I cock my head to the side . . .

"The gay guy will stab you directly in the chest while buying you lunch at Chai and the woman will wait to shove it into your spine as *you* get stuck with the check."

"We had the talk," I smile. "He's officially my boyfriend."

"Then how come everyone thinks you're a corporate hooker?" Josh asks. "And why are the two of you still trying to hide it?"

"David thinks it is better for us if we keep it private. He needs me to help him and . . ." I stop, as I promised not to tell.

He interrupts, "This way only you look bad, Kitten. Think about it."

Reason #5: *If you have to hide your relationship, it isn't worth hiding.*

In reality, David and I have been working on a press strategy to up his profile. I am on the phone twice a day with my best contact, a reporter in New York at the *Hollywood Reporter,* giving him the inside scoop on some upcoming projects that David is trying to get off the ground, telling him about the revolutionary work he is doing behind the scenes. I know that if I can get my favorite reporter to do this story, things will change for David. He knows it, too. So we must keep our love a secret or it will look like I am trying to help him for purely unprofessional reasons and that I am not unbiased.

David and I go to New York for the weekend to meet with my guy from, the *Hollywood Reporter.* Ahhh, holding hands and drinking champagne in first class on the plane is heaven.

We check into the Carlyle Hotel on the Upper East Side. It is romantic and incredible, filled with tapestries, paisley prints, and antique furniture. Our room has a huge claw tub for two. I call down for room service and the hotel guy calls me Mrs. Jenkins. Mrs. Jenkins, I think out loud.

Mrs. David Jenkins.

We see a play on Broadway and then dance at the Rainbow Room. Flawless. Flawless. Flawless. Yet all the while denying any sort of contact with each other to the outside world. I don't care. I am blissfully happy. I have set up the lunch meeting with my contact from the *Hollywood Reporter* for David and me on Monday. It's all going to work out beautifully.

My real problem is that my boss and mentor, Avery, the woman who brought me into the fold, promoted me, championed me, hates David. Really hates him. I became aware of her loathing during a meeting before I left for New York when I overheard her talking to David's boss. She called him a, what was it? "Cocksucker."

You know what? A lot of people at the company hate David. He's not making any friends. Since the merger, we have a new CEO and *she* really doesn't like David.

It has been almost two months and David still thinks I, we, shouldn't tell anybody about our relationship. Perhaps he will change his mind after we get our media strategy plan implemented. Yet I can't help but think, just ever so slightly, that he is screwing me in more ways than one. That I may be running the risk of throwing away my career for a guy whose days are numbered and who won't admit he's my boyfriend . . . Yet everyone knows that we're having an affair.

What is wrong with me? It's as if I am watching a plane start to sputter, lose engine power, and plummet toward the ground. My career is about to take a downward spiral. I can feel it.

Reason #6: *If what you're doing for your boyfriend can get you fired, stop doing him.*

"Shit, I had doubts then." I shake my head at Dr. D. "I was smart, but I couldn't help how I felt. How did I fall for someone in the office?"

"We're getting to that," Dr. D. says.

"Frankly, I think I got sick and tired of people thinking I was the happy corporate hooker. It got on my nerves."

Home from NYC, back in the office, Avery came into my office waving the *Hollywood Reporter* in my face. She slammed the door behind her. Perhaps now is not the time to come out about our love.

"How in the HELL did they get this story about David? Someone had to plant it, it fucking has our entire pilot schedule leaked. Jesus, Emily, it has your fingerprints all over it. The guy is an asshole. He's making you look like a novice idiot. This story could cost both of us our jobs. Do you realize that? You can't get press on the president without running it by me so I can run it by Joyce. This is a mess. Just tell me you didn't do it."

To lie or not to lie?

"I did it. I am so sorry. But I didn't think . . . it's a positive story for the company. A puff piece. David really needed some good press for a change."

"My dear, there are things you don't know, one of which is that he is FUCKING using you. Why don't you see that? This is an absolute nightmare." She finishes by throwing the *Hollywood Reporter* in my face and storming out of my office.

Using me for what?

Reason #7: *If your friends, mentors, and co-workers think your boyfriend has ulterior motives, he probably does.*

As Avery left my office, I sank in my chair of delusion and thought to myself . . . it's no problem if I get fired. Soon enough I will be with the man I love and we will tell everyone how happy we are, be a power couple, start our own company, live at the beach, sip Starbucks on a Sunday while watching our beautiful children swing graciously on Santa Monica beach while Sam chases seagulls in the background. My life will soon be complete.

I am on the slippery slope of metal health and denial.

David stands in the doorway of my office. "I'm sorry, Em, I'll talk to Avery and she'll calm down. I'll tell her I trusted you to do the story and that I asked you to do it confidentially. It'll blow over."

I lift my head off my desk and look at my perfect power man. "Dinner?" I ask. "I'll bring pizza and we can have a carpet picnic."

"Can't, gotta work. Maybe this weekend," David says.

Can't? Gotta work? Since when has working become more important than romantic interludes with me? Can't we work together? Or perhaps his work with me is done. I feel him pulling away. Not that I know for sure. I try to stay calm, but I know something is amiss. Perhaps it is the way he looked at me, or rather, looked past me. The way the eye contact tries to convince me, but is empty. Maybe it's the tone of his voice. Or maybe I just instinctively know. I know. I always freakin' know. Yet I am still trying to believe everything is going to be super-duper.

Josh is coming over for dinner. Pizza with Josh substituting for the man of my dreams. See the pattern beginning?

"Why is David behaving so strangely? I called him three times today and he didn't call me back. Why isn't he returning my calls?" I question Josh, who is paying the pizza guy at my apartment. "He's pulling away. I can feel it."

"Em, there's something I need to tell you." Josh takes a slice of pizza out of the box.

"Please let it be that you're straight and you want to save me from this dating hell."

"I am leaving the company to work for MGM as the new vice president of features."

Great! It's not David that's leaving me. It's Josh. He's leaving me in the office without a buffer, confidant. I was once a well-liked, well-respected up-and-comer. My boss called me a up-and-comer. I had supporters. Now my only supporter is about to go to MGM.

"NO! Absolutely not. You can't leave me alone in the office."

"Congratulations might be nice. This is a great career

move for me. Plus, you very well could be fired by next week and this way I can give you a job."

I should be happy for him. I shouldn't make it all about me. But I need him. And *this is* all about me. The slope is getting slipperier.

"You know I love you, Josh, and I am happy that you got a big, bloated job, but my life is falling apart here. Can you help me for one second?"

"Have a drink and a slice, Kitten. It's all going to be fine." Josh hands me a slice and a glass of wine.

After two bottles of wine, Josh tucks me into bed and lies next to me. "Will you stay over? 'Cause I am having the shittiest day."

Josh lies down and puts my head on his shoulder. "Oh, how did it go from blissful, perfect dances, perfect forearms, perfect power plan to 'putter, putter'?"

"Maybe I am overreacting."

"Sure, Kitten, anything you say," Josh says, petting my head until I fall asleep.

Tuesday through Friday I do not see David. I stand looking at myself in the mirror of my office. He is NOT dumping me. Relax. Breathe. In. Out. In. Out. David is not dumping me.

I call Grace from the office . . . get her machine.

I leave a message that goes something like, "David and I were supposed to have dinner twice this week and he canceled. I am going to die. Slowly, but definitely die. Call me. Hurry. It's getting ugly."

Two weeks with no David. Three calls, ALL returning my calls, on my home machine, when he knows I am at work. One canceled lunch. Feeling fucked.

Friday-morning meeting. Ten o'clock A.M. Take my normal seat to the right of David, who sits at the head of the table. Play footsie with him. Run my shoe up his pant leg— he kicks me in the shin.

"OW!" Everyone at the conference table looks at me.

On the brighter side, I am not fired, yet, and I hired a nice new assistant from Ohio who now has become my only ally in the office. I had to do something with Josh gone. Thus, I am paying to have a new confidant. She listens to the gossip and reports back to me. She's loyal, young, and eager.

I am a mentor. A bad, dysfunctional one, but nevertheless, a mentor.

My protégée, JJ, short for Jenny Jacobson, is on the go. She has befriended the other assistants in the office and gotten into the hip pocket of David's assistant only to discover . . .

"He has another girlfriend," JJ says, kind of cringing like a dog about to be hit.

At what point did he start sleeping with another woman? Ugggghhhhhh! Why does the thought of him kissing another woman make me want to hurl myself out of the building? I should want to hurl HIM out of the building.

I throw my head down onto my desk . . . "Am I unattractive?" I ask. "Really, am I?"

"No, no, you're very pretty," she says, trying to make me feel better. "Really."

"There's no real hope for the normal ones in L.A. JJ, I think it would be smart if you went back to Ohio now. Before you start to round up to thirty. Who is she?" I ask. "Just the facts. Be gentle."

I lay with my head on my desk, like a beaten dog, repeating into my headset what I had learned to Reilly.

"A one-hundred-and-five-pound, five-foot-nine—actress—with beautiful brown hair to the middle of her back. A daytime working soap opera goddess." I try not to shout into the phone.

"No-talent slut," Reilly says. "She's not even on prime time."

"I hate her. I hate him. What am I going to do?"

"Nothing. You're going to do nothing. Just finish your day with dignity."

I plot my strategy in the stall of the ladies' room on the third floor. I will remain calm and professional. I will play hard to get and not return any of David's calls. If and when he reaches out I will no longer be available to "help" him. I will grow into a powerful, self-reliant executive who is too busy to be bothered by a no-good, scummy boyfriend with a new girlfriend. Damn good strategy. As I sit plotting, I find myself privy to a nasty conversation between the anorexic casting director, Iris, and the VP of marketing, Julie, about some bimbo.

"She's sleeping her way to the top," skinny casting VP Iris says.

Poor girl, I think to myself, pulling my legs up so they can't see me.

"She's only in her job because she gives great blow jobs," marketing VP Julie adds.

If I could only find this girl and warn her. There is no sleeping your way to the top, only the bottom. Someone in the stall next to me flushes, and I wish I could go down with the water.

Then as they are leaving, the marketing chick mumbles, "It's too bad, because I think Emily could have had a great career here."

Reason #8: *People will talk about how well you perform in bed versus how well you perform your job.*

Tears, hot, salty tears, burst from my eyes and pour down my cheeks.

Reason #9: *Crying at work is unacceptable.*

But I can't help it. Overwhelmed. Alone. Tossed aside. My work discounted. My love unrequited. What am I going to do? I call for major backup . . . my mother, Bitsy, short for Elizabeth.

Two hours later I feel slightly better. Moms are great for reinforcement. My mom is particularly good at reminding me that I am perfect and the rest of the world is fucked, that men predominantely let you down, as my father did to her, yet someday I will meet my prince. She is also taking me to St. Croix for Valentine's Day. Great, only ten months away.

With the girls drinking at Fowz' . . . again. "All I know is that half the day I mope around, the other half I want to kill David, the rest I just fantasize that he is going to show up at my door and beg for forgiveness. Then I will forgive him, after torturing him. Really torturing him. It's official; I have hit the bottom of the slope."

Reilly nods understanding. "When you start fantasizing about what you'll say or do when they come crawling back, you've hit bottom."

Grace adds, "He's never coming back."

Drunk, laying on the hardwood floor next to Sam at home. Dial David. Hang up. Dial again. No answer.

At work I e-mail David, just a simple "Hello," and get nothing back. One month of brief smiles in the hallway and all the while I drown myself in martinis with the girls. I am, however, maintaining the appearance of dignity and self-respect so as not to show that I am dying inside.

Grace is leaving to go out of town with some guy named Mark, who apparently went to college with us, but I don't remember him. Reilly is going on a business trip tomorrow. Josh is superbusy discovering the world of his new job.

I am left with Sam . . . alone, Friday night, without my protective wall of love and friendship. I pour myself a glass of wine and am reduced to another Friday night of bad TV. Take a deep breath, in, out, in, out, and the phone rings . . . probably Grace making sure that I haven't started the drive-bys on David's house.

HOLY SHIT. It's DAVID! He called. He wants to meet.

See, it's all going to be okay. Just like in every movie, they come back. I have faith. He just needed to work his way through a bimbo to come back to the one he is supposed to be power-coupled with. It was one last fling. One last tryst. Right?

I have a sick feeling in my stomach.

I have totally mixed emotions. Here is my chance to tell him that he doesn't deserve a woman like me. Tell him to piss off. Tell him . . . to "come on over"? How did that come out of my mouth? Have I gone off the deep end? Why am I letting him come over? Why can't I say . . .

"GO FUCK YOURSELF!"

Why do I have no self-preservation when it comes to men?

Bath, shave, hydrating mask, finger- and toenail polish touchup, slather makeup, perfume, blow-dry, mist with Evian, squeeze into 501s and a tight white sweater—with apron—as to appear to be cooking. Wine, dinner, candles, fireplace—all going.

I open the door and we stand there gazing, he holds me in his arms, then he pushes me away.

"We have to talk," he growls, only now it's not sexy anymore.

Sitting in my office the next morning, all I can see is David from the night before telling me he was marrying the soap star.

Phrases like "*This is the hardest decision I ever had to make and you'll always have a special place in my heart*" play on a looped tape in my brain.

BULLSHIT . . .

I open the *Hollywood Reporter*, take the lid off my Starbucks and begin reading. There on page one is a picture of my ex-power prince, David, shaking hands with the CEO of our competitor . . . the headline reads:

DAVID JENKINS THROWS IN WARNER TOWEL TO JOIN THE MICKEY MOUSE CLUB

This has to be a mistake!

At the moment I think I am going to throw up, JJ comes in my office. "Avery wants to see you." She puts her head down and walks out.

I immediately call Josh. He'll know how to deal with Avery.

"You never really realize how much someone is shielding you until they're gone," Josh echoes out of my speakerphone. "The mere fact that you were dating—associated with—someone of power meant you were . . . well . . . protected."

"So what happens now?"

"You're fucked. No longer an endangered species and it's hunting season in the PR department. But don't worry, Kitten, you've got a job here."

"I have to go. Anything I should or shouldn't say?"

"My advice would be to throw yourself on her mercy. Good luck."

As I walk through the hallway toward Avery's office, assistants look up at me as I pass their desks. One woman actually peers out her doorway.

I walk past David's office, which is dark and locked up. He is nowhere to be found, Josh was right. I am totally fucked.

"Fired?"

Reason #10: *You get fired.*

Did Avery just say fired?

"You can't fire me for this! That's reverse sexual harassment. I'll sue," I respond. My boss produces a five hundred-page corporate handbook on policy and procedure and sets it on her desk with a THUMP.

I took Josh's advice and begged and pleaded. My boss, a woman, an angry executive . . . my mentor, Avery, gave me a second chance. Maybe it is just a woman thing to grant second chances. I went back to my office with my tail between my legs because it was the only option I had for my future.

Dr. D. hands me a Kleenex. Hmm, I don't remember when it was that I started crying. I blow my nose.

"Why didn't you just quit and take the job with Josh?"

"I had to face the people who stereotyped me and change their point of view that I was the corporate hooker or I'd have no chance. I would be forever whispered about as the woman who slept with David Jenkins. The town's too small. It could be at a party, convention, or in a boardroom, but that is how all of my peers would have remembered me."

"Smart. You didn't run away. See, there's hope for you yet."

Los Angeles is known for many things, but one of its more famous qualities is the ability to change your image. Whether it is a face-lift, new boobs, or your reputation, if you want it bad enough, you will get it in L.A. I needed major corporate image surgery.

"I spent the next year wearing flat shoes and pantsuits to the office, but kept working. No Gucci stilettos, no sexy *Melrose Place* suits, no late lunches. When David got brought up, I admitted my mistake versus screaming at the top of my lungs that I had been duped by the biggest asshole alive. Self-deprecation, humor, and hard work got me through.

"Avery is the one who told me to invest in pantsuits and flats. Thank God for female mentors. Who knows, maybe Avery, like me, had made this mistake and she knew how to survive it. I wasn't alone. I can't be the only one who ever slept with the boss and had the ugly office affair."

"I assure you, you're not. But time's up. I want you to do this again for the next man who didn't work out. Okay?"

I nod.

Blowing my nose in the bathroom of Dr. D.'s office, I study my face in the mirror. Closer, closer. Pat some powder on my red nose, take a deep breath. David hadn't killed me. David hadn't kept me down. I am still here. I smile to myself. Still the same Em, hoping for love, knowing it's coming. I turn and wad up my tissue and shoot it from the three-point range of the sink, and it lands in the garbage. I hold my hands in the air . . . "ahhhhhh!"

Reason #10: *You get fired.*

Reason #9: *Crying at work is unacceptable.*

Reason #8: *People will talk about how well you perform in bed versus how well you perform your job.*

Reason #7: *If your friends, mentors, and co-workers think your boyfriend has ulterior motives, he probably does.*

Reason #6: *If what you're doing for your boyfriend can get you fired, stop doing him.*

Reason #5: *If you have to hide your relationship, it isn't worth hiding.*

Reason #4: *If helping your boyfriend makes you lie to your friends, boss, and mentor, don't help him.*

Reason #3: *That which is considered scandal in a relationship is bad, really, really, bad.*

Reason #2: *If there are kitschy little sayings about the guy you're dating, there is probably a universal reason why it is a bad idea.*

Reason #1: *If your boss is bigger than life in your company, that doesn't necessarily mean he is bigger than life in real life.*

chapter three

Leave It in St. Croix

The Mustang pulls into a spot on Barrington and I run into the Starbucks on the corner of San Vicente for a quick, triple-venti, nonfat, no-foam, three-Sweet'n-Low-latte, stopping for a moment to listen to a boyish troubadour with a guitar praising the notion of sleeping the day away. How decadent, what a wonderful idea. I think for a split second about how opposite that is from my life right now as I shotgun and brace for the boost of energy. The latte goes down hot and fast, like I wish my new boyfriend would, and in moments I am . . .

In Dr. D.'s waiting room.

The door opens and he's right there with that soothing voice, wrapping me up in his Xanax tone. His voice should be a prescription drug. I'm eager to know, "Do you think it's weird that Stan, after three dates, doesn't want to get naked? Doesn't even try?"

"*Weird* is not a behavior adjective I like to use."

"Well, we need to talk about it," I say.

"Where's his list? Have you even thought or tried to write one for Stan?"

I interrupt, "He wore trunks to the beach, which was cool, but when he took them off he was wearing a little tiny Speedo. Granted, he did swim in the ocean for a while, but he was wearing a . . . banana hammock. I think that will bother me after a while. But I am not sure if it qualifies as a reason, it's kinda like the waxed brows."

I change the subject. "Here's my list for St. Croix guy."

I hand it over and slump back on the couch. It feels nice to relax, if even for a moment. My life has been a little hectic lately. My work has become my reason for being.

I can remember a time when work was the furthest thing from my mind.

The time machine races back in my brain, past late nights alone and days spent working off the repercussions of almost a year without David. The white fur fades out of Sam's face back to a time when he was still spry. The stress lines magically dissolve from mine as if Botox had already been approved by the FDA. It had been one year and nine months since I'd had a vacation. I was twenty-seven years young and over the train wreck that was David Jenkins. Prick. Almost a full year spent working late, working early, working overtime. Never complaining. Sucking ass. Being a corporate team player. Believing and creating propaganda was my mission statement. Generous listening was my motto. Only to be promoted to a higher volume of exploded egos and greater stakes.

Grace finished her doctorate in psychology with me as her subject for dating people you work with. I feel very proud to be the topic of her thesis. On our limited incomes, she needed the practice and I needed the therapy. Fortunately her thesis passed. But I am still single. Reilly is dating Bob. She's got a new job, working with Clinique, so she's keeping me rolling in free lip liner and facial skin care products.

Flying to St. Croix, my eyes gaze over miles of blue-green water and white sand beaches dotted with red umbrellas that change to navy followed by green ones. From the air they represent the flags of each resort. I watch a couple riding horses along the surf, sigh, and feel myself slipping into the land of make-believe until I remember that my mom is sitting next to me. Her bright red lipstick reminds me that it's VD, Valentine's Day, as she reapplies after the eight-hour flight from Los Angeles. I shake the ice in my plastic cup and down the last of my Bloody Mary.

This is the perfect escape, just mom-and-daughter time. Beach time, drinking time, playing time. No beefy forearm distractions, tight buns, or tan abs with water dripping off that curve above the hip, that yummy male muscle. God! A year is too long to go without affection or at least heavy petting.

Jesus, enough already! Needless to say, there will be none of that. Just yo-ho-ho and a bottle of rum . . . with Bitsy.

I pull my Ping ball cap down low over my bangs, slip on my dark shades, and tighten my seat belt for landing. A yellow 1970s VW van from the resort picks us up on the tarmac. Mom and I pile in behind the driver's seat with our luggage. The driver, a tan American kid, listens to Bob Marley on the stereo as he drives and looks me over in the rearview mirror. He glances at my mom and smiles back at me. I smile at him, as I don't think he is old enough to be dangerous.

"Welcome to St. Croix. First time?" Driver Boy questions.

"Yes," Mom says. "Do you live here?"

"Yeah, I moved down after college. My parents thought I was going to Georgetown Law, but instead I ended up in St. Croix and never went home. They think I'm in my third year of business law," he chuckles.

Correction, law school age is definitely old enough to be dangerous. Trickery on his own parents can 100 percent lead to trickery on women.

The oceanfront goes by with surfers, locals, and couples lying on the beach. My eyes hidden behind my glasses eventually land back on Driver Boy.

"Are you babes single?"

Just shoot me now. Why does my dating status have any relevance to the boy driver of our van? Why is that any of his business?

"Yes, and we're looking to get grrrooooovy," Mom says, nudging me in the side.

Oh my God. What is going on here? Did my mom just say

"looking to get groovy" to a horny schoolboy? I am not looking to get groovy. I am looking to hide. I am looking for peace and quiet, nurturing from my mother. I am looking for a calm inside, not to get groovy with some trickery-filled slacker on an island who drives a VW.

"You shouldn't have any problems, the scene is full of guys like me willing to show you a good time." The VW comes to a stop. I look at my mom.

"Groovy?" I ask, eyeballing her.

Driver Boy, whom I notice is six foot one, lanky, and hot in his Hawaiian shirt, slides the van door open for me. I grab my bag and jump out as he hands my mom his card.

"Call me if you need," he raises his eyebrows and glances at me, ". . . a ride."

I slam the van door as Mom looks him over. "Thanks, we will."

We walk up the wooden steps to the most beautiful place I've ever seen, Mom wraps her arm around my shoulder and gives me a good squeeze. "I know you wish you were here with a boyfriend, but let's make the best of it," she says as a pretty, tan island girl puts flowers around both of our necks and welcomes us to paradise.

Is it too early to drink?

As if reading my mind, she points to the small bar nestled in the middle of the pool. "Neat."

A tropical paradise, with cool breezes and the sound of the ocean waves crashing on the shore. I am in heaven. I float around the pool on my blue raft with a frozen strawberry daiquiri in hand. Mom plays bunko with a few older women around a bar table.

This is what I needed. Rest. No men, no drama, no problems. Just alcohol, more rest, and more alcohol. I close my eyes and drift off to la-la land.

Second day in paradise. I awake to the sound of a *BEEP-BEEPING* alarm clock, roll over, and look at the time, 7:00 A.M.

I smack it off the nightstand, pull the covers up, and roll over. Scrunching my eyes closed, I pretend that my mother is not scurrying around the room with her long khaki shorts, large straw hat, 35mm camera, video camera, knapsack, and purse in hand.

I scratch my eyes and roll over as she rips the sheets off my body only to realize that I am naked. "Jesus!"

"Up, up, up," she says, on too much coffee.

Did I mention we were sharing a room? My eyes are dry and burning. My head is pounding. Wow, rum should not be put in the same fat frozen glass with fruit juices.

"We are going on a hiking tour of the island. I signed us up yeterday," she adds eagerly.

"No way. I am on vacation, Mom. Leave me alone." I grasp for the sheets.

Thump! My body hits the floor from Mom shoving me off my twin bed with her feet on my bare bottom.

Why, why didn't I spend the two hundred dollars to have my own room?

"It's a hundred dollars a person for the tour and hike.

We're prepaid and I can't get my money back . . . now get your butt out of bed."

She stands with her hands on her hips at the end of my bed. "Your naked butt," she cocks her head at me. "Where are your pajamas?"

I bury my head in the pillow on the floor. "I'll give you two hundred dollars to leave me alone," I moan.

She sits on the end of my bed looking down at me. UGH! I know what's coming. A change in her tactics. Anger and rules never worked with me as a child. Guilt did, and continues to be the way to get me to do anything I don't want to do.

"Em, I don't ask for much. Please, won't you go with me? Spend some time with your ole mom. I want to share it with you. You're my girl." I stand up and my mother looks at me from head to toe.

"Honey, what's happened to your pubic hair?"

"It's a Playboy wax," I say through my teeth in a huff to the bathroom.

"Looks painful," she yells back as I slam the bathroom door.

On the tour bus Mom holds my hand and I have to admit, it's kinda nice. My daughter time. I look around at the people crowded on the seats. A *couple,* middle-aged, snapping photos out the window. A *couple,* elderly, on their forty-fifth wedding anniversary. I know this, as they are wearing T-shirts that say, *It's our 45th anniversary . . . can you believe it?*

Then there's a lovely gay *couple* . . . Thad and Tom, the two Ts. I borrowed sunscreen from Tom in the pool yesterday after mistaking him for straight. The rum dulled my gaydar.

Just my karma that the guy I try to pick up on my "escape" weekend turns out to be gay. I miss Josh. Finally, my eyes narrow on what must be a *couple* having an affair, as I can't see her face. They have had their tongues in each other's mouth for the past twenty minutes. That leaves me . . . and Mom. Jesus, am I going to end up with my mother? Alone, with two dogs, a guest house, and my mother making me breakfast when I am fifty? Perhaps that is it. I'll just enlist for this life with Mom and call off the search for love.

Then my blind, deaf, and dumbness magically vanishes as I notice a tan, blond, mid-thirtysomething guy sitting ALONE at the back of the bus. I look over my shoulder, subtly as not to be noticed, place my hand on my hip, twist, and pretend to crack my back. Wedddddding band? No! No ring. Single. BONUS!

He pulls on a Ping baseball hat. Heeeeellllllo, the same baseball cap I'm wearing. He must be straight with that golf hat on. A single babe on my bus. Why didn't I notice him?

"Say hello, honey," Mom says, pointing the video camera an inch from my face. "Tell everyone at home where we are." I want to smack that camera right out of her hand!

"Hi. We're in St. Croix." Did that just come out of my mouth? Mom hands me the video camera and proceeds to *SNAP.* She takes my picture.

I look back at the babealicious guy and he's smiling at me, giving me a knowing nod . . . like all parents, at any age, were put on this earth to embarrass and humiliate us.

I am struggling to strap on my backpack and Mom's video

camera when Mr. Single-Over-Six-Foot walks past and says, "Nice hat."

Flutter, flutter.

I almost fall on Mom. She shoves me forward down the bus aisle.

"Was he talking to you?" Mom says, watching him through the window. "He's kind of cute. Sweetie, where's his wife?" She has a point. Maybe the wife, girlfriend, gay lover was sick and they didn't want the tickets to go to waste.

Maybe his perfect, size-six girlfriend with long beautiful hair and perfect legs minus any visible signs of cellulite is waiting naked in their bangalow bed for her prince to come home.

The hike begins up the curvy, rocky slope. Mud flies up from Mom's sneakers and lands on my sweaty shins. Bugs and mosquitoes buuuzzzzzz around me. Panting like a dog, I am anything but glamorous at this moment. I hate hiking. I hate this mountain. I hate this island.

Crack! Mom's hand lands hard on my sunburned thigh. "Spider," she says, showing me the gooey remains on her palm.

"They're not poisonous," Hot-Babe-in-Matching-Hat says. "I'm Craig, Craig Kautz from Montana."

Nice green eyes, white teeth. His forearm brushes against me as he helps Mom up a steep, rocky slope.

"Bitsy Sanders, and this is my daughter Emily," Mom adds, wiping the sweat off her brow. "Do you mind taking our picture?"

I wish the spider had bitten me and it was poisonous. Wish I would die. I wrap my arm around Mom and smile. "Sure."

He takes the camera from Mom, looks through the lens, and stops to look at me for a good long while.

I stand, confused, looking back at him. He slowly steps closer, his face next to mine, his green eyes looking deep into me, studying my face, then he wipes a yellowish-brown smudge of something that resembles horrible tropical insect poop out of my hair.

I feel my heart tighten and constrict as I collapse on the ground and die of humiliation. This trip has become a lesson in humility.

"Wouldn't want to tarnish that pretty hair," Craig says, looking back through the camera lens. "One, two, three, say—we're almost off this godforsaken hike."

"We're almost off this godforsaken hike," Mom and I both say, laughing. *Click.*

That was the best picture from the entire trip.

I am pulled back into Dr. D.'s office by the smile on his face. "What?"

"Nothing. I'm just listening. Please continue."

I guess therapists can enjoy a story, too, from time to time. It dawns on me that Dr. D. is human, a man, sitting there listening to my intimate life tale. I file the thought and jump back in.

On the bus ride back to town I learn that Craig is not married, but I hide my curiosity and refrain from digging any further, as I would like to be kissed at least once on this trip. So much for denying my need for men.

"Do you play golf?" he asks, pointing at my Ping hat.

"I played with my ex-boyfriend. He loved to play and I

found after he dumped me that it was the one thing I still liked about him."

"My ex-fiancée hated golf. Hated it when I played. I think it's awesome that you learned," he distantly replies.

Did he say *ex-fiancée?* What makes a person commit to marriage and then decide to call it off?

I realize that I have let too much time go by, and there is now an awkward silence. How could there not be when he just threw that word *fiancée* out there like a damn grenade into my future of eleven days in paradise with Mr. Ping Perfect?

"Well, after I broke up with my boyfriend I kept playing golf. You figure there's thirty-to-one odds guys to girls on the golf course, I like the ratio. And if you're remotely 'okay cute' and can play, it's a great place to meet the other half."

Then there was . . . laughter. Humor, the saving grace for any awkward situation.

"You're absolutly cute, not okay cute," he says, looking directly at me.

Yeeeaaahhh, cute isn't how I feel, covered in dirt, bug poop, and sweat.

But there is something nice about Craig's compliment. Must be the Montana in him. I take a deep breath as Bitsy turns with her camera and hollers, "Smile!"

I feel like an eighth grader. "Have dinner with me tonight?" Craig asks through his frozen smile, waiting for my mom to take the picture. I turn and look at him. He is still looking forward.

"Okay."

Mom's flash goes off.

Sunset over the ocean and Bitsy and I stand at the maitre d' stand, waiting. She fixes the straps on my white, flowy sundress and kisses me on the cheek. "You look very sweet." She smiles.

I give her a little hug. "So do you." Moms can make us feel good about ourselves, but I think we know that they are biased and thus we're less likely to believe them. Bitsy and I walk through the bamboo-and-wildflower-decorated dining room of the resort. We follow the maitre d' to the balcony, where I see Craig sitting alone. He stands when we approach.

He's wearing black linen pants and a cream linen shirt with a white T-shirt underneath, black belt, black casual loafers. No socks. His tan face and green eyes are highlighted by a blond, sun-kissed crew cut. His teeth are great; one of the bottom front left ones is just slightly chipped. Rugged in a cute kind of way. It makes me want to run my tongue over it. He's way hotter and stylish than I ever would have guessed a guy from Montana could be.

I mean, isn't Montana all about open prairies, cowboys, and John Deere tractors? The waiter opens the second bottle of Chardonnay as I watch Craig charm my mom. ". . . from Duke in eighty-six and then got my MBA at Stanford." His eyes catch mine for a long beat while Mom cuts her salmon. "I lived in L.A. for a while and did my time on Wall Street before I got tired of the crazymaking and went back to Montana. Now I help my father manage our family business. It's funny. I spent my entire childhood wanting to get out of Montana and small-town life, but these days all I want to do is be there in the comfort of it. Of my family, friends."

At that moment I knew exactly what he meant.

"What do they do?" Mom seems riveted, as if she's already planning our wedding, and he doesn't even notice.

Like mother, like daughter.

I can barely hear a word. I just want to reach over the table at this point and kiss that incredible mouth. Wow, I need to ease off the wine.

"Real estate, mainly. We own and manage property in Idaho, Montana, Utah. Mainly ski resorts." He turns and looks at me. "Do you ski?"

"Yes, I do, but I really want to try snowboarding," I answer.

"I'll teach you." He cuts his steak. Did he just say he'll teach me? When? When will he teach me?

Reason #1: *Beware of promises made in paradise. Men talk about the possibility of a future with you on a romantic island when you are tan and easy-breezy, but it never makes the flight home.*

"I'm pleased you said that. I was just about to interrupt," says Dr. D. "Be wary of a man who talks about the future when he has no idea who you are, or where the future will take you as a couple when there is no 'couple.'"

"At the time Craig said it, I could see us laughing, snow-boarding, having snowball fights, mauling each other in front of a roaring fire in his mountain house. I snapped out of it, but the damage was done."

"Where'd you go?" Craig studies my face.

"Oh, ah, nowhere." I shake my head, almost embarrassed that he knows I have him naked on a bearskin rug. When the check comes, Craig takes the bill.

"Don't be silly," Mom says, handing him her credit card.

"Ma'am, ladies don't pay," in his best John Wayne.

As Craig walks us out, Mom stops in the lobby. "I've got to meet some of the ladies for late-night bunko," she lies. "Thank you for dinner, Craig. Take care of my girl."

"I will." He kisses Mom on the cheek, and she gives me a good-night wink over his shoulder.

The sand on my toes feels cool and soft. The waves are slushing up onto the beach. The sound of steel drums floats in the distance. We walk for a long time without saying anything, just watching the clear sea brush against the soft white sand under the moonlight. Craig carries my sandals. He stops and looks up at the moon, lays our shoes on the sand, and takes off his linen shirt, leaving his white T-shirt covering his shoulders and chest. He looks even tanner and hotter. "Wanna sit for a while?" he says in a soft whisper.

Yeah! I almost scream. I wanna sit, roll, strip, kiss, and stroke that beautiful tan body.

"Okay." I ease onto the shirt and dig my toes into the sand.

He sits next to me. "How come you haven't asked me why I am here alone?"

I lean back and look up at the stars.

Because I don't want the answer. Because you're about to ruin a perfectly good evening. Because whatever you might say could infringe on my ability to put my lips on yours and my obsession with running my tongue over that jagged tooth.

Reason #2: *When you don't want the answer, it's probably bad.*

"I am just glad that you're here." I smile.

He cocks his head at me.

"I figured you'd tell me when you wanted to. And maybe I didn't want to know the answer."

He leans back next to me and says flatly, "This is my honeymoon."

I roll onto my stomach and run my fingertip in the sand, drawing a "K."

"I met my fiancée at Stanford. She was from Boston. We dated for three years before I proposed. Two of which I lived in New York and she lived in California."

I draw an "I" in the sand.

"Too much distance," I murmur.

"Too much everything," he murmurs back.

I draw an "S" in the sand. Silent and listening. Not sure what to say. Wondering where this is going and when exactly I am going to have to pry his foot out of his mouth. Just wishing he'd shut up and do what men are supposed to do. Where's the pawing? Where's the overt gesture? I am on vacation, for God's sake. I make another "S" in the sand.

"She moved to Montana and hated it . . . hated me," he says reluctantly.

Huh? Wonder what he did to make her hate him?

"I don't know you very well, but 'hate' seems like a pretty strong word." My finger traces an "M" in the sand.

"I wanted her to be happy, not to worry about anything. I told her she didn't have to work. She thought I was too old-fashioned." He leans back.

"Nobody really wants to work," I sigh, "except movie stars and professional athletes."

"That's what I thought. I figured that I would take care of her. And she'd love and take care of me, but she thought . . . hell, I don't know what she thought. Then out of the blue she tells me she thinks my family is too involved in our lives. As if being close to your family is a bad thing."

"I can't really say too much on the whole parent thing, being that I am on a romantic vacation with my mom."

"Yeah, but I like that. I think it's great."

"And, she called me cheap. I watch my spending, but I am not cheap."

Cheap is unacceptable. There will be no cheap. There will be no penny-pinching while dating me. It ranks right up there with not opening the car door on the first date or making your wife take out the garbage. Men need to pay. Pay now, or pay later. But pay they must. It's chivalry. It's courting. It's the fire hoops a man must jump through to prove that he thinks his date is worthwhile and valuable.

"You did buy dinner tonight, so there again, I think the ex is wrong," I dispute.

"I don't know, one minute she's wearing my grand-mother's wedding dress down the aisle and the next she's running out of the church. So I came on the trip alone. To try and sort it out. Maybe have some fun."

"Are you?"

"Am I what?"

"Having any fun," I say, finishing my sentence with an "E." He sits up, letting the moon light hit my little drawing in the sand . . . "KISS ME." And at that point, he finally leans down, scoops my head into his hands, and . . .

He lays a wet, soft kiss on my thirsty lips.

We laid there kissing in the sand all night. We shared all of our war stories of relationships gone bad, of the crazy people out there.

The sun comes up, the light of day, and I can't help feeling like I really, really like him. I have only known him twenty-four hours. What's wrong with me?

Reason #3: *He's not who you think he is.*

Need help. Need distance. Need sanity. Instead I got Mom. She is thrilled, overjoyed that I, her permanently single daughter, the ultimate shitty man-picker, has finally found somebody nice to date her.

My country-to-country call won't go through to Grace and

Reilly. I wonder how Sam is doing at Grace's. I wonder how I am doing. I try to go over it myself. This guy is on the rebound. He's given me warning signs that his ex thinks he's controlling, old-fashioned, and has a buttinsky family. Plus, he lives in Montana. That is so far from L.A. that I am not even sure where it falls on the map. I certainly don't know what twenty below zero feels like. Let alone how it feels day after day for at least 200 days out of 365. Not to mention my friends, who I am NOT willing to give up, or my job, or my life. 'Cause that's where my little "Oohhh, I can't eat, can't sleep . . . Craig this, Craig that," is taking me. Wake up, Emily! I pinch myself. The guy is on his honeymoon . . . alone! Ooh, there's that word again, ALONE. It sounded nice when he was alone on the bus a day ago.

Although it must be hard for him. I can't imagine how I'd feel being alone on my honeymoon. My heart goes out to him and the pain he must be feeling. I could relate to the being-dumped factor. Fucking David the king of Prickville. Hmmm, maybe I am judging too quickly. Maybe I could help, maybe I could fix his pain and . . .

Have fun, have sex . . . use a condom, I think to myself, but don't try to turn Craig into my future husband. This is a fling, a tryst, a booty call. That's all.

"Why didn't you listen to yourself?" Dr. D. probes. "Why couldn't you just leave it in St. Croix?"

"Couldn't tell you," I say. "I guess the 'happily-ever-after' dream was just too strong." I continue my story.

The phone rings. "Hello."

"Wanna go snorkeling?"

A warm glow just washed through my body, making every doubt-filled thought about him disappear like a nightmare in the daylight. "Yes, I wanna go snorkeling."

"Meet me on the beach in a half hour. Oh, and bring Bitsy." He hangs up.

Bring Bitsy? Bring my mom? Ok, a nice gesture, but how about some underwater love? How can I do that if I bring Bitsy?

I realize that Bitsy is standing in the doorway of our bedroom.

"I see your night went well," she says with a smirk and a hint of slur from her triple Bloody Mary brunch.

"Get your bathing suit, we're going snorkeling," I say, jumping up and down on the bed. I launch off and land directly in front of her, doing a little touchdown-end-zone dance. "We're goin' snorkeling." I thrust my hips. "We're goin' snorkeling . . . with my new boyfriend."

Snorkeling with Mom and Craig near the shore, we point at blue-and-yellow-striped fish swimming past us. An eel dangles out from beneath a couple of rocks on the ocean floor. Conch shells grow among the blowing sea grass. It is silent and perfect underwater. Craig grabs my leg and pulls me toward him. Taking our snorkels out of our mouths, we put our heads above the surface and before I can say anything, he kisses me. I wrap my legs around him and we float, just kissing and more kissing . . .

"Do I have those really horrible lines around my eyes and face from my mask?" I squint painfully, waiting for the answer.

"Yeah . . . but it's hard to make them out from the traces of mascara all over you cheeks and under your eyes," he laughs. "But it just makes you cuter." He kisses me. "Sexier." I look up and Mom is back on the beach, packing her stuff. She motions a big thumbs-up at me with both hands. I wave back at her and she heads to the bungalow. "Come on, let's go in." He starts to swim to the shore.

"I'm going to swim just a couple more minutes." I paddle away from him. He looks almost hurt as I stare back at him and mouth through the snorkel, "I . . . have . . . to . . . pee."

"You gotta pee?" I shake my head yes and he swims toward the shore.

The reef is covered in incredible turquoise coral. I want to touch it but am a little afraid it might reach up and grab me. Silly. I float at the top of the water looking down through my mask, studying the pools of bright purple fish next to me. The only sound is the slow, easy rhythm of my breath through the snorkel.

Finally I poke my head above the surface and see Craig standing on the beach in his trunks, and a tingle rushes through my body. I tug down my mask and snorkel and start to swim toward shore. After a few minutes I realize that I am further out than I was when I started back.

I start to kick a little harder. My fins seem heavy. The sound of my breath is a little faster. The current is stronger, and for the first time I realize I am being pulled out.

My breath races faster. I am caught in a riptide. *Try to relax,* I think to myself.

I look back at Craig and can barely make out the concern on his face. His hands rest on his hips. His head is cocked. He turns and races to put on his fins.

I am further out and my breath is sprinting. So this is panic. My God. Now I know how it happens, how people drown. My obituary is going to read: *Drowned in St. Croix, 27, SINGLE, with a few close friends, a renter, and a dog named Sam.*

I am losing the fight to live when Craig's arm reaches out and cradles my lower back, lifting me above the surface. "Relax! Relax! It's not going any further out. It's heading south, to the side. Go with it," he yells sternly.

"I can't."

"You can. You're all right. Trust me!" He holds onto my arm more tightly.

Trust? Trust a man? Now, in the middle of a life crisis? It's trust him or die? Fuck it. I'll trust him. But if I do drown, I want it written that I died because I trusted a hot guy in St. Croix.

I am not sure how long we were in the water. Maybe a half-hour, maybe longer, but it seemed like days. When we finally get to shore, we're a mile and a half down the beach. The muscles in my legs and arms feel like they're full of hot coals.

I sit on the sand motionless, silent, watching the sun go down, unable to think. Then I'm crying, crying with my head between my knees. All the while Craig strokes my back.

"I thought I was going to die," I finally choke out. "I really thought it was over. I mean, all those things people say about your life passing before your eyes." Shaking my head . . . "I didn't have that. There was nothing. Just that, that, I was going to die on a romantic vacation with my mother."

"I wasn't going to let you drown." Craig pushes my hair off my forehead and tucks it behind my ears.

"You saved my life. Oh my God, you saved my life." The realization hits me. A real hero.

We walked down the beach toward the resort, Craig wrapped his arm around me, and I melted into his body. I felt safer than I ever had in my entire life.

"Women often fall in love with policemen, firemen, even doctors who save them due to posttraumatic stress disorder or a superman complex," Dr. D. interjects.

I shoot back, "That was not a superman complex."

"It was."

"I could have died and never told him that I thought I was falling in love with him. Then I thanked him for saving my life and we had sex."

"Of course you did," Dr. D. slowly utters.

"I was in shock, for God's sake!"

"What did he do?" Dr. D. ponders aloud.

"What do you mean, what did he do? Like, did we have foreplay and all of that? Or did we just go right for it?"

"No, after you said you loved him, what did he do?" he pushes.

"Why?"

"Let's pause for a recap, shall we? You can tuck it in your mental files for next time. You had all the information you needed to leave this guy already. Think of these as your dating Cliff's Notes. He's on the rebound, hard. Plus, remember what his ex had to say about him? These are clues, as she obviously knows him. Then he has sex with you at your most vulnerable and weakest emotional point. Afraid of death is about as vulnerable as you can feel. Yet instead of holding you, finding your mom, or better yet, talking you through this, your new boyfriend decides it is time for you to consummate your vacation relationship."

I look at him like . . . what's your stinkin' point?

"Emily, let me ask you a simple question. If you're at home in L.A. and a guy you've had one, count with me, one date with says he's falling in love with you, what do you do?"

It dawns on me. "I'd run."

I'd run scared and fast from the emotional cripple who could fall in love after twenty-four hours.

"Oh shit, I'm that girl. Aren't I?"

"The question is, if Craig didn't run, what type of man did that make him?"

Reason #4: *Beware of the love bug on vacation.*

"Got it," I say before diving back into therapy.

Holding hands with my new boyfriend-to-be at the airport, I can barely say good-bye. Kiss, hug, kiss, kiss . . .

His tan forearms, white teeth, and perfect hair. He saved me. My Prince Charming saved me.

"I'll see you in exactly one month," he says, lifting my chin.

"I'll call you tonight. Okay?" I say, sadness choking my throat shut.

Here is the guy I have finally waited to find. Strong, handsome, funny, single, successful, and I am leaving to go back to L.A. Why? Every night in L.A. is a damn costume party.

Day one without Craig: Sad, lonely. Two hours this morning spent talking long distance to Craig, still in St. Croix. One hour before bed. Then, fifteen minutes more, I had to call back.

Day two: Sad, lonely. Not going out with Grace and Reilly as I am waiting for Craig to get home to Montana so I can call him. Talked to him for thirty-five minutes on his cell phone on his way home from the airport. Later, two hours and fifteen minutes are spent on a call to Montana while he unpacked.

Day three: Sad, lonely. Not going to the movies with Josh. Instead I am waiting for Craig to get home so we can talk. Hurray! He called early. I can take Sam for a pre-mugging-hour walk.

Days four, five, six and seven . . . Sadder. More lonely. I have missed one fabulous dinner party, one press screening with Josh for MGM's new thriller starring George Clooney, and one board game night at Reilly's.

End of week one. Three more to go.

End of week two. I am running out of things to say to Craig on the phone and am slightly annoyed that I have spent the last two weeks a slave to the phone, waiting for it to ring.

Plus I missed sneaking into George Clooney's birthday party this weekend with Reilly! Ugh! Will feel better after I get to see Craig. Must see Craig. Two weeks to go.

End of week three.

HOLY SHIT! I have just opened my AT&T phone bill. $642.18. Yes, 642 fucking dollars. How am I going to pay for this? I think what I could have bought with this. 642 stinking hard-earned PR dollars!

A small price to pay for love. Right?

Reason #5: *Your phone bills could buy you a new pair of Gucci loafers every month.*

Will call Craig and see if he offers to help. I mean, I did pay for my own ticket to go and see him in Montana. He should offer to help with this bill, right?

Just hung up with Craig. My conversation went something like this: "I need to switch my long-distance plan 'cause my phone bill was six hundred forty-two dollars and eighteen cents."

Passive, but what can you do?

"You need to cut down on the calls to your friends," he lets me know in a gruffer tone than I've heard from him before.

"The only long-distance calls are to you." Less passive, more to the point.

"Really, well, then . . . maybe we should cut back on the calls," he says, not offering one red cent.

"Okay, that's good, well, I guess, 'cause I'll be there in a couple days." NO! That's not good. I just caved.

I finish with a squeamish, "Miss you," and he hangs up.

I am pissed that he turned that around on me. I am pissed
that I am stuck paying this bill, that he didn't even offer to
help. I am pissed that I didn't say I was pissed.

Sitting in Dr. D.'s office, I lay back on the sofa and stare
out the window at a hummingbird trying to suck the sweet
nectar out of a flower. "Do you think I should have over-
looked the phone bill thing?"

"No, but more importantly I think we need to look at the
reason you were afraid to tell him you were angry."

Reason #6: *He should have offered.*

In my mind I know the kind of guy I want should have
offered. The fact is, dating is a dance. A dance of courting.
Where men and women are supposed to behave and look
their best. This may not be the way they act in everyday life,
but for the first, let's say, ninety-day period, men and women
are on what I like to call a trial basis.

Driving in Craig's Dodge Ram truck through Montana, I
look from the open meadow to a winding river cutting
through the green valley and I can't help feeling like I have
stepped into a Robert Redford movie.

"I really would love a shower," I say as he carries my bags
into his cozy ranch house.

"Great. I'll show you the way and then start dinner. Would
you like a glass of wine?" he says, cradling me into his arms
and kissing me.

Finally, back in my hero's arms, which are not cheap arms,

but strong arms, loving arms, with lovely forearms. I find myself thinking that maybe the phone bill thing was my fault and at this moment all I want to do is strip off my clothes and lather him up in the shower.

"I am going to throw some steaks on the grill," he says, pouring me some wine and leaving the bottle on the bathroom counter. "Have a bath." He opens the window onto the meadow. "We can eat in an hour." He kisses me one last time, leaving me hot and bothered.

Okay, razor, bath salts, vanilla shampoo, Nair . . . Yes, Nair. Russian waxing lady is out of town. Reilly suggested Nair for all bikini areas in lieu of my *Playboy* wax. I read the directions and apply to sides and top of the "flower" area.

Sitting perfectly still, I pour myself another glass of wine. Two glasses down the hatch and eleven minutes later I gently rinse the "flower" area and like a miracle, I am hairless.

This stuff rocks!

I ease into the bath, pour myself a third glass of wine and begin to lather my hair. As I lay back, I realize that the shampoo smells funny. Not like vanilla at all, more like, well, hummm, like . . .

FUCK! NAIR!

I put Nair in my hair.

Jumping out of the tub, I slip on the floor and bash my shin into the rustic toilet basin. *OW!* I turn on the shower and quickly begin to scrub my hair, slowly looking at my hands for what I am sure will be clumps of hair. I pour half the bottle of vanilla shampoo over my head, rinse, shampoo, rinse, shampoo.

Jesus, that was a lucky call. This, I know somewhere in my heart, is Reilly's fault.

Is this a sign? No. Shake it off. Finish getting ready. I complete the final touches. After slathering, I spray Chanel Number 5 in the air and run quickly back and forth through it. I gloss my lipstick and dab a little lotion behind the ears to insure the powdery smell is everywhere.

I drink the last of the wine, shimmy into a sheer black teddy that barely covers my Naired flower, toss the empty bottle of wine into the trash. Wow, I drank the whole bottle . . . and float down the stairs to the living room. The house is quiet and a slight breeze blows in my hair. I am feeling sexy, confident, horny, drunk. I open the screen to the patio and waltz out to . . .

Craig's . . . mom, dad, two sisters, and two brothers.

SHIT! They are absolutely silent, with their backs to me, all looking though their binoculars at a moose or something in the distance. I slow-creep backward, but before I can get away, Craig's mother has her binoculars pointed directly at me. Craig's dad just dropped his. I am no longer feeling sexy, confident, horny, or drunk. I am the humiliated hooker from L.A. who is now completely sober.

"How could you!" Craig yells at me in the bedroom. I sit on the end of the bed with the comforter wrapped around me.

"I thought we were having a sexy night, just the two of us. I wanted to surprise you."

"Well, that was a hell of a surprise." He shakes his head. "I wanted my family to meet you. You know how important family is to me."

"I just didn't know they were here. How was I supposed to know? We haven't seen each other in a month, Craig."

I can't believe I am defending myself right now. Any normal guy would NOT have his family here for our first night together. Any normal guy would have stuck up for me. Any normal guy would have already thrown me on the bed and made sweet, sweet love to me.

Reason #7: *It was the best it's going to be on vacation.*

I chew my steak silently as I listen to stories about Craig's stupid family all night. I listen about feeding the trout farm, whether it will be an early spring, and to top it all off we have to be in church Sunday morning. Baptists. I am trapped in the backwoods with the Clampetts.

Days two, three, and four are pretty much more of the same. I think he is still mad at me for the naked family exposure incident. At least one of his family members has been in his house at all hours of the day, every day. I have cooked with his mother, cleared the table and washed the dishes with his sisters, while all the men in the family sit in their BarcaLoungers watching reruns on the Game Show Network. Tomorrow is church. I think I have entered the twilight zone somewhere circa 1950.

I am going crazy! I never thought I'd say it, but I have become a California woman. I need my Starbucks. I need drive-through Taco Bell. I need my apartment with Sam. Gay guys, Grace, Reilly . . . I need to be home. Please, someone tell me I am going to be fine.

Reason #8: *If you are rooted, choose carefully where, when, and with whom you replant.*

Breathe. Calm. In. Out. In. Out.

After church Craig's entire family came over for Sunday brunch. Still, no time alone with Craig.

I know one thing for sure. We have nothing in common and I am wondering what we talked about on a beach somewhere in paradise.

Where did that guy go?

Reason #9: *You will spend two months trying to get back to those few perfect days in paradise.*

I change out of my sundress from church and put on jeans and a T-shirt when Craig's mother comes into my room. She is carrying a large white box. "Honey, can you try this on?" She lifts the lid to reveal a WEDDING DRESS. "It was my mother's and I wore it and I expect any woman who is thinking of marrying my son to wear it." But she didn't say it in a sweet way.

I pull the dress out of the box and it looks almost Puritan in style. I force a smile and hang it close to my body. This is not Vera Wang.

No, never. Not going to happen. What the hell is going on here? I look around the room for cameras.

"It's very lovely and quite an honor, Mrs. Kautz, but I think that I would like to pick out something more . . . *me*," I say, gently laying the dress back in the box. "And I think it's a little early to be thinking about marriage anyway."

"It certainly is. I will say, whomever marries my son WILL wear this dress. Got it?"

Momma Kautz stomps out of the room and down the stairs. Moments later I hear Craig stomping up them.

"What did you say to my mother?" he demands.

"Nothing. I said nothing."

"She said you refused to wear Granny Kautz's dress, and that you were, well, rude."

I have had it with this mama's boy asshole.

"I wasn't rude, I just said that I'd like to pick something out for my wedding if and when I ever get married. Why are we even having this discussion? And while I am at it, why is your family still here? Why haven't we been alone in four days? I've cooked you and your family dinner, done the dishes, folded the laundry, and gone to a Baptist church. I can't take it anymore. I want to go home."

I am out of here.

I jump into something that resembles a country cab, Craig leans down in the window and for about one second I think I see a glimmer of the guy from St. Croix . . . Maybe he is going to kiss me, maybe this is all some sick joke. Maybe it is some freaky test or bad reality show . . .

"What will I tell my family?" Craig asks angrily.

Shock. I am feeling utter shock.

"Tell them your fiancée was right!"

Reason #10: *Face it, we're all different on vacation.*

On the plane home I watch square patches of states passing 30,000 feet below and am glad to be above it all. Away from Montana, away from Craig, away from vacation illusions and on my way back to reality and real possibilities.

Reason #10: *Face it, we're all different on vacation.*

Reason #9: *You will spend two months trying to get back to those few perfect days in paradise.*

Reason #8: *If you are rooted, choose carefully where, when, and with whom to replant.*

Reason #7: *It was the best it's going to be on vacation.*

Reason #6: *He should have offered.*

Reason #5: *Your phone bills could buy you a new pair of Gucci loafers every month.*

Reason #4: *Beware of the love bug on vacation.*

Reason #3: *He's not who you think he is.*

Reason #2: *When you don't want the answer, it's probably bad.*

Reason #1: *Beware of promises made in paradise. Men talk about the possibility of a future with you on a romantic island when you are tan and easy-breezy, but it never makes the flight home.*

chapter four

Don't Go Pro

I sit in the outer lobby of Dr. D.'s office with my journal on my lap. I am fifteen minutes late and trying to scratch down ten reasons why it didn't work with Reese. Hmmm, let's see . . .

Reason #1: *He "plays" for a living.*

Reason #2: *He will be sleeping in eighty-one different hotel beds in six months . . . possibly with eighty-one different women.*

Reason #3: *He owns more than one cell phone.*

Reason #4: *By design, he is going to be constantly leaving me.*

Reason #5: *He lives in two different cities.*

Reason #6: *He doesn't read, except for the sports page and the highlights on ESPN at the bottom of the TV screen.*

I giggle, thinking of what Reese's reaction would be if I e-mailed him the list tonight.

Reason #7: *Too much competition makes me batty.*
Reason #8: *Waiting, knowing the game will soon be over.*

Collecting my thoughts, I write again in all seriousness.

Reason #9: *Wondering if I was the only one or a priority at all.*

I stop at reason 10 . . . My pen freezes and I know that I will write no more. I am suddenly angry at the whole idea of writing these lists. All at once I see, through the paper, that I am writing on top of that damn bridal magazine. This is fucked. I hate these lists. I rip the sheet out of my journal.

The doorknob turns and I jam the reasons into my bag before Dr. D. steps out, talking in that Xanax tone of his. "Hi, Emily. Did you bring your reasons?"

"No."

"Ohhhh . . ." he drags it out and finishes with a stern but questioning ". . . kay. You've had enough therapy sessions to know what we need to work on. The lists are important."

I shrug, in full don't-give-a-damn defiance. I must be PMSing.

"Come in. Let's talk."

"Maybe there aren't any reasons for Reese." I stall, know-

ing damn well there are, and plop down into a stationary position on the sofa.

"Of course there are reasons. There are always reasons.
Don't go backward. We are trying to move forward."

"There are lots of reasons, but not like reasons-reasons,
okay? I don't know. Why does it matter what the reasons are
for him? It's," I sigh, "over."

"Is it? Then why are you getting so upset?" He sets his yellow pad to the side.

He knows what I know, that I don't want to put the reasons down. That if I do, it'll kill all hope, that writing all ten
reasons is the same as shooting an arrow through my own
heart and possibility.

"If you're not here to do work, you shouldn't be here at
all. You have to want to be happy, Emily, and getting there is
sometimes painful. I'm not capable of doing some magic
trick that will make you miraculously able to fall in love with
the 'right' guy. I'm not Oz hiding behind the curtain. *You*
have to figure out what you want and go after it."

I remain stubborn and catch him looking at the list, poking
out of my purse. Defiantly I stuff it down into the darkness of
my new Tod's bag, pick it up, and hug it close to my chest.

"Go, then. Take the afternoon. Think about whether or
not you want to be happy."

Wow. Can he do that? Kick me out of therapy when I am
obviously in need of mental help? Even my therapist is now
abandoning me. I'm getting stood up for my therapy date.
This sucks. FINE, fuck him.

I climb into the Mustang and take off for the beach, I can't help but feel like a naughty ninth-grader ditching school in hopes of getting caught so she can get her parents' attention.

I get to Manhattan Beach, a sleepy coastal town a stone's throw from the rat race of L.A. I sit on the sand and watch the waves pounding at the shore the way they have for a million years. I can't help but think that the ocean is God's cardiovascular system keeping us all going. It helps to clear up any confusion I may have had about my own permanence. A jumbo jet takes off from LAX in the distance. A twelve-year-old boy plays fetch with a lab and a tennis ball, hurling it as far as he can each time. A couple of late-twenties women do volleyball drills in the distance.

I look back at the strand behind me and see people gliding by on the bike path. A man pulls a baby in a two-wheel canopy stroller behind his beach cruiser bicycle. His wife roller-skates beside him.

In slow motion I watch her lose her balance and begin to tumble. I gasp a little, knowing she is about to hit sand on slick concrete He reaches out for her, but misses by a fraction of an inch. But as quickly as it all began she catches herself, does a little spin, and skates out of it.

"Nice recovery," I hear him say as they roll away.

"Thanks," she says, and for a moment they hold hands.

My body is standing up. My feet are walking across the warm sand. The key is sliding into my Mustang ignition. It doesn't start. I pump the gas and she turns over. I drive back to Sunset Boulevard and get to Dr. D.'s office just as he's locking up. He takes one look into my eyes. Maybe he knows we are close. Maybe he pities me for the hour-and-forty-five-minute drive back through Friday traffic. Whatever the reason, he decides that now is the time. We are on to something. If not a breakthrough, then at least a meeting of the minds. I hand him the list. It still ends at nine, but at least it's something. My eyes say please. He looks into them and sees the wordlessness coming from my heart. It is time.

So here I am, back on the couch. "That's why I came back," I tell him. "The man on the beach cruiser tried to rescue his wife, he tried to catch her, but he couldn't and then right when I thought she was going to eat it and take out two skateboarders she recovered on her own and skated on. That's me, at my best, on the verge of disaster with help at my fingertips yet somehow I must right myself, I must skate on of my own volition and accord. I can and will stop myself from eating the concrete of life. Sounds weird, but I had some strange connection to the entire episode. Her starting to fall, him trying to save her and missing, and her ability to save herself. It all made sense, like fate's own personal movie for me."

He sits silently, understanding and at the same time looking puzzled, which is the perfect frame of mind for the unfinished story I am about to unload on him.

I look in his eyes. "I want to avoid the fall and help myself recover."

So I begin.

Baseball is supposed to be America's favorite pastime. The players are the darlings of pro sports, those tight pants, great

butts, strong upper torsos—not to mention the forearms—
the legacy of men like Babe Ruth, Ty Cobb, and Roger
Maris. A bat, balls, ins, outs, and apple pie, right? Plus they just
look so nice swinging that wooden stick at ninety-five-mile-
an-hour fastballs in front of all those fans. The crack of the
bat. The smell of fresh-cut summer grass. White chalk on the
dirt. Home runs. Grand slams. Perfect games. Makes it hard
to remember that it's only a game when you read about it in
the paper every day with all the other facts of our time.

Nine months ago I was relaxing with my computer open on
my lap in a small hotel lobby that looked as if it was decorated
by Laura Ashley herself. The drapes, carpet, chairs, and couches
were covered in pale pink, yellow, and green prints of flowers
and paisleys. Lovely on first glance, but after a while I began to
notice the smaller details, like the cigarette burn next to my
black Prada bag resting on the arm of the chair. Hotels, even
really nice ones, are different when you stay there for weeks on
end. You see the stains left by the people who came before you.

I am in Pittsburgh. Avery, my boss, has sent me to handle
the on-set PR for one of our network's low-budget movies.
It has no stars other than a fifty-foot suburban river snake
who feeds on the homeless as part of a government conspir-
acy to rid the city of its unwanted. Need I say more?

I am glad to be out of Los Angeles, even if it is Pittsburgh,
which isn't half as bad as I figured it would be. The people are
friendly, and at 130 pounds I am considered thin where in L.A.
anything over 110 is pushing the high end of the blimpometer.

I haven't had the flutter, been kissed, or had sex with another *person* since Craig nine months ago. Nine months with no physical attention other than hugs from the girls, Josh, and Sam. More than anything, I think I just miss being touched. God, I miss holding hands. But . . .

I am feeling healthy and strong in my independence. By myself and okay in my hotel, where I have plenty of good conversations with Beth the concierge. She's twenty-two with purple spiked hair and thinks that it is "totally cool" that I get to work on a movie set.

After three weeks and four days in the hotel, I find interesting places to work on writing the press kit other than my room. Today I lounge in the lobby after saying good morning to Todd, the front desk manager, and Alan the doorman.

Clicking away on my laptop, I look up from the glowing screen in time to see a six-foot-two, 220-pound all-American dreamboat with dark cropped hair and blue eyes walk off the elevator and head toward the Starbucks at the entrance of the lobby. My eyes follow his strong, beefy, thirty-something shoulders across what must be a fifty-inch barrel chest. Tight abs are clearly visible through his white T-shirt leading down to yummy hips. From the backside, his baggy Lucky Brand jeans add a nice touch to his perfect bubble butt.

Holy . . .

Flutter, flutter.

Batwoman!

I thought I'd be safe in Pittsburgh, but instead I'm stuck, motionless, simply blinking in awe. Cozy in my overstuffed chair, I watch him slip out of sight into the coffee shop.

I am suddenly feeling very, very thirsty for a latte.

Standing in the Starbucks line behind him, I smell his hair, still wet from the shower. I want to reach up and run my fingers through it. I close my eyes and take another deep breath. He smells like hotel soap mixed with sweet Paul Mitchell hair gel and maybe a hint of Hugo Boss cologne. I exhale and open my eyes.

"Your usual, Emily?" the Starbucks girl asks me.

"Yep. Thanks, Jen." I look down, a little embarrassed as Jen yells "triple-venti-nonfat-no-foam-three-Sweet'n-Low-latte."

I step to the side and Mr. All-American turns and smiles at me.

I am taken aback by his boyish face, which has the most perfect, deep dimples and cleft chin that I have even seen. My mouth is agape. I may have shoestrings of drool falling from the sides of my lips. Not sure. Mesmerized. Transfixed.

His cleft could give Kirk Douglas's a run for its money. It isn't that he is model gorgeous. It is about the entire package, equipped with special features that seem to jump out and scream "sexy and sweet and blessed by God."

I am weak in the knees. I haven't felt weak in the knees, well, since David over two years ago. But even when I first met David, it didn't feel like this. There seems to be something unique, something that feels familiar about him, something that just clicked inside me. Weird.

I get my triple-venti-nonfat-no-foam-three-Sweet'n Low-latte before his mocha frappicino is ready.

"It must be helpful to know people," he says with the slightest hint of a Boston accent.

"And be a good tipper," Jen pipes in.

"With a nice smile," Ted the coffee guy adds as he hands me my drink.

Group support! Couldn't have planned it any better.

"Thanks." I can feel the blood in my cheeks. I wonder if I am red. I can't help but give an ear-to-ear smile at Mr. All-American with the man-boy face and walk away.

Be calm, subtle, coy, not too flirty.

I look back over my shoulder at him and . . .

WHAAAPPPP! My nose hits first, followed by my forehead, as the door to Starbucks is closed and I have just schmooshed into the glass. I am the crash-test dummy in the head-on collision minus the airbag plus the piping hot coffee. It shoots all down the front of my white sweater.

Fuck! Fuck-n-A!

"Hot, hot, hot, hot, hot! Ow, ow, ow!" I grab a bunch of napkins as American Pie Dimple Man watches me try to shake the coffee out of my sleeve.

"Are you okay?" he asks.

"Yep, perfect. I think it's more of a second- than a third-degree burn. I'll be fine."

He walks toward me and I nervously scoot out of his way. Jesus, he must be six three. Wow! He reaches for the glass door and holds it open.

I am frozen, looking up, studying his blue eyes like a schoolgirl with a crush until I realize he is holding the door for me.

GO! my self-respect silently screams. I read the sign like a runner on second heading for third. The third base coach is sending me home. I hit the bag and run for it. The throw is on the way. There's a play at the plate. Did we win or am I, more than likely, once again out?

"Thanks," I say with coffee all over me.

He stands outside Starbucks, sipping his cool frozen frappy, watching my knee-length jean skirt and coffee-stained sweater cross the lobby.

Slumping back into the chair with my computer, I feel defeated. I blew it. Head low, I eye the brown stain growing on my favorite white sweater.

Carefully, I rest my coffee between my thigh and the inside arm of the chair, then begin again to read my computer screen.

Unbeknownst to the homeless who use the river to bathe in, a scientifically designed river snake has been covertly added. It has become a game of cat and mouse as Walter, the mayor of the river shantytown, has learned that the government is responsible.

Wow. That sucks. I hit the delete button, look up, and Mr. All-American Perfect Dimples is peering down at me.

I smile back. He sits in the chair across from me.

All is not lost!

I wonder if he knows that his smile could melt Cruella De Vil's heart.

He drinks his coffee, opens a *USA Today,* removes the sports section, and begins to read. His eyes glance over the top of the paper. I can feel him looking at me. I continue to type on my computer.

jflhalgklhdkljalkhdgljalkhglkhalkhglhljak

I stop typing and glance up. We are looking directly into each other's eyes, separated only by three feet of oak table and four feet of bad carpet.

He doesn't look away. He just keeps gazing into my eyes as if he knows me. Our moment of eye contact has gone on many seconds too long. Yet neither of us look away.

"R-r-r-reese," a Cuban guy says, approaching, rolling the R. "R-r-r-r-reese."

My future Mr. All-American boyfriend looks up.

"We going hor-r-r what?" the Cuban guy demands.

Reese looks back at me, flashes a pearly-white grin with just the slightest hint of shyness, and gets up with his paper tucked under an arm. Fidel Castro's cousin leads him away. UGH!

This is that defining moment, the moment when you pass a perfect stranger in the crosswalk or perhaps waiting for a cab and . . . you know.

You know somewhere in your heart and soul that you are connected to that stranger. Maybe it is because we are all connected in some way. Perhaps we knew them in a past life. I am not sure what gives us that feeling, but it was definably there with Reese. It was powerful, and it was real. The question that must be answered in a split second was to play it safe and just stay silent, walk away alone in the metaphorical crosswalk of life, left to wonder, "Was that my soul mate?" or risk making a total fool of myself and get shot down by a complete and utter stranger.

"Make it a great day," I say as he walks away.

Slowly, he turns and looks at me. I glance at his back foot as it twists unconsciously into the carpet.

"What?"

"I said, make it a great day." I'm feeling really stupid now.

"What's your name?" he says, low and sweet and slightly bashful.

"Emily. Emily Sanders." I stick out a hand over my computer.

He shakes and holds it.

Electricity just shot through both our bodies. I giggle.

"Reese Callahan. And Emily Sanders, you have already made it a great day."

He lets go of my hand, shakes out his arm, and then grins that grin that says, "Yeah, I felt it, too." "Nice meeting you." And walks away.

"It has been two days since my lobby encounter with Reese Callahan. What kind of name is that?" I ask Jimmy the bartender as he sets down a martini in front of me. I look up at ESPN *Sports Center* on the TV above the bar.

"Irish," says a voice behind me. I don't turn around. I just look at Jimmy.

My face scrunches. "About six foot, dark hair, nice smile?" I ask Jimmy. Jimmy nods.

"Emily Sanders." Reese pulls out a barstool. "May I?"

I gesture to the chair like Vanna White turning a vowel on the letter board.

"Corona," he says to Jimmy, "with a lime, please, if you've got one."

That was how it started between Reese Callahan and I. The beginning.

Sitting at the bar, 1:14 A.M., Jimmy is putting the chairs on top of the tables. Reese asks him for two Coronas and we head upstairs. He is walking me to my room.

I open my hotel room door and can feel him brush against me as he holds it open.

"Do you want to come in for a minute?" I try to sound like Marilyn Monroe, but it comes out sounding more like of a low-talker. Who am I kidding? A minute. An hour. A night. A lifetime.

"Sure." He follows me in and looks at the pictures of my mom, Grace, Reilly, Josh, Sam, all framed next to the computer on my makeshift desk in the corner.

"Great dog. What's its name?" he says, studying the picture.

"Sam." I pop my Corona and open his.

"Thanks." He sits down on the edge of the bed.

I sit down next to him. Both of us drink our beers on the foot of my king Serta as awkwardly as high school freshmen. "So, are you in town on business?"

"Yes, I am. Three days. I leave tomorrow."

My face must have changed because his expression turns sympathetic and knowing. "I'll be back in two weeks. Will you still be here?"

"I've got three weeks and five days left in the lovely

William Penn Hotel. Then it's back to California, and maybe Arizona to visit the family."

He starts laughing.

"What?" I'm embarrassed I might have said something wrong.

He pokes himself in the chest. "Iiiiii live in California and Arizona." He shakes his head in disbelief. "I knew there was something familiar or, hmmm . . . I dunno know . . . something about you"

"Where?" I ask.

"San Diego part of the year and Scottsdale the other part."

"Almost perfect. I live in L.A. and my family is in Phoenix. Why do you go you back and forth?"

"Work," he says. "I work in San Diego and live in Scottsdale."

"That's one hell of a commute."

He sets his empty Corona down on the night table and gets up. "Can I call you?"

"Are you leaving?" I quickly stand and throw my body in front of the door, blocking any possibility of his escape. The door is now to my back. There's one way out and that is through me. We are face to face. I look up into his blue eyes. We stand for what seems like an hour in an instant.

Is he going to kiss me or what? I can't take it anymore. I move to the side because if I don't, he may sense my need to rape and pillage him. He touches my hand, wrapping it in his. "Where ya goin?" he asks as he gently lifts my chin, leans down, and presses his lips to mine.

Wet. I am wet. I am frozen, hot, and bothered. There is no other kiss that has ever been better. Slow, tender, my breath in his. Breathe. I almost fall back onto the wall. Yet he pulls me close, catching me, keeping me safe, engulfing me in his body, his huge, strong, perfect body.

I sooooo want to throw him on the bed even if just to cuddle into him for a lifetime! But I must appear to be a nice girl. Wait, I am a nice girl. I just want these feelings to keep tingling me that way!

His smile grows on his perfect face with the perfect dimples. "Emily, I'll be back in two weeks, but we have tonight. Let's just take it slow."

He eases me down on the bed and lies next to me. He props himself up on his elbow, and we begin a conversation that keeps me listening and asking questions for hours. Who is he? Why do I feel like I've known him for a lifetime?

Reese grew up outside Boston, in a small town with three brothers and one kid sister. He loves dogs and kids and romantic movies. I can't really explain it, but he feels like the yin to my yang. We stayed up kissing, talking, and hoping all night that the sun would never come up. Hoping that this connection would never go away.

When the sun finally did come up, I wasn't tired in the slightest. We had talked, laughed, and kissed all night. I roll out of his arms to pee and brush my teeth. I shut the door to the bathroom and look in the mirror. My cheeks are rosy and glossy. My eyes have a hint of sparkle. I sit down on the toilet thinking to myself, *This is it, finally.* I flush, wash my hands, and stroll out of the bathroom.

He is gone. "Reese?" The room is empty and deadly silent. Sun peaks through the heavy drapes. My pulse increases. My shoulders drop. I sit on the edge of the bed feeling an overwhelming sense of abandonment. Did I dream it? Then . . .

A knock at the door. My heart leaps. I jump up, swing open the door, and there he stands, holding a Starbucks coffee.

"Triple-venti-nonfat-no-foam-three-Sweet'n-Low latte." He holds out my drink. "Oh, and don't think your buddies at the coffee shop didn't know who I was buying this for at six A.M."

The best. He is the best. I stand in the doorway, not wanting him to go. I take the coffee and he kisses me one last time. "Make it a great day," I say again, for the second time. He smiles, hugs me, and walks off. "Wait." I pull on his sleeve. "You never told me what you were doing in Pittsburgh."

He waited two or three good long seconds. Jesus, these pregnant pauses of longing eye contact are going to kill me. Then, almost afraid of all of the stereotypes, all of the questions, all of the innuendos, he throws it out there. "Playing the Pirates."

"Huh?"

"I'm a pro baseball player. First base, San Diego Padres."

And just like that, he was gone.

The door to my room shut, my head was racing, and my heart sank.

I lay back down on my bed, feeling miserable.

Looking up at Dr. D., I plead with him for insight. "How did I shove a lifetime of dreams and who I really am, or better yet who Reese really was, or who I wanted him to be, into one night?"

"Keep going," he says. "We'll figure that out later."

"For me, the worst thing in the world is being left. I don't like to be left. I hate it, despise it, would rather face anything than the fear of abandonment, and Reese, as great as he seems, was destined to be leaving me ALL OF THE TIME!"

"You're not still in touch with him, are you?" Dr. D. asks, interrupting the flow of my thoughts.

There it was, out there, the defining moment of whether to lie to my therapist. Truth. I choose truth. I choose good mental health.

"No. Not technically, at least. We e-mail sometimes. Mainly just jokes. I think it is his way of just making me laugh as somewhere inside he knows I am still hurt."

"But it's over?"

I nod a sort of yeah, I guess, YEAH, it's over, nod.

"We'll figure out why you're still e-mailing, then." He writes a note and encourages me to continue.

I was completely enthralled with a man who was destined to be shutting the door on me seven months out of twelve. I knew what it meant to me. For me.

This created "issues." I know this. My friends know this. I need a man who is home, someone normal, someone who isn't leaving all the time. And there are all those stereotypes about ballplayers having a woman in every city. Eighty-one road games. Eighty-one nights in hotel beds. Eighty-one nights left to wonder if your boyfriend has his penis in another woman.

That night I get home to my hotel room after shooting scenes of the river snake eating locals, open my door, and smell nothing but roses from the moment I walk in. The entire room is filled with red roses. There must be six or seven dozen. I leap over the bed and rip open the card in the vase on my desk.

You make my day great. XOXO, Reese. Roses. I haven't gotten roses, hmm, ever. He is too amazing to be true.

Reason #10, *and although I try to shoot it down as pessimism before it can form, it pops into my head: If your man seems too good to be true, he probably is.*

Maybe we were just destined to fall in love. I have finally found my soul mate.

I dial Grace. "Hi, it's me. What're you doing?"

"What's wrong?" Grace says with worry in her voice.

"I'm in love!"

Grace questions, "I talked to you two days ago. You're not in love."

"Love, love, love."

"Lemme guess. An actor? A Clooney lookalike." She pauses.

"Nope." I smell my roses.

"Director?"

"Nope."

"Producer, camera guy, best boy?"

"Nope, nope, nope."

"Em, what's a best boy?"

"I dunno know." I plop down on the bed, spinning a rose in my fingertips. "He's a baseball player." Ow. A thorn pierces my thumb. I stuff it in my mouth and suck it.

Silence.

"Did you hear me?" I ask.

"Oh, I heard you. I am just trying to figure out at what point I need to get on a plane and come out there for an intervention. How far gone are you?"

"He lives in Scottsdale."

"Oh shit, you're planning the wedding. What happened to taking it slow?"

Maybe she's right.

I instantly hang up on her.

What the hell am I doing? I've known this guy less than twenty-four hours and I'm planning our retirement in Arizona. Mental. I am mental. Two hours, one bath, and one Band-Aid from thorny rose later . . . my phone rings.

"Hello."

"Emily? It's Reese." I can hear the other players on the bus talking and celebrating in the background.

"I just got the roses. They're beautiful. You didn't have to do that."

"Well, I figured they'd live in your room long enough for me to at least get back. This way you won't forget about me."

As if that's ever going to happen.

"That's so sweet."

"You deserve them. I gotta go. We just got on the bus and

we're heading to the hotel. I gotta call my parents and I'm beat, so I'll talk to you tomorrow."

"Well, thanks again for last night and today and the roses."

"No problem. I'll call you tomorrow, bye."

"Bye." I hang up.

Why do I feel sick?

The phone rings again. I pick it up halfway through the first ring. It's Grace and Reilly three-way-calling me. They sound like they've got a game plan. I can tell they've conferred and strategized.

"You should have known, you big fat bonehead," Grace says into the phone. "Better yet, you should know now. If you know your issues, which you do, Em, and the guy you date pushes these buttons knowingly or unknowingly . . . Don't date him! 'Cause he's going to make you batty."

"Ahhh, but I can still smell him on my pillow," I counter. "And the room is full of . . ."

"I sense a train wreck," adds Reilly on the other end of the three-way call.

"I haven't figured out what about Reese is making me nervous." I flop back on the bed and write the plusses and minuses of dating Reese while I listen to the girls.

"Nausea, headaches, and sleepless nights are your body's way of telling you what's going right, or wrong," Grace says. "Your body is the first thing to warn you, and in nine cases out of ten, when you feel nervous energy, there is a reason to be nervous."

My focus moves from her ever-more-frantic voice to my

list. Plus column: Hot, sweet, funny, seems family-oriented, tall, dark, handsome, calls, sends flowers.

And the minuses: Is not here, could have an account at 1-800-FLOWERS, is too hot, and has a job where senseless women hurl themselves at him, thus making my ploy to "hold out" not productive.

". . . Wait and 'suss it out,' " Reilly finishes.

For the next two weeks, Reese and I talk on the phone twice a day, once when he is going to the field for practice at around 2:00 P.M. and the other time when the game is over and he is either heading out on the town for the night with the boys or to his hotel room, depending on whether they win or lose and whether he hits or strikes out.

Day fourteen. Exactly 336 hours and 24 minutes since Reese left.

Is it love or obsession when you know how many hours it was since you last saw him?

I am delusional. But, on the phone I have learned every detail about Reese's three brothers, one sister, their wives, husband, families, and his parents, who are still married. A bonus, as it means he knows that commitment and relationships take hard work and love.

Of course that could all be wrong if, say, Reese's parents HATE each other, sleep in twin beds on opposite sides of the house, and never talk.

Other tidbits I have learned . . . He had trouble in school with academics, yet graduated from college. Had one serious girlfriend in high school, another when he got drafted, and a psycho girlfriend who currently wants to kill him because he broke up with her and, apparently, she didn't think the game was over.

Another reason breaks through my mental defenses while I sit on the couch in Dr. D.'s office. Is it bad if an old girlfriend, ex-wife, or even female friend has cause to want to shoot my new boyfriend in the head? The thought happens before I can stop myself from thinking it. But it never gets vocalized. The ex knew everything I had to learn. Just like with Craig. Remember, not every ex-wife, ex-girlfriend is a crazy, drama-filled, needy, money-grubbing, lying slut. Be wary of men who hate their ex and be warier still of an ex who hates your man. I learned that one already. I'm starting to see more patterns.

I will say here, just as a side note, that Reese and I have something. I am not sure if it is the "flutter, flutter," or if it is chemistry, history, past life, something, anything, but there is a connection. A familiarity. A strange, cosmic connection that we both feel and share. Is the connection enough? Or is it just the universe recycling past love? Whatever the answer is, it has me totally convinced that this guy is going to steal my heart.

And unlike Craig, he isn't boring on the phone, nor will I ever run out of things to say to him. Another bonus.

He's supposed to get in at 7:30 P.M. They had a day game in Milwaukee.

I go through my mating ritual. Take a bath in vanilla bath salts, shave legs and armpits, Nair bikini line, pluck the brows, slather in lotion, makeup, hair, Evian mist on face so as to appear to be moist with translucent skin. Jeans, gray sweater, Ping ball cap. My typical trickery.

6:56 P.M.—in the hotel bar, waiting. Ordered one glass of red wine.

7:35 P.M.—in the hotel bar, waiting. Finished the glass of red wine that has turned my teeth purple. Switched to Kettle One martini, dirty.

8:01 P.M.—in the hotel bar, waiting. Have moved from the bar stool to the couch to get away from scary, bald Pittsburgh cop who is hitting on me. May appear to be call girl.

8:55 P.M.—feeling kinda good . . . and warm and fuzzy. On my third martini.

9:40 P.M.—I am sleepy.

1:10 A.M.—head pounding, hair stuck to the side of my face, shoes off, laying on hotel couch, passed out as Reese shakes my shoulder. He's blurry. Ow! My head. I am filled with a mouth of cotton.

Where's the Kool-Aid guy when you need him?

"How long have you been down here?"

"Not long. I am thirsty, very thirsty," I say as I roll up off the couch and look at the mirror on the wall. "AAAAHHHHH!" I have mascara under my eyes, lipstick on the side of my face, lines imprinted on my cheeks from uncomfortable polyester pillows. My eyelashes are bent and I'm pale. Very pale.

This isn't at all how I planned it in my head.

That night Reese walked me to my room and gave me two Tylenol and a bottle of Gatorade out of his bag before he tucked me into my bed, alone.

My phone is ringing. Or maybe it's my head.

"Hello."

"Hey, I was just checking to see how you were feeling this afternoon." Reese says.

"Afternoon? What time is it?" I roll over and look at the neon clock radio.

Twelve forty-two P.M.

"Wanna grab a coffee before I go to the field?" Reese asks.

"Sure, just gimme a half-hour to shower and I'll meet you in the lobby."

"I'll come get you. I don't think I want you in the lobby alone again," he laughs and hangs up.

In the elevator, I looked him up and down out of the corner of my eye. Something about him warmed me inside. Made me feel alive. I realized I was smiling unconsciously. I looked away, and he took my hand in his as if to say, I am glad to see you, too. I was happy we didn't have sex yet. At least one thing is going slow. We made a date for that night and he got on the bus to the field.

We met in the lobby at 10:15 P.M. They lost, but somehow I felt found. We shared a vegetable beef soup and some cheese bread, then went back to my room and kissed and rolled around. For three nights he is in Pittsburgh and it is awesome . . . but I am afraid because in the back of my head, his leaving is looming. He is always going to be leaving me after four perfect days. He is going, going, gone.

The river snake is dead. The movie is wrapped and I have not seen Reese in one month, but we have talked on the phone every day, twice a day, since he left Pittsburgh. Almost seven weeks of sharing every intimate detail of our lives and five days of smooching, but no sex. Both of us are dying to do it, it's just, well, I think it might push me over the emotional well-being line, and he understands that.

I am heading to see him in San Diego. I am going for it! I am putting my fear aside and giving love a chance.

I sit on the aisle seat of an American Airlines M80. I choose the aisle seat to get off more quickly so I will not waste a second of time with my man. I am consumed with excitement.

I walk the jetway. My legs are weak. I hit the open terminal and see him. I am suddenly aware of the blood surging through my body. He is perfect. Smiling. There. Real. Mine. In the flesh. We have a giant hug, followed by a long, wet kiss. We are that couple in the airport terminal, stopping the flow of traffic, that everyone hates.

We barely make it into his apartment in San Diego before tearing each other's clothes off. We fall onto the living room floor and make love for the first time, and it is amazing, sensual, and intimate.

I wake up at 3:10 A.M. and look at him. His eyes are open and he grins at me.

"I am so happy that you made the trip. You make me, well, feel like, like I want to hold and protect you. I felt it when I first saw you," he says, spooning me close to his warm body.

"I know, me, too," I sigh and think this is what heaven must feel like before falling back to sleep.

Walking on the beach in La Jolla with Reese, we stop at a

cute Italian restaurant and have lunch. It's nice to relax. It's his off day, so we get to play without him hurrying to the field. We order a bottle of wine and hold hands in silence as little kids build sand castles. After a bowl of cream-filled fettuccine alfredo pasta with garlic bread and polishing off the bottle, we walk along the water's edge, letting the cool, salty water hit our toes and sober our thoughts. I sit down in front of him on the sand, in between his legs, and he wraps his entire body around me as we watch the sunset.

The next days are equally blissful. I usually drive him to the stadium in his Range Rover, drop him off, and return later for the game.

Tonight as we pull into the player's parking lot he makes me stop an extra second at the security booth. An old black man emerges.

"Hey Earl, I want you to meet someone."

Earl leans into the driver's side and looks at me in the passenger's seat.

"This is Emily. Can you keep an extra-special eye on her? She's my girl."

Earl stutters, "Weeeeeellll, Re, Ree, Reeesse, anan anny girl of of of yours, is pp pp pprecci prreicous precious cargo."

"Thanks, Earl. All my best to your kids."

"Nice meeting you," I say.

"Y, y, you, too." He smiles a big, honest good-bye.

Being at the games is amazing. It is a different perspective than just being a fan. There is a desire to cheer just slightly louder. Sitting in the "family seats" isn't as bad as I thought it would be. Mainly I just go alone and keep to myself. After listening to the wives talk about vacations to Bora Bora and Rolex watches, well, I don't seem to have much in common with them. Mainly, I have a job. Which after this two-week break is over I will need to get back to. For now I just sit in the stands watching Reese make play after play, feeling lucky and proud. He's a good man.

End of week two. Things I have noticed:

1. Woman's hair clip in bathroom drawer. Which, okay, he could have had a girlfriend before me. Completely normal.
2. One thank-you card inside drawer from someone named Molly. Molly could be a fan, a friend, or a sister-in-law.
3. Two cell phones. I only have the number for one.

Reese has two cell phones. Why? Why two? I mean, who the hell needs two cell phones? Why is the one that I don't have the number to ringing all the time? Why doesn't he answer it? Is that my fear? My innate womanly instinct, insecurity, or is it real?

More important, my nausea is back. Maybe Reese isn't doing anything and I am just a paranoid freak judging a guy who has been nothing but loving to me. Yet something is eating at me.

I drop Reese at the ballpark, arrive back at his apartment, and call Reilly, who can at the very least sympathize with me for my obsessive suspicion or, well, inability to feel *good enough*.

"He has two cell phones and it's making me crazy," I say, digging into his drawers.

"Lemme call you back. I am on with the stupid cable company. Two minutes. I'll call you right back. Gimme the number at Reese's," Reilly says.

"Call me back!? I am having a situation here!"

I give her the number and proceed to go off the deep end. I start looking, digging, really. Inspecting. I have been long-distance-dating him for one month, in San Diego thirteen days, and I am now acting like a jealous wife. This is how the terminology "acting like a woman" became negative.

Seriously, someone help me. I rationalize looking at the return addresses on his mail by thinking that everyone has, at one time, felt the madness I am feeling. Fucking condoms in the bag. Searching the drawer in the nightstand I find books. Books I sent him . . . inscribed and signed, xo, can't wait to see you. Emily.

Why are they hidden under the pillowcases in the night-stand?

KY JELLY!!!

Where's his overnight bag? I rummage through the closet.

Ahh, relief, pictures of me on the movie set, in the hotel, pictures I gave him of Sam and I . . . WAIT. An envelope. A card. More pictures . . . the card reads . . .

As the sun sets I am reminded it will be another day without you. Maybe I'll see you in Houston. Love, Molly. It's fucking dated two fucking weeks ago! And if that is not enough, there are pictures of MOLLY at her house, at her work, and with her dog. SICK! I am going to throw up!

Where's Reilly? RRREEEIIILLLLLLYYYYYY! I sit, shaking on his bed. I call Reilly back and start to pace.

"Piccturress. He has picturreees."

"What? What pictures? Calm down. Breathe. Breathe," she says.

"I found pictures of another girl, a card, and condoms in his . . . his . . . his fucking overnight bag." I take a deep breath.

"Is that why you didn't answer the phone? I've been calling every five minutes for the past half-hour," Reilly says.

"What?" I sit down, thoroughly confused. "The phone didn't even ring."

We both sit silent for a second, then Reilly blurts out in a low tone, "Check the ringer on the side of the phone."

I roll the phone on its side, and the ringer is turned OFF. "Em, Emily, are you there?"

"Hold on."

I run through the apartment checking each phone, and ALL of the ringers are turned OFF!

"They're all off. Every fucking last fucking one of them." My tears are turning to anger.

"Fucking cheating, lying piece of shit!"

"Ballplayer," Reilly says. "Get out of there. Call a cab. Go to the airport in San Diego and fly home. Call me back. I'll pick you up."

I sit there silent. Maybe he is trying to protect me. Maybe

there aren't other women. Maybe I misread him. Maybe I don't have the right to be jealous. But what he said about holding me, protecting me . . . confusing. I am scared. I am angry. Heartbroken.

"Emily, GO!" Reilly yells at me.

I am now officially awake from the dream. My fight-or-flight instinct just kicked in and I am all out of fighting. It was a dream I so wanted to be true. I pack my bags and call a cab. Am I wrong? Am I running? Am I just afraid? Am I giving Reese a fair shake to explain himself?

As I hang up with the cab company, the phone rings . . . as the fucking ringers are now turned on!

"Hello," I say tentatively.

A woman's voice timidly responds, "Is Reese there?"

"No. Lemme guess. This is Molly," I say with disdain.

"No, it's Hillary. Tell him to call me on my cell."

I do not leave an explanation. I simply leave Molly's card and pictures out, scattered on the living room floor, with a Post-it that says, *Call Hillary on her cell*. I think he'll get the point.

He doesn't deserve to see my puffy, red eyes.

I step off the Southwest shuttle and the sight of Reilly and Grace standing there is overwhelming. Tears burst from my eyes. Grace wraps her arms around me. Reilly takes my bag, wraps her arm around my other shoulder, and together the girls walk me through the airport like security guards flanking their fragile bundle.

That night I rub Sam's furry muzzle, resting on the side of

my bed, and look over at the phone, secretly waiting for Reese's call, his apology, his explanation.

I make Sam climb up on the bed so I can spoon him. I run my hand over his barrel chest and find a lump underneath his thick coat. I sit up and examine him. He looks me in the eye with an "I'm okay mom" look. I study my pup for a minute. There is something perfect between people and their dogs. He licks my face and rolls into his spot next to me. The phone rings. Once, twice . . . Sam and I stare at it.

I hesitantly reach to pick it up, and it stops in mid-ring.

I lay there motionless, staring at the phone.

Sam runs his snout under my hand to pet him. I give him a scratch on each side of the muzzle and click off the light.

In the darkness I wonder if it was him, I wonder if I didn't give it enough time, an explanation, or an ending. I mean, there is something about him.

I guess a better question is, I wonder why I still care and how long that's going to last?

chapter five

Gay/Straight

I pull into the parking structure beneath Dr. D.'s office, multitasking on the cell phone with Reilly, discussing final preparations for Grace's Halloween-themed bridal shower while applying lip liner. This is the moment of truth. We know that Grace will either think we are incredibly clever or in horrifically bad taste to have orange-and-black invitations that will ultimately land in some wedding scrapbook to forever torture her.

Walking into the office, I am sort of giddy at the thought of Grace's reaction.

"Where's your list?" Dr. D. asks.

"That's it. No more lists. That's how I got here, a guy in the office, a guy on vacation, and a baseball player (my soul mate whom I ran away from having no idea if it's his fault or mine, but then again, does it ever really matter?). Can we talk about my new guy?"

"How's work?"

"Good. I had my review last week. They made me a vice president. I got a raise, gave JJ a promotion, and have what may be a potential new boyfriend," I ponder out loud. "There's only one reason I can think of right now that it may not work with Stan."

"What's that?" he asks, as flat and clinical as a cold stethoscope on my warm chest.

"Can I start at the beginning?"

"All right, fine."

"I've given you tidbits, so you already know a little, but let me start from the first time I saw him again after the fundraiser . . ." I lean back on the couch.

Official date number one: We meet outside of Rebecca's for lunch, an upscale Mexican restaurant on the beach in Santa Monica. He's wearing khaki shorts hanging low on his hips, a blue T-shirt, and flip-flops, beachy, cute. My favorite white sundress flutters in the breeze, conforming to the curves of my body. It's that rare moment when I believe I look good, instead of weighty at 133 pounds, and he is missing the moment.

We eat fish tacos wrapped in corn tortillas, salty chips, and salsa with green chili peppers. My mouth is on fire, but I wash it down with Coronas and limes. Which of course reminds me of Reese. Ugh! I love Mexican food; must be the Arizona girl in me.

After lunch we walk across Ocean Boulevard and head toward the Santa Monica Pier. The lights of the rickety wooden Ferris wheel sparkle and reflect off the dark blue ocean, adding a magical contrast to the orange and purple sunset. Pine, tar, and salt water are in the air. We play skee-ball and shoot water guns at balloons in carnival booths. It's a date, straight out of *Happy Days*. But is he the Fonz, or Potsie? Not that Potsie wasn't cool, because he had that whole singer gig going, but he was always just a little soft compared to the Fonz. Maybe that is what is wrong with me. I am attracted to the Fonzes of the world instead of Potsie or Richie.

Am I silly by still having the faintest hope that I could find a man to love who is both kind and cool? That the connection I felt with Reese can happen again? Are there loving yet cool guys out there? Could Stan be that guy?

A cool breeze blows off the shore as he walks me back to my car. The valet revs up in the Mustang and I feel like Sam must when he watches me pack for a trip. As if the lights are going down and my longing is just beginning. I don't want the day to be over.

I thump the door lock to the Mustang. Up, down. Deciding. There is a moment of awkward silence and I can't help but blurt out, "Do you want to, maybe, come over for dinner tonight? It's already six-thirty and you did, well . . ."

I search for a reason.

"Buy me lunch."

My God, I sound needy. Let him go. Play hard to get. Let him call. Don't be so available. Be patient. Play the waiting game. Let him seek me out. Men are hunters, cavemen. They want to work for the kill. They want to feel like they properly brought down their meal. They want to earn it and here I am lying down in the tall African grass like a horny lioness.

"Sure. I'll follow you."

Holy shit!

In the kitchen I add spices to my marinara sauce and pasta while tossing in the scallops and shrimp. Heat from the wet, boiling penne fogs the window above the sink. I breathe in the steam. I set the Caesar salad down as Stan lights the candles on my old, barn-style dining table.

"I love this table," he says, blowing out a match and uncorking a bottle of wine. He pours me a glass with flawless style.

I am traipsing around on clouds; harp music surrounds me in my head. I look to my back for the wings. Yep, there they are. My feet dance above the ground.

Built-in, well-mannered boyfriend, already at the house having dinner.

Around 11:00 P.M. I am sleepy and cuddled on the couch, watching Stan watch the highlights on ESPN. Jeter hits another home run. Ho-hum. Then wait. Reese, at the plate. The pitch. He swings. Misses. He never swings at the first pitch. I subtly ease up a little and watch the second pitch. Low and fast. Crack! The ball SAILS into deep, deep, deep center field. It could be. The outfielder runs to the warning track. It might be. The outfielder goes up for it, but the ball sails over the fence. Home run. Reese pumps a fist as he rounds first. Padres win by one and I am flutter-flutter-flutta-flutta-fluttering!!!

I shoot my gaze back to Stan. "You need to go," I say.

He looks at his watch. "Emily, it's eleven thirty-five. We've had three margaritas, two Coronas, and a bottle of Pinot. I live an hour south on the 405. Driving isn't wise."

He wants sex, wants to strip off my 501s like Reese should be doing right now, like he *is* most definitely doing with some baseball bimbette as I think about it. He is throwing her on the bed and . . .

What am I thinking about? Stan doesn't sound so bad. Why not? Go for it, a perfect distraction.

"I know what you're thinking," he says. "Don't worry. I'll sleep on the couch." Stan looks down at me with his big, gray-blue eyes.

Too late. The thought of having a body to spoon me when my head is spinning around with thoughts of Reese sounds like a great way to forget the highlights. No couch! It would be nice, even for just one night, to have him hold me. Besides, I can use some hot kisses, maybe an hour of over-the-clothes groping.

"I promise to be a perfect gentleman," Stan says, taking off his shirt to reveal six-pack abs. YUM!

After putting on my pajama bottoms and T-shirt I lay, hoping that a new, hot lion can replace the potential of the old kill. I don't feel awkward at all. It is almost comfortable, considering I am climbing into bed with a near stranger.

Stan crawls under the covers next to me wearing only his boxers. He leans over on top of me, gazing a long time into my eyes, and proceeds to give me one small, uneventful kiss on the lips. He pulls me toward him, cuddles me in the spoon position, and promptly falls asleep.

I lay awake, watching this uberhot male specimen breathing in and out. I couldn't help but scream inside, "Hey, wake up and do me!," but instead I lay motionless like a good girl, wanting. Always wanting.

Can't sleep. I get up, shuffle into the back room, turn on my computer, call Reilly, and explain the situation.

"At what point did it become the woman's job to provide shelter and lodging for her date?" she fires at me. "Doesn't he have all those friends in West Hollywood he can call?"

"I like it that he's here. I just thought maybe I would at least . . ."

"Get some action and put a Band-Aid over your broken heart," she interrupts.

"Well . . . yes. I just invited a stranger into my bed and he is getting a better night's sleep than I am. Plus, I wanted to call you in case they find my body dismembered in a Dumpster."

"Love you. Go try to get yourself some," and with that she hangs up.

I click on my e-mail and draft a message to Reese.

Dear RC,

Nice homer. Saw you on the highlights, but that's not really why I'm e-mailing. I guess I can't escape my thoughts of you. And even when I do, I see you on the TV. Don't you think God has an ironic sense of humor? I guess I'm just

wondering how you are and if you ever think
about me. Because I think about you.

I look at the computer screen, shake my head "no," and
press delllleeete.

After slipping under the covers and wrapping Stan's arm
around my waist, I sleep until he gives me a hopeful morning
kiss. I shut the front door behind him and I sigh at the
thought. Does no sex mean he really likes me?

Why does this theory keep proving itself to be true over
and over when all I want is someone to roll in the hay-ho
with whom I actually care about?

"I am not even going to get into the marathon of concerns
this raises," Dr. D. interjects. "You invited a stranger to your
house. You let him sleep over hoping he'll help you get over
your ex. And you're complaining that he didn't want to have
sex with you, which I clinically find unrealistic."

"It just leads me to wonder why he didn't want to, well,
you know, do it," I say

Reason #1: *You should never have to wonder why a man
doesn't want to have sex with you. Because no matter what
the answer is . . . it isn't good.*

Dates two through five are equally lovely, but lack any mashing, mauling, chemistry, or naked behavior. We golf, surf down
south, camp out on the beach. We basically do everything but
penetrate. In fact, no real sexual anything goes down. Literally.

But sex isn't that important, is it? Perhaps I can live without the actual lovemaking, as it is the love that truly matters. There are so many things about Stan that lend themselves to a future behind a white picket fence.

Reason #2: *A man/woman relationship without sex is called . . . "just friends."*

Grace, Reilly, and I meet at Atlantic for a drink after work. The place is empty, so we pretty much have it to ourselves. Bellied up to the bar, Ian the bartender pours us another round of Presbyterians, a cool, refreshing vodka drink made with Absolut Mandarin and half-and-half Seven and club soda.

"He hasn't touched her flower," Reilly says to Grace. "They've had like ten dates or something." She rolls her eyes.

"Five." I look at Grace, dumbfounded, in hopes that she can give me some doctorly advice as to why my potential mate has no built-in mating rituals.

Grace swishes her Presbyterian and questions, "Nothing? Not one stroke? Fondle? Lick? Nothing?"

Reilly and I shake our heads in confusion.

"Plus, Sam hates him, won't go near him, and has had diarrhea ever since I started dating the guy. Weird, huh?"

"Dogs know." Reilly drinks. "Then again, I knew when I met him and his creepy friend Adam."

"How does that make Stan feel about Sam?" Grace asks.

"He doesn't like dogs."

"You have your answer." Grace's face fills with shock and dismay. "Two words, buh-bye."

Reason #3: *Animal haters need not apply.*

Date six. Still trying to liberate Stan's libido. Early in week three we are having a few of his friends over for dinner. I am cooking. Fresh flowers and good wine abound. I peer out from the kitchen over a hot pan of lasagna and notice Stan bending down to pick up Sam's tennis ball off the hardwood floor next to the couch where Adam is sitting.

Stan moves in slow motion with a face scrunched in torture as if a proctologist has his hand up his ass. He eases the semi-slimy ball between his thumb and forefinger, holding it as far away from his body as he can, and then . . . drops it with a thud into the magazine bin. His body sort of shivers with disgust and he looks to Adam, who lowers my Pottery Barn catalogue. Adam and Stan share a mutual "eeugh, gross" wince.

I get an image in my head of him leaping four feet in the air to pirouette like a ballerina and for the first time come to terms with the fact that my boyfriend has issues. I am not exactly sure what the issues are, but they are 100 percent there. Germ issues, dog issues, slime issues, sex issues. Gay issues?

He turns and sees me standing, head cocked, looking at him in a bewildered state. My eyes squint and question.

He breaks the stare and comes to me out of Adam's earshot and murmurs, "I just, ah, don't like things that are . . . wet."

Did he just say he doesn't like things that are WET? Whoa, mental tailspin. I am a woman, for God's sake. I am self-lubricating. How can he not like things that are wet? What does it mean?

"It's a big deal," I explain to Dr. D. "He is afraid of my flower. Believe me, there's no problem in the garden. It is a nicely tended, weeded flower."

Dr. D. shifts uncomfortably. "Why is sex so important to you?"

"Besides the fact that it feels really good when done properly, it's the one male/female thing we do in a relationship that we *don't do* with anyone else. It's the intimate closeness that bonds and connects us. It is what narrows our field of focus, the thing that is hot and beautiful and out-of-body and can only be fulfilled by another person. Of course, as with everything else, I can do it alone. It just isn't the same."

"Your boyfriend may be gay-straight," Dr. D. says, leaning in and touching my knee with sympathy. "Or he may just be a handsome, impeccably dressed straight guy with a plethora of issues. I'm not sure yet."

"I was sooooo hoping he was Mr. Right. We look really sweet in photos together. Although he is more attractive than I am. Thinking back, he keeps 'fixing' me right before each photo (that's when I noticed the whole eyebrow thing), my tousled hair, crooked sweater, complaining that I never wear socks with my Keds. Oh my God, he's a fag! My boyfriend is a fag. Not that I have a problem with fags. I love gay men. *I love Josh. If I was a guy I would be gay.* But I don't want to date one. I should have known. I should have seen this earlier when he tried to change my wardrobe, my hair, my style. He just seemed like, well . . . like he cared. No wonder I was so comfortable in bed with him."

"You shouldn't change your style." Dr. D. reinforces. I pull the stupid red bow that Stan gave me out of my disheveled ponytail. "Granted, there is compromise we all make to have a successful relationship. Some people quit smoking and ease up on the alcohol intake, but style? Never change who you really are, as sooner or later the old style just creeps back in, leaving your partner to wonder who they fell in love with. It is what makes you unique, special, and it is part of what makes you Emily. Habits yes, style never."

"So, what do we do?"

"The first thing," Dr. D. says, "is to find out if he's phobic of women or germs. If he's just a Howard Hughes type, then there may be hope. Well, if you can live with that."

I leave Dr. D.'s office with at least a glimmer of possibility and a list of potential ways to decipher my man's issues.

On the way home, I dial Grace on the cell and she asks me about my promotion. "Did you get it?"

"Yeah," I say, aware that my tone falls somewhere between depressed and comatosed. I don't know what my problem is. Maybe it is the fact that another potential boyfriend is biting the dust while the one I really want is sliding into home somewhere.

"So, what's your first move in your new position?" she probes, as if searching for a pulse.

"I'm promoting JJ to manager, directly reporting to me. Won't win her any friends, but she doesn't need to worry about friends. I do."

"What are you the VP of?" Grace asks. "Busywork?" she laughs.

"No," I shoot back at her, defenses bristling.

"Jesus, lighten up. I know you're climbing the corporate power ladder. I am just trying to get a laugh. What's up?"

"I just came from therapy."

"Ohhhh."

"Sorry. The job's good, I mean I am spearheading all of the PR on original movies, which are terrible but hell, it's TV. We're on our fourth installment of the Bible. I'm supposed to make Ben Kingsley look cool as Job. If I can get him nominated for a Golden Globe, my bonus will be huge. I took on the extra stripes and drama in hopes that someday I'll get to do something, anything, with Clooney. Plus the extra cash is much needed on the house-saving road, as God knows when or IF I'll ever meet someone to buy a house with so I need to start planning for my life now. The tradeoff is a lot less 'life' and a higher volume of tyrannical egos to deal with."

I take a breath.

"Here's an example of my typical day. I get my ass chewed by an executive who thinks he's superimportant and should be on page one of the *Hollywood Reporter,* instead of page seven, when in reality nobody gives a shit about him because he makes bad B movies. To top it off, his name was spelled wrong, which he is completely pissed about. So my conversation with him after he saw the magazine went something like this . . . me patronizing him for an hour, explaining I know how he feels, telling him that I'm going to read the editor the riot act, a lie, and somehow slipping into the conversation, nonchalantly, that his name was spelled right when I sent it out in the press release. Thus covering my own ass while making him feel like he is completely justified for acting like a total prick. Then I pick up the phone, call the editor, and the first thing I do is apologize for calling, explaining that I'm just calling because my executive is an idiot and he's making me call. We share a knowing laugh and I tell him that I am grateful that the story was ever written in the first place, which I am. I throw myself on his mercy, 'cause I realize he's my bread and butter for future good stories. I mean, without the editors and writers, we're fucked. They won't write anything we want, and then I beg him to do a correction . . . which I might add is simply the fact that the *E* comes before the *I* in Weinberg. The editor agrees, as hack-n-flack (journalist/PR exec) must get along, which I do with my guys, as I have more in common with them than the dick in Armani who works at my company. It's not like the editor demoted Weinberg or called him a he-she or something."

Wow, that was one long rant about work.

"Speaking of gay guys," Grace interrupts, bored, ". . . how's Stan?"

I switch gears and take a deep breath. "He's coming over after golf Sunday afternoon to celebrate my promotion. I am going to put him through Dr. D.'s sponge test."

Seeing Stan one week after the wet ball experience gives me pause. Breezing through my front door in golf attire, Callaway visor, carrying his clubs, I realize that I have been overreacting. Maybe Stan is not gay. I see him walk across my living room and want to maul him. He sets his clubs against the wall and gives me a hug and a kiss on the . . .

FOREHEAD. FOREHEAD! FOREHEAD!!!

That afternoon I try a sponge test on him, as recommended by Dr. D. First, I wet a brand-new yellow sponge and leave it in the sink. Then in the middle of cleaning the table I holler to Stan that I need a sponge. He makes his way to the kitchen and I peer from the hallway, and I peek around the corner to watch him take one look at the soggy sponge, basking in a sink full of what he must imagine contains a sewer of bacteria, before he . . .

He searches through the contents of the cabinets until he finds a fresh sponge, which he promptly brings over and hands to me.

"Honey, could you get it wet for me?" I singsong like Mr. Rogers.

Reluctantly, he wets the half of the sponge that he is not touching and brings it back. Weird. He's weird, but hot.

Reason #4: *Tests of any kind set your partner up to fail.*

After dinner, he takes a shower while I plot with my girls on the phone about how to get my boyfriend to visit my secret garden.

Stan walks to the kitchen with a towel wrapped around his waist, pops the cap off a Corona bottle, passes me in the hallway with a little smile, and settles on the sofa, flipping between two baseball games.

"Beer? Baseball? Couch potato? This is so confusing," I say under my breath to Grace. "I gotta go. I'll call you later." I click off the phone and walk into the living room, where I lay on the couch next to Stan and gingerly place my head on his lap so as to appear to be napping, when in essence I am trying to tease him a little—my head on his LAP. I playfully kiss him on the tummy.

He looks down at me. "What's on your mind?"

The question is what's not on my body. "Honey, I need some passion, intimacy, followed by bonding." I blink as innocently as I can.

"We're having dinner with my mother tonight. I got up early for golf. Let's just have a nap." He says this ignoring that I am silently screaming out for sex. Sliding his body down on the sofa, he proceeds to cuddle me and fall asleep.

I see the problem, feel it deeply, but somewhere inside I want to go to dinner with his family. I want to have a handsome boyfriend who comes over at 3:00 P.M. on a Sunday after golfing and naps with me on the sofa. I just want the nap following vigorous lovemaking. I want this to work. I close my eyes to sleep and something bigger than anger or frustration hits me.

Rejection.

I am lying in the arms of my new boyfriend and he won't

do me. I feel shitty, so I get up and call Josh. He'll know what to do.

I explain every sordid detail, of which there aren't any, of my potentially gay-straight boyfriend. Josh listens carefully before saying, "Kitten, speaking strictly from a guy who posed as a straight boy all through high school and two dreadfully wasted years of college, it sounds like you have a lot of signs, but gay or straight, it doesn't matter. You're not getting what you need."

Josh and I hang up and I stand over Stan while he sleeps. I want to whack him with the phone, hard, right in the middle of his forehead.

Reason #5: *Rejection from your partner is unacceptable.*

I lay back down with Stan, wrap his arm around my waist, and spoon into him. I study his sexy forearm and think to myself, Why can't I listen to my friends about shitty men? Josh told me everything I need to know, yet here I lay, trying to make my fluffy poodle into a macho German shepherd.

Sam nuzzles his muzzle into my leg on the couch and I give him some love. He's been sick. I thought it was Stan-induced diarrhea, but I know it's more. I search beneath his thick coat of fur, rubbing his frail body, and find more lumps. I hug him for a good long second and he gives me a little howl. Damn, he puts on a great façade for a sick ole boy.

Sam lies back down next to the couch and I think to myself while lying motionless with my sleeping gay/straight boyfriend. I always ask my friends for their opinions only to discard any good advice that they may throw out. Why? These are the people who only have my best interest at heart, and I ignore them. Why is it that we never listen to the people who love us?

I decide at that moment that I will have a party, a dinner party, a judge-n-jury party. I will invite my entire gay circle of friends, Josh, Gary, Bill, my lovely lesbian couple friends, Dena and Natalie. I will pepper them throughout a crowd of about ten or so straight friends along with a few of Stan's friends and let them determine what I am afraid I already know but refuse to accept as I will not be dateless, loveless, and futureless when my best friend walks down the aisle. It will be like group therapy, only with an insular friend posse. No matter what happens, I will listen to their advice and act accordingly. I have a plan, a good plan.

The plan rattles around in my brain all through my Sunday nap. I am STILL lying awake looking at the clock as I scoot my hips and butt into him, coy, literally pivoting into his package. Oh my God, something stirred. I feel stiffening. Wow. He is kissing the back of my neck. He has my hips, his towel is open, and voilà. We have consummation!

As soon as he is done and I am barely started, and not a second later, he gets up as if disgusted by himself and leaves my house in a huff. "What about dinner with your mom?" I shout after him as he gets to the door.

"I'm not feeling well, I gotta go," he shoots back.

I immediately call Grace and Reilly. "He's not gay. My man's not gay. He's a frickin' weirdo, but he's not gay. Or is he? I am conflicted as we did it, but he ran away. It was okay, quick, sorta good for about forty-five seconds, so why do I feel bad?"

"The only reason you gave him a boner is 'cause your ass was up against his unit," Reilly reminds me. "Try to see the visual."

OH GOD!

I hang up with my girls, take a long bath, and then log onto the e-mail. I see mail from Callahan26, Reese, the ultimate temptation. I click on, open it, and begin to read.

```
Dear Em,
    I'm in Pittsburg at the William Penn hotel, ex-
actly one year since I watched you dump hot cof-
fee all down your white sweater. I couldn't help
but laugh in Starbucks. There are a new round of
college kids behind the bar. I couldn't get you
out of my mind during the game against the Pi-
rates. One thought seemed to be clear. You were
not at the hotel waiting for me and it made me
sad. Just wanted to let you know I was thinking
about you. Hope you're well, your friend, Reese.
```

I reply . . .

```
Dear RC, hmmmm . . . friend. Are we friends now?
```

In the morning I tell the girls that Reese e-mailed me and I e-mailed him back.

"What are you thinking?" they ask in unison.

"You're probably on a mass e-mail list," Reilly ally-oops.

Grace slam-dunks, "Everybody gets the same 'I miss you' form letter."

"I'm not letting him in, it just feels nice to be thought about. Don't worry, it's not like I'm going to call him or anything."

The girls cast a gloomy doom over my thoughts of Reese. Like reverse Nike marketing, they urge "Don't do it!"

After Grace's bridal shower, the girls and I sit on the couch looking at horrible orange-and-black crepe paper and balloons strung around the room.

Grace says, "It was a nice idea to theme it. There was just something amiss, though."

"Sort of like Stan." Reilly yanks down the orange strip of paper.

"Perfect teeth. Impeccably dressed. Hates Sam. Hates slimy dog balls," I add. "I will not be dateless to your wedding, no matter what's wrong with him."

"Uh-huh . . ." they say in unison, taunting me, like "We'll see."

I walk into Dr. D.'s for my next session with five solid reasons not to date Stan even though I know that there are at least seven, but I refuse to give him the rest of them.

"You made it through the shower. How was that for you?" asks Dr. D.

"It was great."

"It didn't make you sad at all?"

"No, I am happy for Grace. I love her. I'll just be glad

when the wedding is over. If I can hold on for two more weeks, I've got a date." Even if it is a fraud.

The night of the dinner party quickly approaches. This is the ultimate test. I don't know why I'm doing this *before* Grace's wedding. I should have this party afterward. What was I thinking?

Candles burning, the caterer finishes the last touches to the stuffed mushrooms, salmon, and assorted crudités. I watch Stan fluff the pillows. He stands back and arranges the lilies perfectly in the tall vase. To his credit, he takes as much pride in the small touches as I do. I'm not even surprised.

Reilly stands next to me in the kitchen doorway watching Stan push each lily away from the next so they are not touching in the vase. I hold my martini, subtly scrutinizing his obsession with perfection and think to myself, *No straight guy follows the caterer tasting Brie and saying, "fantastic."* He might as well have clicked his heels and said "fab-u!"

Reilly doesn't say a word. She just watches, then lets out a huge belly laugh, doubles over, and walks back into the kitchen. Stan begins to arrange the magazines alphabetically in the magazine rack.

Throughout the night I witness Stan grow more and more agitated as Josh and Stan's *friend* Adam are getting along famously. I look from Stan's stewing anger to Josh. Josh gives an eyebrow raise, followed by an "isn't this funny" smirk.

Fast-forward to . . . I blow out the last burning candle as it drips wax all over the white linen tablecloth.

I take a poll from my friends as they leave: sixteen gay, nine straight, four undecided. Grace is convinced, Reilly just doesn't like him, and all, ALL of my gay friends kiss me on the cheek while handing me their empty glasses and whispering in my ear things like . . . Gary: "He likes cock." Bill: "Honey, he's not on your team." And Josh handed me his number to give to my boyfriend, so when he decides to come out of the closet he can call him!

That night, tucked under the covers of my bed, I say to Stan, "Honey, I think we have intimacy problems."

"Don't be silly," he says as he rolls over with his back to me, "just cuddle me."

Done. I am D-O-N-E. First of all, women shouldn't spoon men. Women are on the inside of the spoon. Always. No exception. Well, unless your boyfriend has shoulder or back injuries, like Reese, who still would never ask me to cuddle him.

He senses that I will not drop it. He opens his eyes and sees me staring at him. "What?" he defensively barks at me. "Emily, I work very hard to be intimate with you."

Reason #6: *You don't need any more reasons when they won't have sex with you.*

Wow. I hate this. I know what's coming.

"And it isn't easy," he continues as if somehow I am unlovable. "I just can't believe I'll ever be myself with you and I think we should take some time," he finishes.

Wait a damn second! "All right," I mumble as I whack myself in the head over and over that a gay man, pretending to be straight, with "wet" issues, just broke up with me. I want to scream, "You're totally gay-straight and you're never going to be happy in a relationship unless your partner has a penis!"

Reasons #7, 8, 9, AND 10: *No sex.*

But I say nothing. Instead I just nod, roll over, and go back to sleep. The SLAMMING door was a little unnerving, but not as bad as sharing my bed with someone who wouldn't kiss me good night. All in all I feel relieved, and then a sudden panic strikes me.

"I am dateless for Grace's wedding," I tell Dr. D., "and you are not helping enough!"

"I am teaching you to hone your radar skills so you can see through the wrong men before you waste months only to find they are nothing but a cubic zirconium in a good golf visor with a nice smile, when what you need is the real thing."

Dr. D. can be so poetic sometimes.

That night I sit at my desk, log on to e-mail, and see Callahan26. I rub Sam's sore hips as he stands eyeing me with those old yellow wolf eyes. He is on new medicine from the vet to help him ease his aches and pains. I click on to Reese's reply e-mail to me.

Silly question, Em. Of course we're friends.
The question remains, are we more than friends?
How are you? RC

I type and respond to his e-mail . . .

RC,

    I picture you writing your e-mails to me with the same expression on your face that I see when I watch you on TV, playing baseball. The look on your face right before you are about to steal second.

    We are sorta friends, with a hint of connection and remembrance of fear.

    I am glad you're well. You'll be happy to know, another boyfriend bites the dust. But he wasn't worth keeping. He had "wet" issues and reasons. I'll leave it at that.

    Wish it wasn't the season, you'd be a potential "friend" date to Grace's wedding. Hope you're surviving the Midwest road trip.

    Your friend???XO Emily

I delete the XO and press SEND.

Reasons #7, 8, 9, AND 10: *No sex.*

Reason #6: *You don't need any more reasons when they won't have sex with you.*

Reason #5: *Rejection from your partner is unacceptable.*

Reason #4: *Tests of any kind set your partner up to fail.*

Reason #3: *Animal haters need not apply.*

Reason #2: *A man/woman relationship without sex is called . . . "just friends."*

Reason #1: *You should never have to wonder why a man doesn't want to have sex with you. Because no matter what the answer is . . . it isn't good.*

chapter six

Arm Candy

riving to Malibu from L.A. with Grace, I get lost in my thoughts of my life itinerary. It is either stable or out of control. For now I am leaning too far in the direction of loveless and under control, suffering from P.B.W.D., Post Best Friend's Wedding Disorder. I don't want to sink any deeper by thinking about it too much, but the petals are wilting. There is no ship on the horizon. It has been 156 days without the touch of a male or even the possibility of interest. It is a major dry spell, a sexless Sahara desert. And the most excited I get is when I log onto my computer hoping to see Callahan26. Even Dr. D. is struggling to stay awake during my therapy sessions.

Speaking of ships and Dr. D., he just pulled up next to me in my brand-new navy blue Land Rover at the stoplight. He's to the right of me in a mint-condition 1978 Bronco, hunter green with a tan top, towing a beat-to-hell-and-back sailboat. He notices me at the light, staring out my window at him. I am gawking in full, mouth-gaping awe. He points up at the light, which has now turned green. Cars *HONK* behind me as I pull away.

For a spilt second I almost didn't recognize him. It's weird. I don't think I have ever seen him out of his office building. How can you tell someone your most intimate secrets, then when you see them out of their element, barely recognize them? I didn't even wave. Come to think of it, neither did he, just a finger pointing at the green light, as if to say, "get going forward, Emily, keep it on the road."

"That was Dr. D.," I say to Grace sitting in the passenger seat.

"I hate seeing my patients out of the office. No matter how many times it happens, I never get used to it." She looks back out the window.

Dr. D. I think to myself, *What must he think of me?* I'm sure I promised to be an engaging patient at first, but I fear I have turned into a weekly appointment with disappointment. I got there ten minutes late this week and left five minutes early after finishing the session off with a bout of silence. I am considering liposuction or a tattoo, considering running through a supermarket naked. I am wearing forties dresses and heels. What is wrong with me? I haven't had a period in two months. Not to worry, there isn't any possibility of a bun in my oven, as it's been around five months with no physical attention. So, is that it? Is that how it all ends up? Maybe I should ram my Rover into the next hot male I see on the 405 freeway before all my eggs die of loneliness.

Fortunately there is a distraction for this, if not a cure. Here I am at the beach with the girls, hunting for prime real estate to plant our umbrella, chairs, and blanket. Grace and Reilly walk in the summer heat of Malibu staking our claim.

"I'm exhausted," Reilly says, dropping her chair and Chanel beach bag in the sand. She recently got promoted to western sales rep for Chanel, so she is keeping Grace and I rolling again in the hippest shades of overpriced frosty mauve and lavender.

"Guess this is it, then." Grace tries to dig a hole in the sand for our oversized, checkered Burberry umbrella.

The beach is crowded with eighteen-to-twenty-four year old tan, muscular, sun-worshipping men playing volleyball beneath a rainbow flag. Why do I live in L.A.? My eyes drift over the polka-dot-bikini-wearing nineteen-year-old silicone-stuffed babes and then to my own friends, equally attractive, but desperately trying to stay OUT of the sun.

The easiest way to tell if a woman is over or under thirty is to watch her at the beach. The 20-year-old will be toting a bottle of 2 SPF tanning oil and the thirty-year-old will be reapplying 35 SPF, antiwrinkle sunblock under an umbrella, large floppy hat, and some sort of wrap that covers her ass.

Post–sunscreen slather, Grace, Reilly and I unpack our bags. Labor Day weekend is closing out the summer. The girls and Mark, Grace's husband, and I rented a share in Malibu for the month of August. I miss just girl time, but must admit it is nice having Mark around, especially when the garbage needs to go out or the DVD player needs to be hooked up.

The arrangement was flawless until Reilly, in a drunken stupor, hooked up late one night with Mark's friend Goz, whom we all know better as the Roach, justifying his nickname with the fact that if a nuclear bomb were to explode and we were all disseminated, at least his gelled hair would survive. Roach looks like a cross between Wayne Newton and an all-black-suit-wearing throwback to the eighties who thinks he is really, really cool in his red, leased, overpriced Lexus. It wouldn't be so bad, but his incessant need to bang every stripper in L.A. and tell us about it has given the girls and I a not-so-secret loathing for him. He made the moves on an inebriated Reilly at 2:30 A.M., and woke up the next morning and proceeded to tell everyone over bagels and coffee how she likes to have her nipples twisted. Needless to say, he was promptly banished from the beach share.

Our little summer house isn't too fancy, but it is down the beach from Chuck Woolery, who, I might add, is still as hot as he was on *Love Connection* despite the fact that he's pushing sixty.

After having no sex with Stan, I find myself on the prowl. I can't stop undressing every surfing, swimming, jet-skiing, boogie-boarding hottie. Currently in my sights, a twenty-something-year-old surfer with sun-streaked hair and brown puppy dog eyes carrying a long, long board. His board shorts, hanging low on his hips, accentuate that oh-so-delectable male muscle, that hip/abdomen bulge that's usually covered by love handles on any guy with a respectable desk job.

His eyes have wrinkles from years of squinting at the sun in the rock-ock-ock-cocking ocean, waiting for something to surf. Surfers have an innate sense of sexiness. Perhaps it is their infinite patience. They don't rush. They just enjoy the water, the taste of the salt, and the warmth of the sun . . . then, as if God put a quarter in the machine, they take off, paddling with those well-defined back muscles, springing to the erect position in a single fluid motion so they can cut loose from all boundaries known within the flat, unmoving, two-dimensional world. They play with energy, gliding and carving through an alternative, liquid dimension with a balance of fear and joy.

I prop up on my elbows and eye him from behind my blue-tinted Dior glasses. He turns around, revealing the best young, rippled back I have ever seen. Tan shoulders to die for, with soft supple skin, glistening with salty droplets screaming: "Emily. Lick me. Love me. Look away. Quick. You're gawking, girl." AGAIN!

He swings a towel around his waist and pulls down his wet trunks, replacing them with dry ones and tying them like the laces of a corset on a Danielle Steele cover.

Drool. Physical drool wets the corners of my mouth as Grace leans up and whinnies, "Eeeaaaaasy, girl. Doooowwwwn, girl."

I turn and look her in the face. "He's just the tasty treat to get me back on my horse."

"And judging by the way those trunks are hanging, he's definitely a thoroughbred," Reilly says as she rolls over onto her back.

I get up, in my surf trunks and powder-blue bikini top, and head for the water.

The tan surfer treat pours fresh, warm water over his face from an old gallon juice container, blinks the salt water out of his eyes, and begins to peel an orange.

Subtly I stroll toward the water, pretending not to see him. I never look down. I am almost past him when he reaches backward in the sand for his beach towel and his arm trips me. I stumble, falling, landing face-first in the sand.

I hear Grace and Reilly howl and clap in the background.

"Jesus, I am so sorry." His eyes widen.

I watch his face, and a twinge of mortification flashes through my body as I look down and see that one of my breasts is out of my bikini top and in full view.

"Nice," sweet-treat guy says, staring at my exposed areola . . . "Really nice," he smiles.

His compliment fills me with relief as I readjust myself.

With one nipple pointing west and one pointing east, I try to rearrange them to at least semipoint in the same direction.

"I'm Lance. And, uh . . ."

I nod while appearing to fondle myself. "Emily."

My nipples are both going in the same direction. A victory!

As he hands me a towel to wipe the sand off my face, Rilke's *Letters to a Young Poet* falls from the pouch in his faded red backpack.

This small novel is my favorite. It was the first read that somehow validated my own personal perception of love, obsession, and passion. It is my all-time favorite book!

My gaze darts from the book to his eyes. They appear "knowing"—can I describe these young eyes as "knowing"?

"You should read this," he says. "Wait."

What? I think to myself. What did I do? What's wrong with me? Besides that I am old. Why is he looking so deep into me?

"Something tells me you already have, haven't you?"

How did he know that?

What I want to say is . . . Lance, would you mind if I threw my sandy frame onto your young, wet, buff, tan, soft-skinned-surfer, tasty morsel of a body, as my last boyfriend didn't like things that were wet, and I really, really need to have some validation.

My relationship with Stan left me thinking somewhere deep down that I'm not desirable.

I sit for a second in the sand, watching Lance wax and stroke that lonnnnng boaaarrddd, with his forearms that have sun-kissed blond peach fuzz on them. "Can I help?" I say, wanting to be that surfboard.

"Here." He hands me the melting sex wax. "Like this." He puts his hand on top of mine and shows me exactly how his board should be rubbed. After a few moments he smiles, a big smile that looks as if he just got his braces off.

Flutter, flutter.

With that he invited me out into the water for a surf lesson. And I said the least likely thing, "yes." It was cold on my feet, but not ice-water cold, mostly refreshing, and the air was hot. He sat behind me on his knees and I lay on my belly as we paddled out to where the other surfers were all sitting up. One guy nodded at Lance, the silent surfer speak. I felt immediately safe with my legs straddling this boy's board.

Sitting out there, waiting for our wave, we somehow bonded without talking. The motion of the ocean kept me writhing this way and that, trying to keep from falling in, but he helped me keep my balance. Then it was our turn. We paddled and caught the wave, and he helped me to my feet with the confidence most men show when they open a car door or lay their credit card down to pay for dinner. As soon as I was standing, balance came effortlessly. We were flying.

His hands guided my hips as we flew beneath a dozen drifting seagulls. The wind blew my hair back and I'm pretty sure he took a deep breath of it. Then it was over. We popped up over the back of the wave and I jumped off into two feet of water on soft sand. The most honest emotion filled me.

Walking into Dr. D.'s office, I want nothing more than to show him that I'm not the hopeless bore he saw the week before.

"You look tan," he says.

"Yeah. We had our last hoopla at the beach this weekend . . . I saw you on the road."

"Yes, you did. I saw you as well."

"I like your boat, but it looks like it needs a lot of work," I say, taking the awkwardness off my blatant pry into his life, as if I'm not supposed to know about his life outside the safety of the wall at 20002 Sunset Boulevard, Suite 402.

"It's a great boat, a 1968 classic, all wood. It just needs some TLC." His eyes light up as he leads me into his office, as I can tell wants to tell me about the boat. Hmmm . . .

"How are you doing?" he quickly regroups.

"Good, I feel really good."

He crosses his arms over his chest, which to me should be forbidden as a therapist for it is Bad Body Language 101.

"Well, I was starting to think I was never going to have sex again, with another person, and then I met someone."

He nods. "Did you have sex with him?"

"No, but I'm going to."

There's a silence as I am waiting for feedback, judgment, approval, something!

"I know what you're thinking," I say.

"Do you? What am I thinking?" he says, poised to write it down.

"You're thinking that I'm jumping into another relationship. But I'm not. This is simply *arm candy.*"

He says nothing.

"Arm candy, you know, like men who have trophy wives. A young, hot, firm, guy who looks good and tastes even better."

"Someone you can boss around," he smiles.

"No. Hmm, maybe," I tease, "but only in bed. I am NOT making him into a boyfriend. I am simply going to have an easy-breezy dating adventure filled with a ton of sex to make up for the last seven months."

More silence. God. I hate his silence. I should have gotten used to it by now. I am never quite sure if he is just reevaluating the situation, waiting for me to talk, or planning what he is going to make for dinner tonight. UGH!

"What?" I finally blurt. "You think it's a bad idea, don't you?"

"No, I think you should do what makes you happy. But sex or no sex, I think you need to be careful about the men you let in, particularly *into* your body, because you and I both know that there is no easy-breezy for Emily. Did you make a list?"

"I don't *need* to make a list, as I don't want him to be my boyfriend," I reiterate with an authoritative tone.

"How young?" he asks.

"Young."

I can see this is going nowhere, as Dr. D. is predisposed to thinking that I am, as I always do, making a bad decision with Lance. But he is wrong. For the first time, I am not looking for Lance to bring something to the table other than his naked body, so I spend the rest of my session talking about the potential of changing jobs, apartments, or possibly hairstyles.

Dr. D. didn't bring up Lance again until I got up to leave. "Make a list. At least try."

At home I dig through my bookshelf desperately looking for Rilke's *Letters* . . .

"Do you think he's too young?" I ask Grace and Reilly on a three-way call.

"Young-shmung, men do it every day," Reilly pipes in. I

reach to the top of the bookshelf . . . there it is . . . almost got it . . . when I catch a glimpse of myself in the living room mirror.

I raise my arm in the mirror and watch the skin on the bottom jiggle. I cringe, grab the book.

"Look at it this way . . . you won't have to go to spinning class—he's totally exercise," Reilly laughs. "After gay-straight Stan you should go for it."

"You deserve it, honey," Grace chimes in. "I say, go work up a sweat! I gotta go. Mark and I are going to his parents' for dinner. Love you."

"Thanks. Love you." I pick up an arm weight and try to flex.

As Grace hangs up, Reilly's other line beeps. "Hold on," she says.

Arm lift. Arm curl. Arm curl. Shoulder rep. OW! Something just pulled in my shoulder. I set down the weight and pick up the book.

"Hi. Sorry." Reilly clicks back on.

"Well?"

"Do it. DO him. For Christ's sake, Emily, you've had sex what, like, once in seven months?

And almost two of those months you were in a monogamous relationship."

"As always, I appreciate your love and understanding," I chuckle.

"I just think it's about time you had someone to be nice to you, 'kay? I gotta go, I have a blind date," Reilly adds.

"With who?"

"Some Brazilian guy that my boss knows."

"Good luck. Love you."

"Remember that you're a great, beautiful woman, who could possibly be mistaken for his mother, but you're a Catholic so don't let it bother you."

When is a man too young? In this day and age, *age* isn't supposed to matter. As a thirty-one-year-old woman I have at this point in life found myself not in *need* of a man for anything other than company and sex . . . maybe love. So why not do it with a young hot guy who worships me. What's wrong with having the upper hand for once?

Friday night Lance comes over for dinner. He arrives in a white, dented, 1971 Chevy Malibu with surf racks on the roof, minus hubcaps. My eyes squint a little and I feel my stomach cringe, as the thought of spending the rest of my life in the passenger side without bling-bling tire decoration scares me. Scares me a lot.

I watch him get out, see his big brown eyes, and remember why it was I wanted him to come over.

The instant negative emotion that his car gave me could be a potential "reason," but that would be *IF* I wanted him as a boyfriend, which I don't. Everyone has different needs in a relationship. This is NOT a relationship. It is sex.

Then why does the car still bother me? Am I shallow? Or is it that I have worked damn hard, taken a lot of bull, put in too many weekends and nights, to have nice things, clothes, and a decent car? So why do I feel like a piece of shit for wanting the man I am having sex with to have the same? Perhaps there is something to be said for not "needing" anymore, but "wanting."

Wow, self-realization without Dr. D. I feel like I am evolving.

But then again, I don't want to have sex with his car, and besides, I drive everywhere anyway.

Just for the record.

Reason #1: *Monetary gaps in the bridge over the river of a relationship make it unsteady.*

I am breaking one of my cardinal rules, never cook on the first five dates. I am cooking dinner. I love to cook, particularly for a man. My mom now says, well after Stan, that I will spend the rest of my life cooking, so date outside of the kitchen for at least a month before going there, that I don't need to prove I am a perfect homemaker, because I am. Which I know deep down, but can't let go of the need to hang it out there like my American flag.

The "right" man will know and eventually get the privilege of seeing that side of me. But here all bets are off, because I *know* Lance is not boyfriend potential. He is a tasty biscuit, plus he is a little strapped for cash, so this is fine. I am cooking.

The candles burn while Miles plays on the stereo. I am grilling halibut and peppers, and almond rice simmers in the pot.

Lance walks around the house inspecting every picture and book, making mental notes. He pulls out a poetry book by Neruda from the shelf. As he flips the pages of *The Captain's Verses* he starts to recite a poem. I stand there, frozen in my living room, as in a hushed whisper he recites a poem. Only toward the end he closes the book, and continues the poem because he KNOWS IT BY HEART!

OH MY GOD! He is such a potential boyfriend.

How is it possible that my arm candy has turned into a cerebral, sensitive poet guy?

"We're studying Neruda in class." He places the book back into its slot.

Class? Did he say CLASS? As in a school classroom? What class, college, my God, he is still in college.

"I'm studying music at UCLA. Our teacher says poetry is one of, if not the best source for lyrical inspiration."

I suddenly have images of him as a teenager while I drop him off in the white Chevy outside of Townsend Middle School in Tucson, Arizona. I shake it off.

I am torn between sending him home and tearing off his clothes.

Maybe it doesn't matter that he's a starving artist in his senior year of college. He is young, yes. Maybe a little naive, yes. But firm, sexy, introspective, dark, and mysterious. Yes. Yes. Yes. Such an oxymoron of a male specimen. And those old-soul brown eyes. Why think about it too much, no need to think, DON'T THINK, IT HURTS THE TEAM . . . no need to make a list. He isn't a boyfriend, he's a tasty treat. I am confused by the whole situation, but I am still very hot and bothered and the night is as young as he is.

Rule #2: *Male or female, dating someone in college is too young if you're in your thirties.*

He lights a cigarette and sits down at my kitchen table to watch me. "Need some help?"

Did he just ask me to help? My arm candy is asking to help with dinner. Ahh, love him already. Housebroken and all, he's not a pup.

He gets up and opens the kitchen cabinets. "I'll set the table."

I watch him set the table and we talk about the fleeting and temporal nature of life as he rounds the table with Sam at his heels. He leans down and scratches Sam under the muzzle as they share a look. He doesn't think we get second chances in life. He doesn't believe in heaven. He thinks it's a place we create here on earth. In the ocean (sitting in the surfing lineup, waiting for the wave, judging the peak, paddling into position, and that moment when you know you have it, when you feel its power accelerate beneath you, when it picks you up and throws you down the face), he has been taught. Taught about love and opportunity. Taught him how to seize the moment. He loves the freedom. He loves knowing that for the next few moments life has nothing to do with the world onshore.

He helps me with the dishes, all the while wooing me with those puppy-dog browns and his knowledge of my favorite poets. I empty the bottle of pinot noir into our quarter-full glasses and he pulls a little cigarette from behind his UCLA backpack and asks me if I want some. Surprise, it's a joint. Mary Jane, Ganga, weed, pot—I am cool with that, but haven't really gotten high since college. Not that I have a problem with pot, but simply that every time I smoked it I got cravings for things like mayonnaise sandwiches, chips, dips, cookies, cake, ice cream, fried chicken . . . anything, and not in small amounts.

When the "freshmen fifteen" turned the corner heading for twenty with momentum, I gave up bong hits for a waist-line. Lance lights the end of the joint and I take a little puff, followed by extreme coughing, eye-watering, and laughter.

It feels good to laugh, to be at ease, to forget about having the upper hand.

Lance hands me a glass of water. "Would you like some ice in that?"

"Sure," I say, watching him make himself at home in my kitchen. He pushes the dispenser and puts an ice cube in his mouth. Leaning down, he lets the ice cube slide from his mouth into mine with a HOT! HOT! HOT! kiss.

That night in bed, I think I am going to have to tie him down like Nuke LaLoosh in *Bull Durham,* but instead we just lie in bed taking turns reading *The Story of O* out loud to each other.

He takes off one piece of my clothing every few pages, and slowly touches every inch of my body. He asks me what I like, and I have no problems telling him. I like it here and there and everywhere and for a moment I feel like Dr. Seuss . . .

Fifteen days later: Living on Macro Bid . . . my prescription for a bladder infection.

"I am not making him into a boyfriend. I am not making him into a boyfriend. Shit, I am making him into a boyfriend," I say, looking at Dr. D.

"Yes, but you have been since you saw your, what was it, lollipop?" Dr. D. smiles.

"Arm candy."

"Yes, arm candy. Emily, if you want to find the right guy, why are you wasting time with someone that you knew was wrong from the moment you met him? Are you somehow setting lower standards for yourself, so you won't be disappointed? Won't be alone?"

Yes, I am. Why wouldn't I? I mean, every time I think that a guy has potential, like Reese, they turn out to be a complete piece of shit. Why not just keep the bar low in my wanting? If I don't want him to be my boyfriend, he can't hurt me. Then if he turns into my boyfriend, well, presto . . .

"Lance is great. Lance is smart and sexy. He's just a little young," I argue. "I didn't know that he was going to be someone that I would like . . . I mean, like-like."

"You're making him into someone you can like-like. Tell him to go home."

Reason #3: *When your therapist flat-out tells you that the guy you're dating is wrong for you, he probably is.*

"No," I say, crossing my arms. "I am happy."

"Do you want to find true love?"

"That's not fair, you know I do."

"Than send *the boy* home!"

"I thought you weren't supposed to tell me what to do. I thought you were, as a therapist, supposed to help me come to my own conclusions."

"You're a special case."

The clock cuckoos and I look up. "Oh, lucky me. Time's up." I pick up my bag and swing it over my shoulder. I do not look at Dr. D., who is still sitting in his chair as I open the door . . .

"Make the list for him," he barks just when I thought I'd escaped.

Maybe he was right. Lance hasn't really left my house except to go to class, as he doesn't really have a home to go home to. He still lives with his parents, but in the guest house.

But he still lives with his parents.

Reason #4: *He lives with his parents.*

Fucking Dr. D. got me all worked up. He did have a point about wasting time. But when is it really wasting time? Tick-tock. I can hear my ovaries dying. If only I were twenty-two again, time wouldn't matter. Am I supposed to sit at home waiting for Mr. Right, Mr. Reese Callahan, to just knock on the door and pronounce us man and wife? Why is it so bad to kill some time with someone who makes me, well, hot coffee before going off to work in the morning? None of this would matter if only I had ten years back. Why can't I just enjoy my arm candy and not worry about it? Tick-tock . . .

"He lives with his paaarreeennttts?" Reilly almost spits out her drink.

Reilly, Grace, and I sit at our usual spots at the bar in Atlantic.

"Wow. How young is he?" Grace asks.

"Twenty-three, but he has an old soul."

"Where is he tonight?" Grace questions.

"Waiting for me to get home."

"Your home?" Reilly asks.

"Yes."

"Nicely trained." Grace tings my martini glass.

"We *do it* a lot. In the kitchen. On the table. Over the sofa. In the shower. In the back room. You name it, we're doing it, and it is amazing. I don't know. I mean, I am not making him into my boyfriend or anything, but . . ."

The girls both roll their eyes, knowing that I am indeed molding Lance into the guy I want.

Maybe they were right. Maybe I was molding him. But so what? There is a fair amount of training that goes into every guy, into every relationship.

"WHICH ONE?" LANCE asks, holding up two shirts.

I feel sick, as both are thrift-store Hawaiians and we are having dinner with my new boss at The Ivy.

"Why don't we jump over to Barney's and take a look around."

"Barney's? The big purple dinosaur?" he says, almost making fun of me.

"No, Barney's the big overpriced trend store on Wilshire, baby."

"I know what you mean, but I can't afford Barney's," he says, pulling on his shirt.

"Yes, but I can," I counter with a lift of the eyebrows.

"Touché," he says, tossing me my keys.

After watching the salesgirls fawn all over my tasty treat, I leave less $400 plus two shirts. But, he looks smokin' hot in Armani! If I could just fix that hair.

Reason #5: *If you want to dress up your boyfriend, buy a Ken doll.*

On our way home I stop in Umberto's to buy shampoo and various products as a ploy to see if my hairdresser, April, is working. April takes Lance's semidirty hair and snips away the curls, giving him a George Clooney buzz cut.

We went to dinner that night and it was like dating a different mannequin . . . I mean man. Can you dress them up and take them out? What was I doing to poor Lance?

"I admit it. I have a problem."

"Thank you," Dr. D. says.

I am successfully changing Lance. I have taken things that were cool about him and sterilized them. I have made him into a straight version of Stan. But somehow I know that deep down, Lance is not Stan. Lance at thirty-four is going to be hot, smart, sensitive, and wow, I will be like . . . mid-forty-something, taking care of him and the kids while he has sex with college girls.

For now, I am still obsessed with the training and validation. I have noticed little nuances that need fine-tuning beyond the apparent hair trimming and new clothing, things like Lance's eating habits. Maybe it is a guy thing, maybe it's a young thing, but why is it that when a man holds utensils he holds them like a sandbox toy? I've seen Lance eat soup, ice cream, and cereal, all with that damn shovel.

"Hey, nice shovel," I murmur as Lance slurps Cap'n Crunch at 6:30 P.M. into his very stoned body.

"Sssssorrryyy," he says, awkwardly embarrassed with his mouth full of milk. He changes spoon position and continues.

This is not a good sign. There are definitely things that I do to make my man the way I want. A fair amount of house-training needs to take place before one says, "I do." But I have become passive-aggressive in my obedience school training. I have become the dominant alpha she-wolf. Which is fine at work, but doesn't work for me at home.

Rule #6: *I don't want to be the boss at home.*

To dress one's boyfriend the way I like him and then school him on table manners has got to be a reason. A penalty somewhere in the Emily dating handbook. Some women want to be the boss, I mean, really, we are the bosses. But at home I just want my man to be the man. And I have a man-child.

But at that moment, while contemplating breaking up with Lance and sending him home . . . he puts down his cereal bowl and makes his way to the sofa, on his knees. He lifts my flowy skirt and kisses my inner thigh with his cool, milky mouth. I lay my head back and lightly moan. All of the buzzers and whistles stop and I am reminded why . . . young is good. Young is nice. Young is . . . oh, God, yes!

11:15 A.M. the next morning. Pop home from the office between a meeting over the hill in the Valley and heading back to the office. I have been up since 5:00 A.M., taken Sam to see another specialist, did yoga, made seventeen calls, one conference call, showered, dressed, and am back home.

I open the door of my bedroom and look at Lance, still sleeping. I smile a sort of GET THE FUCK out of my bed smile. The door creaks shut and his sleepy eyes open and he says . . .

"Babe, can you leave me five bucks for a sandwich at Subway?"

I smile a weird little awkward grin, squint, and close the door.

I am pretty sure that I am not supposed to leave my boyfriend LUNCH MONEY.

Rule #7: *Leaving lunch money for your boyfriend is a no-no.*

Two weeks later: Lance still has not gone home. I'm torn by the fear of sending him off to be alone versus keeping him here to waste time, as we know he is not the right guy.

I truly do love spending time with Lance.

We've successfully visited Banana Republic, the Gap, Hugo Boss, Kenneth Cole, and various restaurants, bars, and day spas. I sit at the kitchen table and balance my checkbook. In exactly thirty-two days I have spent $4,822.42.

"Holy SHIT!"

Rule #8: *Too much paying will end a relationship.*

As I close my checkbook and look up, Lance stands in my doorway in a towel. Wet, ripped, and willing. I look at him and for the first time he isn't hot anymore, he's just young.

Rule #9: *You'll always pay as he hasn't had an adult job . . . as he isn't an adult.*

He holds up a black cashmere sweater.

"*Can* I wear this?"

Did he just say, "Can?"

Rule #9½ *(God, he's so hot I don't want to get to TEN):* *Your boyfriend shouldn't have to ask permission.*

I nod yeah, but a what-have-I-done nod. He smiles and walks into the bathroom to have a shower.

What's next? He asks if he can stay up late tonight. Really, what have I done? I have taken my boyfriend's balls. But he let me. He let me pick the clothes and buy the dinners and he licked me for hours. He liked that I took care of every detail and he took care of my "needs."

I open my computer to pay my bills online. Ugh!
INSTANT MESSAGE POPS UP ON MY SCREEN.
Callahan26

Em, What's new? How's my favorite L.A. girl?

To tell him . . . hmmm, to ask his advice? Favorite L.A. girl. Is there a favorite New York girl, Atlanta girl, Houston girl?

RC,
   Not much, just working hard and paying too much. How goes the game?

Em,
   Good—we're coming to L.A. and . . .

Lance sneaks up behind me and kisses me on the neck. He's naked, fresh as a daisy out of the shower. His towel falls to the floor. I push my laptop screen down. He leans down to kiss me. I roll back in my chair, push down hard with my heels, and the chair falls over backward, sending me crashing onto the hardwood floor.

"Isn't this how we met?" he says as he tries to pick me up.

I squirm and move out of his reach, as his touch is enough to change my mind—which is already made up—and just for the record was made up before the IM from Reese.

I crawl onto my feet and realize that my elbow is trickling blood. Lance looks concerned and tries to help but . . .

"I got it!" I snap at him as I push past into the bathroom.

Maybe it was my tone. Maybe it was my words, but at that moment Lance wasn't acting young anymore.

Before I could put peroxide, Neosporin, and a Band-Aid on my elbow, he was dressed in his tan khakis, thongs and his old Hawaiian shirt.

That afternoon he grabs his backpack and longboard and says he is going surfing. I knew he wasn't coming back.

"Don't you want to take some of your clothes? I mean, in case you want to change." I look into his brown eyes.

"Nope, I got my clothes. Those are your clothes for me." And with that, he smiled and walked out the door.

I stood in my picture window with Sam at my side and watched his white Malibu rumble to a start and rattle away down the tree-lined street as the dead leaves fell and drifted from the maple trees.

Rule #10: *When you're not sad he is not the one, maybe it isn't a bad thing.*

There was a sense of relief. A sense of sadness, but mainly a growing sense of my bladder infection, so maybe it was good that it was over. I needed the sleep.

After Lance left I lifted the computer screen and saw the last IM from Callahan26.

```
Em
Em . . .
Hello. . . .
Hello . . .
Okay, well, I'll call you.
```

Callahan26 signed off at 7:32 P.M.

In bed that night at 9:00 P.M. I turned the light off and for the first time in thirty-six days sighed, and fell fast asleep.

Lance's words came back to me. Words from our favorite poet. "Lord, it is time, the summer was too long. Lay now thy hand upon the sundial and on the meadows let the winds blow strong."

"You seem," says Dr. D., as I sit on the couch noticing the firmness in my triceps from hours and hours of bracing myself on my knees, "healthier."

"I am," I say.

"Are you ready, then . . . to try for what you want?"

"I hope so. I really hope so."

Reason #10: *When you're not sad he is not the one, maybe it isn't a bad thing.*

Reason #9½: *Your boyfriend shouldn't have to ask permission.*

Reason #9: *You'll always pay as he hasn't had an adult job . . . as he isn't an adult.*

Reason #8: *Too much paying will end a relationship.*

Reason #7: *Leaving lunch money for your boyfriend is a no-no.*

Reason #6: *I don't want to be the boss at home.*

Reason #5: *If you want to dress up your boyfriend, buy a Ken doll.*

Reason #4: *He lives with his parents.*

Reason #3: *When your therapist flat-out tells you that the guy you're dating is wrong for you, he probably is.*

Reason #2: *Male or female, dating someone in college is too young if you're in your thirties.*

Reason #1: *Monetary gaps in the bridge over the river of a relationship are unsteady.*

chapter seven

Never, Never, Never . . . Go Back

Rounding the corner with a limping Sam, I drop the leash as my speed-walk with arm weights turns into a jog that turns into a sprint up the steps to my porch panting harder than my pooch, unlock the door, rip off the button-up sides of my Adidas sweats and bolt to the bathroom. Where I . . . Ahhhh . . .

Nothing is better than that instant relief when you RE-ALLY, really need to peeeehhhh. After rebuttoning, I wash my hands and find myself studying a stranger's face in the bathroom mirror. To be gentle, she looks . . . well . . . scary. I can see that a few wrinkles on the sides of her eyes have escaped the Laksy Clinic and Dr. Stevens and Mekelbergs' Botox treatments. JESUS, how many cc's of nerve-numbing poison must a woman shoot into her face to defy the aging process?

How the hell do all those Olympic runners look sexy and flushed after a race? I eye the Xanax in my medicine cabinet and wonder if my exercise did enough for my health to balance taking one now with two quick glasses of wine and an hour of mind-numbing A&E's *Biography* while lying on the couch with the fan blowing directly onto my overheated body. Sounds like a slice of heaven on this Saturday afternoon.

In midcontemplation, the doorbell rings. Sam howls! "Hold on!" I yell from the back of the house, expecting a delivery from MGM of a press kit that Josh wanted me to proof. I dry my face but can't seem to get the mascara out from under my eyes. *Ding-dong.* "Hold on a sec!" I stomp to the front door in my stinky, sweaty old Tom Petty T-shirt and wonder whether the messenger will get the humor in me telling him trick-or-treat. After rubbing Sam under the chin and looking into his eyes smiling back at me, I open the six-by-six-inch, swinging, eye-level, fifties security door and look out at . . .

REESE.

Reese standing before me, through the peep door, in black trousers and a green short-sleeved dress shirt. A double shot of *"flutter, flutter"* shoots up me with a wave of memories. Kissing him. Wanting him. The way he looked naked in bed. His perfect cleft chin. His dimples when they overcame his face after he told a joke. All of it rushes and confuses my body, overcoming me. I feel weak, almost faint, as I hold onto the doorknob for stability.

"Hi, Em," he says.

For the record, I'm not a big fan of the showing-up-unannounced thing, as I don't have proper slather and preparation time. Two thoughts explode through my head: (1) Is my face still beet-red with mascara under my eyes that makes me look like Ozzy Osbourne? and (2) What if I had a new boyfriend? Or better yet, what if I were in the throes of passion with my new boyfriend? Unlikely, but it could happen.

"What're you doing here?"

"I came to tell you I was sorry." He just throws it out there like a perfect forgiveness pitch.

"Sorry?" I say, almost out of breath. "For what?"

I realize I am fiddling with the doorknob from the inside. Still safety-tucked indoors between two inches of solid oak. I am opening it. And there he is . . . towering over me. Sam howls again and jumps all over him, licking and brushing in and out of his legs, acting out my real-world fantasies. Reese bends and gives Sam some love. Sam gives him a good *HOWL* as if the wolf in Sam responds to Reese's alpha-male scent or something, one dog to another. Reese gives him a full belly howl back and they're bonded. For me, all I can think is . . . this is the first time they've met. After all that Reese and I have been through, at least in my mind . . . the movie, Pittsburgh, the relationship, San Diego, the e-mails, the friendship . . . the wanting . . . the reality is . . . he's never even met my dog. What kind of crap is that?

I want him out.

He is definitely not coming into my house. My house is somehow the safe haven to my heart. He is not stepping one big toe inside. No way. My mind is made up. My resolve is hardening.

"You look hot," he says. Then it strikes me that I reek of sweat, my face is redder than a lobster in a boiling tub, and Mr. All-American Baseball himself is in my doorway.

"Can I come in?"

"No."

My nosy neighbor, Beverly, an angry would-be starlet from the thirties, who is now a sucked-tight, hat-wearing, bitter, horrible, rude, vacuuming-at-4:00 A.M., someone's mean old grandma-on-acid type, spies on us.

Reese looks over and gives her his boyish, howdy ma'am smile with a . . . "How are you doing today?"

Beverly starts in with a voice that curls Sam's tail under. "I was fine until that vicious wolf started howling . . . again . . . for the fifth time today. Why don't you go inside?"

"Why don't you?" I shoot back at her. "I saw you steal my garbage cans."

Beverly glares back from behind her glasses. "I can't even carry the cans!"

"You may play this whole ninety-year-old, can't-carry-up-my-groceries, gotta-have-Jason from-upstairs-do-it, but I saw you steal my garbage cans, one under each arm. I've got your number, Beverly!"

Beverly *SLAMS* her door and I yell, "I want my garbage cans back!"

I look up at Reese. "I'm moving."

"I can see why. Do you wanna get a cup of coffee?"

"Sure," I hear myself say, as if one simple cup of coffee means nothing. As if one cup of coffee at Starbucks down the street might give me a better chance of keeping him out of my house.

He starts to step through the doorway and I grab his big, rock-solid arm.

"My coffeepot's broken." I snap the leash on Sam and we stroll down the street past fascinated neighbors. I can almost see the smoke puffing out of their ears as their minds try to process what this gorgeous male specimen is doing with the woman they see solo walking down their block morning after morning, midday after midday, month after year, with only her faithful pup.

The wrong kind of silent nonsingle pride gives me confidence, and there is something nice about not walking alone today. Sam continues to subtly rub his snout underneath Reese's swinging arm. Reese runs his hand across Sam's fur as he arches his back to get a full in-motion body scratch.

When we get to Starbucks, Reese steps to the front of the line past a couple of guys who are reading the sports section. They look up and I can tell they recognize him. One of them whispers something under his breath. I step closer to Reese as he orders in that voice that soothed me to sleep so many nights on the phone, "Triple-venti, nonfat, no-foam, latte with three Sweet'n Lows."

Reese passes go and collects his two hundred dollars. Holy crap! He remembers my coffee. Ali Baba, the magic word is spoken. The key turns. My heart is unlocking. I'm easy. No,

I'm not. He cannot win his way back into my life with a cup of coffee that he remembers from over a year ago. I am stronger than that.

We step outside Starbucks. Sam is tied to a lamppost on the corner, ten feet away from the patrons of Noah's bagels sitting at sidewalk tables so my gentle giant doesn't scare them. They are all laughing, except for the Hasidic Jewish family, because Sam is slowly making his way around the pole in a circle, dry-humping the air.

Should have had him neutered.

His head is wrapped tight against the pole and his hips are shooting back and forth as if he is giving his best lovin' to a giant imaginary poodle who just won first place at the Westminster Dog Show.

Reese and I stop in our tracks and I am instantly horrified, but we can't help but laugh. "SAM! STOP IT!" I say under my breath through clenched teeth. But he doesn't and at the moment I make my move to get him he freezes, HOWLS at the sky, and has a giant orgasm on the sidewalk. Reese doubles over laughing.

Sam lays down in exhaustion, which I also find amusing, as do the other people eating breakfast—until he eats his own sperm off the sidewalk. At which point the laughter dies out and a dozen half-eaten bagels hit their plates. I am dying a slow, embarrassed death.

"He did not learn that from me."

Reese goes to Sam, unleashing him, to save me from any further humiliation and looks at the people, all gagging with astonishment. He smiles with pride and looks back at me as if signaling to catch up . . .

Buzzing on caffeine and high on the laughter endorphins, we walk back to my place and there it is. Out of my mouth it pours, "Do you want to come inside?"

Of course he does. I can see it in his eyes. He wants in . . . to my house, to my life, to my heart. I mean, why wouldn't he? After a year and a half of therapy, two potential new boyfriends, becoming a successful executive, and taking a gourmet cooking class, I have become the healthy catch of the day. I gave him my heart and he did what? Pissed all over it. Took my love and broke it like a wooden bat on an inside fastball, only to get another bat. It wasn't the first time he had to switch wood. In his book, I probably wasn't even a hit, just a long foul ball. Hey, bat boy, grab me another. The show must go on. I probably never even made his own personal *Sports Center* highlights.

He walks to the kitchen sink to wash his hands and I remember the nights I spent alone wondering if I was just insecure or he was a total pig. Nights spent wanting to kill him, wanting to see him, wanting to torture him! Wanting to have him back. Wondering, why? Why didn't it work? More important, was it me?

Now I am two promotions into getting my ass out of corporate America. I am finally at a place in my life, with $34,000 saved, when I may actually be able to buy my own home. I have paid off my Sallie Mae student loan, stopped putting 51-40 oil into the Mustang only to watch it leak out onto the driveway, became a functioning adult, and upgraded to the Land Rover.

I have driven the curvy road of relationships past men, boys, and a nongender. I have grown. Grown as a person, grown as a professional, grown as a woman. I am stronger and smarter and able to see right from wrong. Then why? Why can't I walk away from this one guy? Is there always one bad boy in our lives that we just can't say no to? Is this the ultimate test? Let's see how much Emily has really grown? This is a test of my character to stay strong and flex my self-preservation skills. Or is it a test to forgive?

Reason #1: *If it feels like a test, it probably will be.*

He turns off the water and dries his hands on my kitchen towels. I can't help but think that he's here. Let the past lie. Forgive and forget. We are both different now. Isn't timing everything? Wait. Wait. Stop.

Reason #2: *If there was a reason you left, remember what it was. At some point, if you take them back, they will leave you or you'll leave them AGAIN and probably for the same reasons you left in the first place.*

In this case I can't remember . . . was it his failure to commit or my good sense to walk away before I got bludgeoned?

I remember my fear.

But he looks soooo good, so honest, so open, so "belonging" in my kitchen.

"So what," I finally ask, "are you really doing here?"

"We're in town playing the Dodgers."

"Really? So you just thought you'd drop by?" I say, getting back into the sarcasm that saved me from so many painful situations all throughout my growing-up years. The sarcasm that is intended to block the obvious, that I may be wavering.

Good. Good ploy. Stay strong. Stay focused. Stay witty and in the game. My banter is my private ninety-five-mile-per-hour fastball flying at his head. Duck. Or is it a curve that will break over the plate, making him look like an absolute idiot when he hits the dirt on a called strike?

The pitch I am about to throw, however, may be hittable. He sees it out of my hand, picks up the rotation of the stitches on the ball, and starts his swing. "I just needed to see you. To tell you a few things I should have probably said before you walked, RAN out of my life. I figured you didn't want the answers to your questions then, but what I didn't figure was that I'd think about you, and miss you, every day."

I give him a "suuurrrre, suuurrrre" eye roll.

He's unwavering. "I missed talking to you. I missed the way you laughed with your little snort at the end. I missed the way you made me feel better. But I knew you wouldn't believe me if I tried to explain everything at that time. I guess I just needed to come and tell you that I know what happened when you were at my apartment and that it wasn't what you thought."

What I thought was that he had his penis in ten other girls. He swings and misses. I cock my head, changing my expression to a "likely-story" look as he walks past me and sits on the arm of the overstuffed couch in my living room. He digs his toe in and taps the plate with a rhythmic waggle. "Okay, it was what you thought, but it wasn't. Em, when I met you I was . . . well, you moved me. We were so much alike. But I had other stuff in my life."

"Stuff?" I question.

I'm not a questioner, but there it is. I sound like my neighbor Beverly. He made me do it. Oh, I hate that tone coming out of my mouth. I never want to hear it again.

"Yes, stuff. I had broken up with a girl, Molly, about two weeks before I met you in Pittsburgh, the girl whose picture and card were in my bag. She was calling all the time. It was messy. I should have told you more. And while we're at it, Hillary, the woman who you left the note to . . . hmm, what was it, "call on her cell phone," IS MY SISTER. Look, you're smart and sexy and I wasn't completely honest, but I was honest about how I felt. And I'm sorry if it hurt you."

I stand eyeing the plate. Rock back, glove and ball over my head, kick my leg up, knowing that I am about to throw him the heat and drive toward home. "Okay, I got it, so you were lonely and although I seemed to be perfect for you I just wasn't enough. But I thought I was, so really I was the fool, and that was a year ago! Got it. Thanks. That makes me feel better about me. But what do you want now? Forgiveness? You got it. I gave it to you when we became, hmm, friends. Acceptance? Fine. But if you want back in, forget it. The game for us is over. For the season, hell, for your whole career with me as far as I'm concerned."

He nods, shakes his head a little, stands, and picks an old Ernie Banks autographed baseball off the mantle above the fireplace.

"Boy, you make it tough. Still guarded, I see. Look at it from my side." He's changing his stance. "Did we ever once discuss whether we were seeing other people? Did we ever talk about monogamy?"

God, how could I be so mad and still want to kiss him?

"And Em, oh, by the way, why are you so angry now and nice in your e-mails?"

We both stand there a good five seconds looking each other in the eye. I start with one long breath.

"In the e-mails I am here in the safety of my home with my dog and you are lingering but not imposing. You're in the air, but you're not making a mark. I can't smell your Hugo Boss cologne in an e-mail. And to answer your question, no, you never officially said you weren't rolling in your double feather bed with other women, but Reese, the calls, talks, cards, flowers . . . all those things say you're not calling, talking, and sending flowers to the other women you are screwing."

Fastball down the middle. I had a point, a point men tend to forget: actions speak louder than words. He knows I have him on that one.

He shakes his head. "I wasn't, Jesus." His eyes meet mine. "I missed you a lot." He pulls a piece of grass off my T-shirt. It makes the hairs on my arm stand on end. "You still have your fire," he laughs, almost resolved that I am not budging. "I just came by to see if maybe you wanted to come to the game or see if we could get a drink. Whatever you want."

His boyish charm almost has me. I stand silently, giving him nothing. I run my hand over Sam's tail wagging back and forth as he stands, panting, watching the classic duel. More silence from me.

"Maybe it was a mistake to come, but I still needed to explain to you." He backs up toward the door. "Okay, well, then, I'll go," he says, walking out onto my porch.

He's at the warning track. It could be. He might be. Goooinggg aall theee WAY! Gone.

Reason #3: *If and when a guy who completely wrecked you shows up again and wants back in, he must be willing to work extra hard to get you back. He can't just slip away like a shadow at dusk. He must be tenacious, must prove that he will never, never, never do whatever he did again and that this time it will be different.*

Reese didn't know how to work hard at getting me back, he worked at one thing, hitting a ball. His whole life hung on that single struggle, and women came easily. Way too easily for a relationship. He'd never struggled a day in his life for a woman, love, sex, or happiness. There had never been a slump in any of those categories. For him, if it didn't happen in L.A., his luck was bound to change in Phoenix or Atlanta. He'd get a hit in San Diego or Florida. All he needed was another at bat or seven and he was bound to hit one out of the park. I was a split-finger fastball and he was expecting a slider.

Quick sidebar, almost a reason but not quite . . . if the man you want has 50,000 people cheering him every night, if men want to be him and women want to sleep with him, get out easily and quickly because at some point, sometime, somewhere *you* will not be easy anymore, as relationships take work. And work is nothing a ballplayer is willing to do OFF the field.

I watch him walk away. Stay strong, Emily. Do the right thing. SHUT THE DOOR. My internal warning system is on overload. Every fiber in my body is trembling and my palms are sweaty. My heart is racing . . . I can't control it. I can't stop myself. I STILL want him soooo much.

"I won't come to the game, but . . ."

He turns around.

"I'll have lunch with you tomorrow."

"How about a late dinner or drinks tonight?" he says with those damned dimples blazing.

"Can't. I have a date." A lie.

"Ree-he-heallllllyyyy."

"Yep. So, lunch?"

"I'll take it."

And just like that we were in extra innings.

I arrive at Dr. D.'s office, almost afraid to tell him.

"You're giddy," Dr. D. studies my face.

"Not giddy. More excited, with hints of fear and embar-rassment."

"Interesting choice of adjectives."

Dr. D. seems to know what I am thinking, seems to know what I am realizing, that Reese has the skill set to trick me with the faux promise of picket fences and love everlasting. Should I tell Dr. D. and hope that he goes easy on me, or should I avoid the whole subject of Reese? Well, I don't think it can hurt, telling him.

At what point did I start to believe that Dr. D. was judging me instead of helping me, and more important, why did I care what he thought in the first place?

"I am going to have lunch with Reese tomorrow." Jesus, I am embarrassed. "Before you start in on me, let me just say, he is *the guy*. Okay? The ultimate flutter. Now, I realize that may not sound all that healthy and maybe it isn't. Maybe it is, God, or maybe it was bad timing, or maybe . . . I dunno know. But it is bigger than him or me or therapy. There is still something about the way I feel when the phone rings. It's been over a year since we broke up, and every time the phone rings I still hope that it is him. It's the way I feel when I get an e-mail from him or see him online. It's the way I feel when I wake up at two A.M. and his arms engulf me, the way they make me feel safe, the way that I know he is in the room before I ever see him. It is either fate or chemistry or a fucking cliff that I am about to jump off, but I have to have lunch with him."

"Have lunch, then. Why are you looking for approval?"

I raise my eyebrow. "Approval? I am not looking for approval."

"Yes, you are. You are looking for me, your doctor, to tell you that it is okay for you to go back when you and I both know it isn't."

My tone changes, as if I can somehow take criticism about myself, but not Reese. I counterattack, "Maybe I am just looking for signs of life in you. Signs that you may actually, after all these sessions, understand what I mean by *the flutter.*"

"Emily, whether I understand your flutter or not is unimportant. I understand what you want and I understand the lengths that you will go *not* to get it. I'm not telling you that Reese is not the guy. I am saying that the odds aren't good. I am here to listen, advise, and help you, not validate what your flutter means." He takes off his glasses. "But just so you and I are clear, I do have a pulse, I do notice and hear you. I am vitally aware of how you understand and can tap into your hope for love, and that is rare. I understand that you are special, that you're busting at the seams with energy and that a bright shining light spills from your eyes and draws people to you. But ultimately, you are still just a gentle little girl who wants someone to love you." He slides his glasses back on. "Oh yes, Emily, I am alive and very clear on what you are saying now, what you have said up to this point, and, if your behavior continues in this manner, what we will be talking about when you are forty and still single."

At that moment he gave me a lump in my throat, and I wanted to officially break up with Dr. D., although he did not know it. I smiled faintly at what he had said and decided not to fight him. I changed the subject and he let me.

I continued on about the fact that I had given my resignation at the company and had registered my new PR company's domain and Web site. Tomorrow, after my lunch with Reese, I would be meeting with my corporate leasing agent to look for a small office space for my new company, Sanders Entertainment Media Strategies Group. It was a leap, a leap JJ was taking with me. We were only a group of three, but a group nonetheless.

When I drove away from the office I knew that it was Reese or therapy with Dr. D., as the two could never coincide under the harmonious and perfect union that I wanted my life to be. It made me sad.

I head to Beverly Hot Springs at ten in the morning for a cucumber-body-salt scrub that will loofah off any dead skin and leave me with a sixteen-year-old glow. I lay naked on the table while a large Korean woman scrubs me with what feels like wet burlap and smells like cucumbers. I daydream about what my life with Reese will be like. I am naming the children in my head when something on my calf begins to itch. The scrubbing continues and the itch moves up the back of my knees to my thigh. I reach back and scratch. The Korean woman flings me onto my side and begins to scrub my elbow. The itching intensifies until I can't take it anymore. I sit up, only to discover that I am head-to-toe covered in hives. I grab the water hose and start squirting my arms and legs as the older Korean owner comes scurrying in the back and yells at the woman who has been scrubbing me, "I tell you, you have to change the loofah and scrubs in between." I am suddenly mortified, as they now are yelling in Korean at each other and I am standing naked, scratching, two hours before my date.

I try desperately not to think about the fact that somebody's dead skin is all over me as the older Korean woman leads me into the cold dip pool and submerges me until I am convinced that I have hypothermia. I am torn between freezing to death and scratching to death. Forty-five minutes later, as I am still itchy, fully showered and slathered and ready for my date, I find myself writing a check for $120 to cover the bacteria scrub.

At lunch with Reese we talk and laugh and he scratches me. I remember all the reasons why this man had touched my heart.

Things I like about Reese: (1) He pulls out my chair. (2) He asks me what I am having and then orders for me. (3) He puts his fries on my plate before I have to ask for any. (4) He laughs at my jokes. (5) He asks me about my family, job, Grace, and Reilly. (6) He remembers that I must have dessert. (7) He tells me he likes the way I smell. (8) He never looks at other women. (9) He's here. (10) He's trying.

We leave the restaurant, and dark clouds spark with touches of lightning. By the time we are walking to the Rover it begins to pour and we stand for a second under the awning wondering if we should make a break for it. "Wouldn't it be great if we got a rain day? Just one day to rest, do something other than go to the field," he says, looking at the clouds.

"Wow, for someone who is living the American dream, that almost sounds like a complaint." I reach out and touch the wet drops with my upturned palm.

Crash! Lightning strikes somewhere in the distance and I pull my hand back.

"One, two, three . . ." he counts. The thunder *RUMBLES* on top of us. "Getting closer."

Part of the awning drips on my shoulder and he pulls me into him. "No complaints here," he says, looking down at me. "I love the game," he continues. "You know that. But it's my job. My job is to go out there one hundred and eighty-seven days a year, not counting spring training, and give it all I have, which is the only way you can respect it or earn its respect."

I smile at him. He looks ten years old, talking about the love of his life, baseball.

"It would just be nice if every once in a while we'd get a rain day, and I could do what I want at the spur of the moment."

"Like what? What would you do, Mr. Callahan?"

"I'd go to the beach or play golf, or go to the zoo, maybe . . ." He looks down at my face, which is mesmerized by his entire being.

"Or just lay in bed with you in my arms all day and watch movies." And he kisses me.

RIP . . . the awning tears and spills water onto us. We make a break for the Land Rover.

We shake water off of our clothes in the truck. He kisses

me again, only this time it feels like forever. When he starts the engine of my truck, I turn on my favorite Alana Davis CD and look at him. "The zoo, huh? We'll have to go there sometime."

"How about next week? They have a great one in Chicago."

And just like on the highlights, he hit it out of the park.

GRACE, REILLY, AND I make our way down to the "premiere level" of Dodger Stadium, heading toward the visitors' dugout with our hot dogs, popcorn, and beer.

I stop and check out the tickets as Reilly checks out the players.

"Wow, they have nice asses." She eyes Shawn Green, who is up to bat for the Dodgers. "Which one is he?" Grace questions, sitting and passing me my beer.

"That one. Number twenty-six. There, on first base," I point.

"Cute," Grace says. "Although I find it ironic that we know everything about him and we have yet to meet him. Don't you find that odd, Reilly?"

"He's really cute!" Reilly says, nudging me. Grace eyes her as if they are planning some type of intervention. Reilly's tone changes. "Yeah, odd Emily."

I ignore them both, as I refuse to turn this into another session with Dr. D.

Ahhh, at a baseball game with my girls, watching the love

of my life play first base. The inning finishes and he runs to the dugout, pauses for a second, and looks in the stands. He smiles right at me and gives me a tilt of his head. He stands there long enough to make sure I see him. I give him a little smile and he goes into the dugout!

Everyone within five aisles of the dugout turns and looks at me. Grace and Reilly die! My heart seriously feels like it is going to explode.

"Okay, that was smooth, very smooth," Reilly says.

"Too smooth." Grace shoots Reilly the look.

I set down my beer. "Okay, say it. Just get it over with. Both of you."

"Say what?" Grace puts on her therapist voice.

"That you think this is a mistake. That you think he'll break my heart. That he has a girl in every city. That he'll constantly be leaving me. That I'll be second to baseball. That he'll one day have to quit and go through some midlife crisis at thirty-five and date the beer-cart girl at the golf course."

They both sit dumbfounded, staring at me.

"Well, yeah, that pretty much sums it up," Grace nods.

"Very succinct," Reilly adds, looking at me, almost impressed. "Oh, but wait, you forgot that you will have wasted another two years, dropping you off past your mid-thirties, and you will be single again."

"Look, I got it. Okay, obviously it's already in my mind. It's all there. I am a little scared, but I can't be afraid to love him again. I can't, and if I don't at least try, how will I know?"

"We just love you and want you to be happy," Grace says.

"And if he breaks your heart, AAAGAAIINN, we're here for you." Reilly holds up her beer. "To baseball, Em's favorite new pastime." We all tap plastic Dodger cups together.

The girls dropped me at Reese's hotel, where I had conveniently left my truck. I wait outside near the valet stand, watching the team bus pull up to the Ritz-Carlton. Reese walks off and heads into the hotel without seeing me. I give him a slight whistle and he turns, grins, and heads my way. "You wanna get a beer?" he says.

"No. I just wanted to say thanks for the tickets." I nod at the valet, who runs to get my truck.

"You're going? Why? C'mon, have a beer with me."

I shake my head with an "I don't think so" look as the Rover rounds the driveway.

"I just really wanted to say thanks and well, it was great seeing you." The valet holds open the driver's-side door as Reese walks around to tip him for me, but then he gets in. I stand dumbfounded for a minute. The valet rushes around the front of the truck and opens the passenger-side door, but not before giving me a wink. I sigh and climb into the truck.

"Let's go home," he says.

That night in my bed Reese and I make sweet, sweet love. He treats me like I am a Dairy Queen soft-serve on a hot summer day. "You know," he says after leaving me trembling, "I'm not going anywhere, promise." With the candlelight dancing off my red velvet drapes and Sam asleep on his cozy blanket on the floor, life seems perfect lying in Reese's arms.

We kiss and kiss and kiss, and you know what? I believe in him, in me, and in us. Everything just falls into place like they say it does when you meet the right guy. And for the first time I'm not scared of him hurting me.

He leaves on that Thursday morning for Chicago and then it was the All-Star break and he was going home to Arizona. We're going home to Arizona.

The Western stars are aligned and we can actually spend some quality down time watching the purple, yellow, and pink sunsets over the blooming floor of the desert. I couldn't wait to be in his house. I couldn't wait for him to meet my family. I feel like I am bursting from every corner.

We rent a car at the airport and arrive around 6:00 P.M. at his house, which is sweet and not too big, yet big enough. It's decorated nicely, yet could use a woman's touch. That night we head to Albertson's and push a grocery cart together. I know it sounds small, but it is the small things that I have been longing for in my life. Each aisle is a new discovery about one another.

He likes Frosted Mini-Wheats, I like Frosted Mini-Wheats. He likes Almond Joys, I like Almond Joys. I like skim milk, he likes 2 percent. Okay, you can't win them all. But actually doing something this ritualistic, coming home, putting the food away, is a dream come true. Reese is BBQing his "famous" pork chops and I am actually making my scrumptious apple pie. I feel, well, I don't know. Domestic.

After dinner we lay in his oversized king bed watching *Forrest Gump*. He looks at me and does his best Gump impression. "Emily and I are like peeeas and carrooots. She's my best friend. She's my only friend." My heart officially opened.

We made love that night with his French doors open and a warm summer breeze blowing in after a thunderous monsoon. It smelled like him and me and the desert after the rain, which is beautiful and completely reminiscent of home for me.

7:45 A.M. and Reese heads to the batting cages before it gets too hot to hit a few. He kisses me as I roll over in a sleepy haze and says he'll be back at 9:00 A.M. with breakfast and coffee.

I hear the door slam, jump up, and look at my tired face in the mirror. MUST FIX. I jump in the shower, shave, loofah, and slather. Blow-dry, light makeup, new jammies, and back into bed. Ah, must appear to be perfect woman for perfect man. I look at the phone, wanting to call Dr. D. to prove my point, that Reese isn't a complete dick, that maybe it can work. But will it? Okay, I also want to get a little perspective and may have been a little harsh on him in my last session. Why am I compelled to call Dr. D.?

I dial. Big mistake. I begin to explain my revelation of the smell of the desert and shopping for Frosted Mini-Wheats, but I am subtly reminded by Dr. D. of Reese's failures in the past. Failure to commit. Failure to open his heart, other than to baseball. Failure to love me more than himself. He tells me to go back to easy-breezy girl. Throw on the brakes. Keep my heart in check. And right when I want to hang up on him, Dr. D.'s tone changes to almost, well, warm . . . and he finishes with, "Just give it just a little more time to let him prove that he is worthy of someone as special as you, Emily."

I hang up thoroughly confused. Luckily, I am saved. Reese is back with Starbucks and Krispy Kremes in hand . . .

Damn Dr. D. What does he know, other than the fact that I am special? Hmmm. But the damage of Dr. D.'s words is done. That night after going to dinner at Jillys and shooting pool, Reese and I lay in bed watching the All-Star game. He's still slightly annoyed that he wasn't picked, but he hasn't had the best season due to a shoulder injury in spring training. As I lay there listening to the perils of baseball, I get to thinking, *Maybe Dr. D. was right. I'm not listening to my own reasons. Maybe I need to slow down. Maybe for once in my life I need to breathe. To be just slightly more objective, protective, and just a little less willing.*

So I did. And like a wash of bravery, I remember how I felt when I left Reese's apartment in San Diego a year and half ago. It didn't make me mad at him. It didn't make me bitter. It just gave me the slightest inner edge. A freakin' miracle. For the first time in my life I put it all in perspective and pulled the emergency brake. I *was* learning.

But Reese knew. He sensed the smallest glimmer of protection. Just the slightest hint of guardedness, as if somehow I had moved the outfield wall just out of home run reach . . . he was going to have NO part of this. We lay there kissing.

"What's wrong with you?" he says as he delicately brushes the hair off my face.

I roll off of him and lay to the side.

"Nothing, everything is good, really good."

"I know you and something's up."

Reason #4: *Never listen to a man who says he "knows you" when he doesn't. He knows what he wants to know.*

I want to believe he can see into my soul, but you know what, he can't. He has no idea of the tears I have shed. The days spent wanting to call. The hours spent in therapy trying to figure out what the hell was wrong with me.

"I think we should talk," Reese says with all seriousness in his eyes.

See, I knew it was coming the . . . "talk," which is never a good talk . . . particularly when the man initiates the talk.

"What is it that you want from this?" Reese says, not giving away any idea of what my answer should be.

"I don't know. I am just taking it one day at a time. Easy-breezy."

"That's not going to work for us," he says, propping up on his elbows and flipping off the game.

NOTE: He turned OFF the game.

"If there is anything I learned in the last year, it is that we need to give it our all. I mean, I am not quite sure where it will take us and I'm not making any promises, but I know I don't want to be with anyone but you and I don't want to worry that you are back in L.A. with anyone else. I just think we need to be committed to trying this."

Did he just say "committed"?

The man whom I longed to commit to. The man who juggles the hearts of five women in five different states. Can he change? Has he changed? All questions to save for therapy.

"What's changed, Reese? I mean, I am okay with this now, but how do I know that in a couple of months when the honeymoon period is over you won't be gone?"

It's an honest question.

"I've changed. I wasn't ready. I am now. I know what I want, and it's you." He kisses me gently.

"There are no other women right now that I need to know about? No one you've been dating, chitchatting with, *e-mailing*? 'Cause let's just talk about it now," I say as if opening Pandora's box.

"No one. There's no one but you."

I am not sure at what point I believed him. But I did. He had so much honesty, sincerity, goodness.

"Trickery," Grace says, packing boxes in my kitchen. "It's Trickery 101." Grace, Reilly, and I wrap my dishes in newspaper as Josh comes through the door with two bottles of champagne. "Where's the new homeowner? Congrats on the new beach casa, Kitten." He hugs me.

"Thanks. Remind me of that when I am taking two Xanax a night to stop the anxiety of being a small-business owner with a mortgage. Jesus, renting and working for 'the man' was so much less worry."

"But so much less money and fun," he says, popping the cork. "So what were you dollies chatting about?"

"Can a leopard change his spots?" Reilly says, taking a glass of champagne and lighting a cigarette.

"Whose kitty are we talking about?"

"Reese Callahan. AKA RC Cola . . . not even Coke or Pepsi, but RC imitation Cola . . ." Grace says.

"No fucking way," he shoots back to her.

"Why can't we talk about Reilly's wedding or something? For fuck's sake, she's marrying a Frenchman," I pipe in, knowing good and well he isn't French.

"Belgium," she snarls. "Look, don't be bitter at me."

"Em, how come you have short-term memory loss when it comes to this guy? He's just telling you what you want to hear," Grace continues. "I want to be happy for you. I am. I just feel like I'm watching you make a huge mistake." She turns to Josh. "Emily and RC had the talk."

"Look, I wasn't the one who asked for 'the talk.' I wasn't the one who wanted to be committed, monogamous. He's different. He's more grown up. He's learned." I plead with my friends to understand and support my decision.

"I don't know. I would just be suspicious with this one. I mean, you already know he is a master manipulator," Josh adds with a hint of venom. "The guy has two cell phones."

He looks at me and then says with his "I love you" voice, "I think what the girls are trying to say is, just be careful."

I try to explain how he changed, but they're not buying it. I am just glad to have them to help me pack up the house.

There is something safe about these three people in my life

that makes me feel lucky, as if they've always been a part of me and always will be.

Careful. Careful. Those words ring in my head as I board Mid-West Express headed to Milwaukee for a Brewers game. Careful is with me when I check my bags on United to see Reese in Colorado, on Delta in Chicago, then St. Louis. Careful never leaves me as my frequent-flyer mileage grows like the Reese batting average. Every week, a new city. Every week Reese sends me a new ticket. Between trips we talk twice a day. Like clockwork, he calls on his way to the field, he calls on his way home to his apartment. We talk before bed. We talk all day. And sometimes we fight. Not bad. Just little disagreements that usually end with Reese saying something perfect like, "Honey, we're going to disagree. It's okay. It's not the end of the world."

Heaven. I am in heaven. We are a match and I have found the man I want to marry. His love of kids, family, ethics, Arizona, sports, humor, music. All of it. But it's only been eight months. Too busy traveling to the games, hanging out in the off-season, and being happy—to see Dr. D. I feel good, finally. Maybe I am cured. Safe. I trust again. Wasn't that the plan? Nothing that I thought would be possible with a professional athlete has become my reality. It just goes to show you that timing is everything.

But, I will say, the being-apart thing has gotten harder. The constant ache when he walks away. Even now, I get the slightest empty twinge. It fills me with the torture that maybe, just maybe, he won't come back. But he always does . . . and there are kisses. More kisses. Reassurance. Kind words. Hugs. Laughs. More kisses. And desperate gaps of time in between.

Dr. D. is pissed. Really pissed that I haven't been to see him in six months and thirteen days. I went to see him this morning as a checkup and do you know what he said? "Emily, you've picked a man who by nature pushes every scared little girl button you have. You have picked a man who leaves you every week. He was home for all of four months and now he's off, leaving you again. He LEAVES you. Leaves you. Leaves you. And you can't even blame him, it is his job. But, he's still leaving you." He shook his head. "Not good. We had just gotten past the whole abandonment issue lying under your murky past. Don't you see it? Reese feels familiar and familiar is comfortable, but sometimes familiar is bad for us. You have now traded your major league father issues for a major league baseball player."

Reason #5: *If he's always leaving, he has to go.*

Dr. D. was right. He was always leaving and it did feel familiar, but can we really pick and choose the people we fall in love with? For me, no. It's all about the flutter, the feeling, the knowing, the passion, the happily ever after. And Reese fits that bill. Would it be better if he was a lawyer or a sales guy or a fireman, sure, but the fact that he had a dream and he was living it was so awesome. It said something about his character. So I was willing to put my own issues aside to love this man.

IN A PICKLE . . . between what is right for me and what feels good for me. Caught like a runner between third and home. Knowing that I need to pick and make a run for it. But which way is really home for me? Because if I am smart enough to know I have issues, I probably shouldn't be dating someone who pushes those buttons. At some point wouldn't he leave me for good?

Issues are important. Issues are what you've learned along the way. For me the whole absent father thing is huge. It's always there. Wondering why he left. Wondering when he's coming back. Waiting, forgiving. This is my issue. It's what makes me comfortable in my own skin. It's what makes me NOT make the mistakes I have made before. It is experience, knowledge of self, and, if nothing more, it is thousands of dollars of therapy and countless hours of conversations with the friends who helped me figure them out. Why am I ignoring my issues?

"Hey, I love you," Reese says. I choke on a piece of ice and practically fall off the hotel bathroom sink. He looks at me with shaving cream all over his face. I sit there, my legs dangling off the counter, my back against the mirror, just staring at him. HE SAID IT!

I felt the tears filling, something inside of me that moved deep down because I had finally found someone who really loved me. I took his lathered face in my hands and kissed him, through our kisses I whispered that I'd loved him since the first day he smiled at me. And I meant it.

I wasn't sure when exactly those three little words changed

everything, but they did. Reese left for Atlanta and I went home to L.A. Our relationship had changed into something more, but I didn't know what.

In my new house in Manhattan Beach.

. . . the house is on a friendly walk street exactly eleven houses up from the sand. The navy trim gives the white wooded house a nautical, old beach house flavor, with a white picket fence that surrounds a little grassy area and patio. It has two bedrooms and a den. Two bathrooms and a sweet family room and dining room. It needs a new kitchen but has great wood floors and a working washer and dryer that just got delivered from Sears. Currently, I am still surrounded by wall-to-wall, floor-to-ceiling cardboard U-Haul boxes. Between the travel with Reese and trying to keep my little company running, it seems the home life is still in disarray. Sam has managed to maneuver around the new beach casa pretty well. His hips are still sore but I am more concerned with the lump that we had a biopsy on last week. The vet said it didn't look good, but as long as he is still eating, the meds should keep him comfortable. When I am away he is well loved at Grace's house. When I am home, he stays pretty much glued to my side. I think the boxes have given him anxiety. Must unpack!

I hear the phone ring. I see the cord on the floor and follow it along hoping to find the handset. I kick a box out of the way. It's on the third ring. At four I know it goes to voice mail, but I reach it. "Hello?" There's no one there. I missed it. I wait a second for a message to register and call my voice mail. Instead, "You have no messages." I knew the moment I heard the call that it was my Reese. I knew by the second ring that there was no way I was going to get to that phone on time. By ring three I realized that a call at eight o'clock at night during a game could not be good news.

Why isn't the ugly automated message that's on every personal voice mail telling them they have no messages more friendly and apologetic? And why doesn't it have some self-affirmation at the end like, "But that doesn't mean you're not special"?

The phone rings again. "Hello? Hello?" I answer and stand motionless, listening to Reese.

"W . . . w . . . wait," I stop him. "What does that mean? Torn rotator cuff?"

"It means I jumped in the air for a line drive with a man on third and came down on what's left of my arm. I made the play, but now I'm fucked! Done. It's over. My season, maybe my career," he says in a scary tone that I have never heard before.

Reason #6: *When things go bad you see the real man.*

"I'll come there," I say obviously.

"I am flying to Vail tomorrow to see a specialist and to prep for surgery on Friday," he kinda barks at me.

"Okay, well, I'll fly to Vail."

"Emily, no. I'll call you when I get there."

I ease back in my chair, staring at a framed photo of the two of us in Phoenix, on top of an unpacked box, somehow knowing immediately that something has changed. And it is more than a rotator cuff. It has something to do with the fact that I had now been put back on the shelf with the other less important stuff.

I wonder why it is that if I stub my toe, I want him to put a Band-Aid on it. If I'm feeling sad, he can make me feel better. Why is it when men are at their weakest, they don't want us to help them? Does an injury or a flaw in the armor somehow make them think that we will love them less? Or is it that, like an injured bear, they just retreat into their cave and lick their wounds? Either way, I'm alone and knowing something's different. At least his pain was tangible.

I get in the Rover with Sam and head to Grace's to spend the night. She has no idea that our movie of the week and pasta dinner are about to turn into a therapy session.

"What the hell just happened?" I say to Grace as I plop down my overnight bag and Sam's water dish on the floor of her town house.

"He may not have a job. He may not have a career left. He needs to focus on himself right now." Grace sounds sensible.

"Then why is my heart breaking?"

"You still want a man to need you, not want you. Do you see the difference?"

"But I want him to do both. I want to be there for him and he doesn't want me."

"Let him be," Grace advises as she pours a glass of wine.

"Why the fuck doesn't he want me there? Maybe he thinks the whole I-love-you thing was really a jinx, like love is a hex, or maybe he never loved me at all and this is just a good way out. Maybe he's not even injured."

She flips away from our movie of the week until the TV lands on *SportsCenter* at the exact moment that my noncommittal, abandoning, faking boyfriend dives horizontally in the middle of a full-out sprint for a line drive toward right field and makes a spectacular catch, only all 220 pounds of him comes down on his right shoulder. Grace and I both grimace in pain.

"Oh, he's injured." I shake my head in amazement.

I hit Reese's number on the speed-dial for the third time today and get the voice mail. I figure two messages is enough and hang up. Three makes me a borderline stalker. I pull into the underground parking structure at Dr. D.'s office, hoping to not hear "I told you so."

Dr. D. knows something is wrong the moment I walk in.

"Reese got hurt."

"I know. I saw it last night on *SportsCenter.*"

Hmmm. Dr. D. watches *SportsCenter?* That's not how I pictured him.

"I've called Reese three times and he won't call me back. I don't understand why he's not calling me. Why isn't he calling me?"

"Maybe he needs to focus on his body, or perhaps he can't come to grips with the fact that his career is probably over."

"But if his career is over," I say, "his life with me is just beginning. He has so much to look forward to. We have so much to look forward to . . . together. Why doesn't he want me to make him feel better?"

"Because that's not how men are," Dr. D. states emphatically.

I drive home from therapy and know Dr. D. is right. Everything he said was right. I finally got the number to Reese's hotel in Vail, where he is staying after his surgery, and I call. A woman answers. I knew it. Another woman. Some San Diego, Arizona, Florida slut who's been banging him this whole time. He never loved me. He never cared. And here she was, the proof.

I stumble with hello, but not before managing to blurt, "Who the hell is this?"

"This is Peggy Callahan, Reese's mother."

Embarrassed, I hang up.

Reese never called me from Vail or when he got home. The sad part is I can't even be mad . . . because his life is so shitty. Minutes seem like hours, hours like days, days like fall turning to winter. I can't eat and neither can Sam. I can't sleep. I've managed to unpack every box and hang every picture in my new house, hoping it will both ease my pup's mind as well as keep me occupied. I can't stop watching bad TV. Poop bag in hand, I take Sam on a short, slow walk as he wants to get out but doesn't seem to have the energy. As we meander along the ocean, my cell phone rings. It's Reese on the caller ID. Two long weeks have gone by. TWO WEEKS, and now he calls.

"Hi," I say. "How are you?" As if nothing's happened and my heart hasn't been breaking!

"I've been better. I'm sorry I never called you."

"That's okay I understand." Even though I didn't. "Where are you?"

"At home in Phoenix."

"I miss you."

"I miss you, too, Em. But I've really had to do some thinking these last couple of weeks and, well, I need to concentrate on getting healthy right now."

"But I can help you," I say.

"I have my family here. I have doctors here. I just need . . ."

"I don't understand why you don't want me there and I don't understand why you didn't call me. I . . . I . . . I love you. What's happening to us?"

"Just give me some time."

I sit down on the beach and look up at the full moon with the waves breaking below and Sam by my side. I sit there and imagine what the moment would feel like if Reese were here.

I feel empty. Spent. Worn out by all of it.

It's been thirty-six days since I have seen my man. His baseball season is over and I want my goddamned boyfriend back! Who is this new guy? His voice is different. His caring is gone. His ability to be anything remotely close to in a relationship is unfathomable.

I sit with Dr. D. and wonder how we've hit the wall on a turn at 185 miles per hour. Unloading all of the irrational, angry things I feel and want to say in this small twelve-by-twelve room.

"I called him today to tell him that I wanted to be with him. That WE said we were never going to go more than two weeks without seeing each other."

"And what did he say?" Dr. D. asks.

"He said that he didn't have anything to give, that he needed to concentrate on getting well. That I deserved the guy he knew he could be, and should be, but that he can't be that guy right now . . . and then he asked me to hang in there. Dr. D., I don't need anything. I just want my boyfriend back."

"Emily, come down off the cross. We need the wood."

"What?" I ask.

"You're becoming a martyr and that isn't good in a relationship. You do 'need' things. You 'need' to feel safe, happy, wanted, loved. Reese is being honest with you. He's taking care of Reese, which is exactly what he should do if his career is really over. He's struggling."

I look at my watch. Ten fucking minutes left. I stare at Dr. D. I want to scream. I DON'T LIKE YOU OR YOUR ANSWERS. I know Reese. He "needs" a woman. He "needs" me. He "needs" someone to take care of him.

"I don't understand why this happened," I murmur under my breath.

"You never will. We all want answers to why someone changes, stops caring, stops being there, grows without us, retreats without us . . . but Emily, Reese is just Reese and you're never going to understand what makes him pull away. You just have to accept that it is him. But we'll talk more about it next week."

Driving home I have an epiphany: If Reese isn't leaning on me for love, nurturing, ice packs . . . who was he leaning on? There's got to be someone.

Am I letting my imagination get the best of me?

Let's look back on this . . . He didn't want me in Vail. He doesn't want me in Arizona. He wasn't home at 2:00 A.M. last night . . . said he was sleeping. Likely fucking story. He went out with Mike Jenkins and his wife two nights ago. You just don't go out with married couples . . .

THERE IS ANOTHER WOMAN. Maybe two or three. I mean, this is Reese! There. There is my reason. He's a cheating, lying, injured sack of shit. But I must have evidence. I must catch him.

I must know because if it isn't that, then is it that . . . I am unlovable?

I ring up Dr. D. and give him my newfound knowledge.

"He's not cheating," Dr. D. says in the softest tone I've heard from him, as he knows what I know—that I am going off the deep end. He gives good phone therapy. "But here's what you need to remember. Whether he is or isn't . . . if you feel like this . . . you need to move on. Do you see my point?"

"Yes, I understand your point, but I need to be sure."

So I did what any psychotic, jilted lover would do in this situation. I gathered my girls and hired a private investigator.

The girls bust through my door with wine in tow, Reilly in the lead. "He's a lying, cheating, injured sack of shit," she shouts out.

Grace's sister's friend's husband is kind of a PI. He's in PI school in Phoenix. So he's tailing Reese for us, or rather for our amusement. And we're staying close to the phone to hear how it goes.

Jesus! What am I doing? WHAT am I doing? I am thirty-two years old. I have a great house at the beach. I have a great company and I've lost my ever-loving mind. I have a boyfriend who has been nothing but loving and supportive until doing the thing he loves most got him injured. Now, instead of being supportive, giving him space and being understanding, I'm having him tailed.

The girls are over and we are having my boyfriend tailed! Two bottles of wine later, "Are you sure?" I say in the phone talking to our wannabe PI in Scottsdale.

The girls are riveted on the edge of the couch. I pace, smoking Reilly's cigarette. "What exactly happened?" I then repeat it to the girls.

"A black Altima just pulled into the carport at his house. So, she had his clicker. Fine, I see. And then what? A brown-haired woman, was she pretty? Okay. Yes sorta. Keep going. She got out with a gym bag."

"Overnight bag," Reilly adds.

"Slut," shoots Grace.

"She shut the garage. Well, is Reese's Range Rover there? No. Okay, well. Go see who the hell she is. Knock on the door or something," I command Mr. PI.

"Kick her ass," Reilly says, powering down her last gulp of wine and opening another bottle.

"Okay. We'll be here."

I hang up.

"I am so DONE with him. Done, it's over. This is all I needed. It's over. I'm done. Did I mention . . . I AM DONE. You know, he said he wanted a smart, normal girl. The girl next-door type, but you know what . . . he never did. Men? The normal ones like us never seem to work for them, as we're too much work. Work to be honest, open, show up. Now he's got Hot Lips taking care of him."

I plop down in between Grace and Reilly, and they both look at me as if any minute I may explode. No one moves until . . . I throw my head on a pillow and begin to sob.

"I just don't understand."

"What's to understand? The guy's an a-hole. We knew this over a year ago. We knew this six months ago and now, thanks to Inspector Clouseau, we have conclusive evidence. I say we all get on a plane and go to the dickwad's house. Show up and . . ." Reilly ponders.

"And what?" I ask.

"Torture him anally with a red-hot poker," Grace says with a sudden disturbing tone that makes Reilly and I both stop and look at her. Then, for a minute . . . we engage in uncontrollable laughter as if all three are aware that my life has suddenly become a bad movie on the Lifetime channel.

The phone rings. "Are you positive? 96115 East Tatum Way? Oh my God," I shriek.

"WHAT?" Grace and Reilly say in unison.

"Yes! Stay put. Watch the Rover."

"What happened?" Grace asks after I hang up.

He was at the wrong house, I think to myself, sorta relieved but now thoroughly baffled. "The fucking PI in training has been watching the wrong house for the past three hours. How is that possible? I mean, I am not a PI, but isn't it like the first rule in the handbook, check the address of the house that you have under surveillance? Idiot. I hired an idiot."

"Reese is still guilty. I can feel it," Grace confides.

"Well, he's home now. The PI saw him pass by and pull into a garage two doors down."

The phone rings again. "He's on the move," I say to the girls. "Keep with him . . . Where? He stopped at a bar. Yes. Go in. Follow him. We'll call back."

I down some wine and think of calling Dr. D., as I am now on the express elevator to hell and no one can stop me. It's funny, it all seems amusing and entertaining . . . not like it's really my life, but the sad part is . . . it is my life.

Ring . . .

"One beer. With who? Alone."

The girls shrug.

"Where's he at now? Really, what's he renting? *Caddyshack.*"

"It's not a date movie," Reilly is quick to point out.

"Okay. Is anyone else at the house? No. Well, okay. Yeah. He's in boxers and a T-shirt with an ice pack on his shoulder plopped on the couch watching *Caddyshack,* and the pizza guy just left."

Grace yells from the kitchen, "He's not caught, but I know that pig is guilty!"

"Yeah, you can go home. He's in for the night," I tell the PI. "I'll send you a check this week."

The girls spend the night and we lay in my bed watching Alec Baldwin host *Saturday Night Live.* I am glad for my girls. I pass out, wake up Sunday, and go to church. The girls go home. My freaking head is pounding as I sit in a pew literally praying that my night was a bad dream and that I have not become the insecure wackadoodle that I think I have. Still, I know the dream is real and can somehow sense that it is about to get worse.

If I could just see him. If I could just have him hold me one time, I think that I could magically understand, be patient. His reasons would be clear to me. The problem is that he doesn't want that. Jesus, he doesn't even know that the distance, the silence, the abandonment are making me batty. He wants me to sit tight, hang on. But what was I hanging on to?

The horrible thing is, instead of letting him heal, grow, and get well, I can't help letting my imagination get the best of me, that he is somewhere in the arms of another woman, or he indeed does not need me. Either way, it makes me feel shitty and insecure and that everything is wrong.

Maybe this is a woman thing. Am I the only sane, secure woman who has lost herself in a man—a man who doesn't even understand or seem to care about the effect he is having?

That afternoon I call Reese.

Reason #7: *Hold on to reality or you're choosing insanity.*

"I am going crazy," I say to him. "And it isn't really your fault. It isn't my fault, either. But this situation is bringing out the worst in me. It's making me suspicious, insecure, and stupid. Reese, for all of the reasons that you fell in love with me—that I am smart and independent and very lovable—I have to let this go. Because if I don't respect me, who is going to?"

"I am sorry, Em, and you're right. I want to be the guy for you, but I can't."

In my heart, I thought he might fight for me. But somewhere inside I knew he didn't have it in him. Even though I wanted so badly for him to be able to.

Reason #8: *They absolutely must be willing to fight for you because if you're fighting every battle yourself, then you're still alone.*

I plop down on the kitchen floor, staring up at the pictures on the fridge to remind me that my life is full and wonderful in so many ways. I gather the strength of my life troops, never taking my eyes off the front of the fridge. I breathe in a deep breath and continue . . .

"I am sorry that you got hurt. Really, I am. And I am sorry if this entire conversation is forcing you to deal with one more thing that you can't handle, but the new you is not who I signed up to be with. I have worked too hard and come too far to settle for something less than what I deserve."

He says nothing. Just listens.

"No self-respecting woman is going to sit with blinders on waiting for something that may never come. It isn't enough. I don't need a lot, but I do need to feel wanted and important. Just one sign would have been enough," I breathe.

The silence grows, the light dims, until there is only the slightest glimmer of hope that he will plead with me not to leave him, that he will profess his love for me and my importance in his life.

"I know that you are the woman for me. I know in my heart that I am losing someone special, yet I can't do it right now. I can only focus on one thing and that is getting well and playing next season. I don't expect you to completely understand. Most people can't, but maybe this is just bad timing and maybe you can hang on," he says softly, "again."

Reason #9: *When they ask you to hang on, it'll feel like you're hanging from your neck.*

I wanted to yell at him. To scream, "What about the guy who said he was ready? Who told me to trust him? Who made me fucking open my heart only to watch it get trampled! UGH! I KNEW IT!" But I couldn't. When I picked up the phone to make this call, I knew what was true a year ago. Reese only knows how to fight for one thing, and I could only blame myself for wondering why I thought that he had changed.

"I'll always care about you and maybe sometime down the road, I dunno. I don't want to keep hurting you, but I just can't deal with your needs right now."

"Reese, the only thing I *needed* . . . was for you to love me."

I hung up knowing that I would probably never talk to him again. Yet he had left the hope alive with the whole timing issue. Only this time I know I won't let him back in my house, my life, my heart, ever, ever, again.

It was the moment when I knew for the first time in my life that I was growing up and taking care of myself.

I was strong. I knew that I had made the right decision, because I did have needs. It wasn't that I was crazy. It was that dating him would make even the sanest girl mentally unstable. It was over. I had ended it. I knew it was right, but after I hung up I cried for the next three days straight.

I have grown. I am changed. I finally know that I deserve more.

Sitting on the patio at my house watching the waves gently slide onto the sand, I note that the surf is low today and the ocean looks peaceful. I sip a glass of pinot noir as the sun sets and pet Sam. He is feeling bad today. I can tell his hips are hurting by the way he holds his right back leg in. He isn't really eating and last night he whimpered in his sleep for hours. The vet said I'll know when he's ready, but I don't think I'll ever know.

I try to focus on the good instead of how overwhelmingly lonely I feel, the aching in my heart surrounding thoughts of Reese that never seem to dull. Two more weeks have passed without a word. I have been strong and not called, although I want to every day.

I am working hard at the office from 8:00 A.M. to 8:00 P.M., only deviating to take Sam to the latest specialist of the month. I wonder how it is that I seem to be relatively sensible on the outside. Yet inside I am irrational and crazy. I mechanically move through the day like a robot with most of its guts pulled out. Frayed wires shoot every which way, starting small electrical fires inside of me every so often, triggered by a song on the radio. Little tantrums that flare up, sparking and arcing and shooting through what's left of my heart. The fires are made of questions all starting with why. Why?

Why is it that the one thing that isn't working is 95 percent of my pie in life? Why is it that Reese still consumes every other one of my thoughts? Why couldn't I focus on the good things in my life? My work, my new house? The cute guys at the beach? Why must I constantly wonder where he is, how he is doing, who he is with?

I am living in the memory of him, the possibility of him, because the present sucks. I wonder if all women slip into some sort of vulnerable position of fear postrelationship they really wanted to work. Do we all lash out, mainly at ourselves, when it slowly slips away?

I think it was the not knowing that made me batty.

I head into the house with Sam at my heels. He whimpers as he lies down at my feet. I reach down and give him an understanding look and scratch him on his muzzle. I pour myself another glass and shut my refrigerator door. I stand looking at the frozen images of my life stuck to the fridge with magnets. Grace, Reilly, Mom, Josh, Sam . . . and a small picture of my dad and me when I was five. I study the photo of myself in pigtails and a flowery green dress. He holds me in his arms, and I long for that time long ago. My eyes drift to a picture of Reese and me at his house in Phoenix in the front yard. I am smiling and happy. Then, as if my eyes are playing tricks on me, he fades out and I am standing there alone.

But I am not alone.

I take the picture of Reese and me off the fridge and toss it in the garbage. I open the freezer door and pull out the vanilla ice cream and proceed to give Sam a bowlful. I lay down on the hardwood floor next to him, stroking his fur as he laps up the entire bowl. When the bowl is empty he licks me on the side of the face, and I can't help but bawl.

Reason #10: *It doesn't matter what is happening, it only matters how you feel.*

Dr. D. was right. I did have needs. Wants. Desires. At thirty-two, it was about time I started acknowledging them.

Reason #10: *It doesn't matter what is happening, it only matters how you feel.*

Reason #9: *When they ask you to hang on, it'll feel like you're hanging from your neck.*

Reason #8: *They absolutely must be willing to fight for you because if you're fighting every battle yourself, then you're still alone.*

Reason #7: *Hold on to reality or you're choosing insanity.*

Reason #6: *When things go bad you see the real man.*

Reason #5: *If he's always leaving, he has to go.*

Reason #4: *Never listen to a man who says he "knows you" when he doesn't. He knows what he wants to know.*

Reason #3: *If and when a guy who completely wrecked you shows up again and wants back in, he must be willing to work extra hard to get you back. He can't just slip away like a shadow at dusk. He must be tenacious, must prove that he will never, never, never do whatever he did again and that this time it will be different.*

Reason #2: *If there was a reason you left, remember what it was. At some point, if you take them back, they will leave you or you'll leave them AGAIN and probably for the same reasons you left in the first place.*

Reason #1: *If it feels like a test, it probably will be.*

chapter eight

Good-bye to a Friend

SUBJECT: His Time

Date: Thursday, Sept 8, 2002

From: EmilyS@AOL.com

To: Distribution:

Grace, Reilly, Josh, Mom, Jeff, JJ. . . .

Dear Friends:

My heart is breaking.

I have made the decision to put Sam down tomorrow.

The time I have shared with him. The stories,
howls, walks, hikes, cuddles, and knowing that
he is always here to love me have given me
great joy over the last eight years. I will
miss him deeply.

I know that his quality of life is no longer dignified or pleasant. I know that he suffers daily from hip, stomach, and skin pain. I know that he is exhausted from seeing every specialist in L.A. and being poked and pricked. I know that he looks at me every day before I leave and every night before I go to bed with sad eyes as I slip his cone over his head to stop him from biting himself. I know in my heart, although I tried to ignore it, that he is ready.

Tonight I will feed him steak and ice cream and all of the wonderful people food he has never been able to stomach. I will take him for a long walk without his leash and let him smell all of the flowers, grass, and trees he has marked. I will roll in the yard with him and hug him for hours. He'll rest his fuzzy muzzle on my bed with his huge yellow-green and brown eyes and watch me fall asleep. Then I'll hear the click of his nails on the hardwood floor as he checks the house and eventually comes into my room and settles in his bed at the side of my bed and falls asleep.

Tomorrow morning he will wake, we'll walk, and then he will no longer suffer. The vet is coming to the house at 7:00 A.M. to do it here so it is less traumatic for him. He will go to heaven from the safety of his own house. Surrounded by his friends, family, and me.

Anyone who ever spent time with Sam knows that he is a special dog who came into my life when I needed something to love, and he needed kindness, comfort, and safety. We have taken care of each other and given each other boundless joy and love.

In the afternoon, after he is gone, I will wander around aimlessly for a while picking up his toys, beds, and bowls and know that his spirit is with me and will always be near to protect me.

Please say a little prayer for him, and for me, tonight.

It is so hard to let go of something so beautiful, magical, and something that I truly love so very much, really, truly heart-wrenching... but I know he will be chasing bunnies in heaven and waiting for me to join him someday.

He's been a good ol' pup.

Emily.

chapter nine

Don't Date Your Dad

itting at my desk in my office, overlooking my back yard, the Pacific Ocean, I review the press list for an upcoming MTV party. We're handling the PR. Business is good and this account is going to put me on the map with the cable industry. We need it. I look at my name on the bottom of a press list. CONTACT: Emily Sanders . . . President . . . impressive. I feel like one of those Virginia Slims ads from the eighties.

I can still feel the dull aching hole that Sam once filled. The silence in the house without him is deafening. It hasn't left for even an instant. But is it slightly less razor-sharp every morning.

I wonder if I am grieving over the loss of my pup or still grieving over the possibility of the happily-ever-after life that never was, with Reese. I think it is both. I know for sure that

I am hiding from the knowledge that at some point I will have to go out there again and try.

The last seven months feel like a trip over Niagara Falls in a barrel. Everyone I know has been hard-selling me the hope of "new love." I go out with the girls and end up chatting about spring training and the upcoming baseball season with the bartender. I made it through the holiday season staring up from the murky depths of an eggnog bowl.

I have given up waiting for love, believing in love, or hoping for it. Once upon a time I bought into Santa Claus, the Easter Bunny, and a father who said he'd be there on my birthday. It was hard to see them for what they were, but new confidence replaced the old wonder-eyed amazement. I am a big girl and don't need to believe in such nonsense.

As a bonus, I have gotten on the bandwagon and joined a book club, and all we read is the latest kitschy novels about how GREAT it is to be single. They are witty and sassy and full of great stories, but you know what? I like having someone to hold my hand. I guess that's why they call it fiction.

What exactly is love, anyway? I love my friends. I love my family. I loved my dog. I just don't know if I can love a man, or if maybe they can love me. And what happens if they do? I am now approaching the age when the "I do," is quickly followed by a year of fertility tests, injections, and drugs that will hopefully help us produce two kids before he goes off to play golf. Forever.

I have decided that men, for now, are a waste of time and energy. I am embracing the single life. Does that make me bitter? I am tired of hoping, fixing, being patient, being there . . . when at the end of the day I am really alone. There's that word again.

A lone soldier like, what was her name . . . the nineteen-year-old virgin they burned at the stake. Hmm, I am . . . Joan of Arc. Emily D'Singleville. Doomed to fight the question asked by all, including me: "Why do I sleep alone?"

Will I be one of those women sitting in the bar when they're fifty, bashing men? I'm not a man-basher. I love men, the way they smell, their forearms, their teeth, the way they give me the flutter, flutter.

That's it. My flutter meter is off. It definitely got dulled, bent, bashed, and twisted, like the rest of me, by Reese. Maybe it finally just turned off. After all, the flutter is what always gets me into trouble. Maybe Dr. D. is right. The flutter is my warning system, not my love meter. So far, every wrong guy has had the flutter in common.

The phone rings in the office and my assistant, Karen, a twenty-two-year-old UCLA grad, answers, "It's Grace."

I push the speakerphone and that dear, trusted voice rings through. "Okay, I'm in."

"You're in?" I say, excited. " 'Cause it's really a big deal for my company. You know landing MTV was huge. This launch party is the kickoff for my national promotion campaign."

"It'll be great. You'll be great. You know Reilly and I will be there for you! A fun girls' night out. Gotta run." Grace hangs up.

That night at my party for MTV, I stand with my girls on

the balcony looking out onto the garden. From here it looks almost make-believe, with its fairy twinkle lights shining off the passing silver trays.

"Look, look . . . it's Britney," Grace whispers in Reilly's ear.

"C'mon, I've got to get back," I say as we walk down the stairs into the main party room, which is covered wall-to-wall with video screens, rock stars, music executives, composers, and record-label types, music blaring, shrimp on cocktail trays, memorabilia from rock over the last thirty-five years, champagne, and caviar.

My eyes dart across the party and I smile at the marketing executive from MTV, who gives a nod of approval.

I feel relieved and happily reach for my first glass of champagne. "Well, this month's house payment is made."

"And then some," Reilly says.

"Bar's open," I say, grabbing my girls' hands. We glide across the living room, through a sunken billiards room past Luke Wilson playing George Clooney. George gives me a "hello" wink, as he doesn't know my name, but has seen me enough over the past five years to not be a stranger. Funny how times have changed—although he is still uberhot!

"There's that guy, the guy who dated Sheryl Crow. He sang that song . . ." Reilly ponders.

"AH! 'Tears in Heaven,' yeah, 'Tears in Heaven.' What's his name?" Grace continues.

"Eric Clapton," a man in front of me at the bar with a lovely British accent says, without turning around.

Nice shoes, black trousers, black T-shirt, with camel-colored suede jacket . . . can't quite see his face. "Citron martini," the still-mysterious gray-haired guy says to the bartender.

"Two." I saddle up for a better look at the mystery guy.

"Make that three," Grace pipes in as Mr. Mysterious turns around and looks at us and smiles at me with his full lips and white teeth shining.

Flutter, flutter.

Damn it! Just when I thought my flutter was dead. Now the question is, to risk or run? Sweet green eyes, strong jaw, over six foot, and definitely over fifty. Strong, deep laugh lines around the eyes and mouth. Hair short, all gray, and slight gray stubble on the chin. Sexy. Very sexy.

He hands me my martini with some good long eye contact, hands Grace hers, and Reilly steps up already holding one. "Three women who like martinis," he says with his European charm. Babe, older-guy babe.

Reason #1: *If his age is old enough to notice, it's old enough to matter.*

Maybe an older guy is what I need. Someone more mature, someone who can spark my intellectual curiosity. Someone who's learned the lessons of life. I'll benefit from all the shit that he has had to go through with maybe an ex-wife or two. Maybe he's had a couple of relationships where he was actually schooled on how to treat a woman.

When is an older guy too old? It seems when you are younger, say sixteen, eighteen seems too old. When you reach twenty-one, thirty may be too old, and at thirty-two, fifty-seven is way too old. Wow, did he just say he was fifty-seven? That's what fifty-seven looks like? Maybe it's the music business, maybe it's the clothes, or maybe he's had some work done, but he looks like an older, gray-haired Tom Selleck. Tom Selleck, who will always be the hottest TV actor of the eighties. Even now, that frame, hair, smile. I have my fifty-seven-year-old Magnum standing in front of me.

"He's cute, kind of weathered, but cute," Grace says as we get the Rover from the valet.

"Is he too weathered? I mean, do you think he is too old for me?" I look at Reilly for any support that he is indeed too old and I should continue my weekends as a safe shut-in.

"Em, I always pictured you with an older guy. You need someone who gets you, appreciates the humor, and isn't afraid that you have an opinion, a career, a house. Plus, you're young enough that the old guy is going to worship you. What the hell is wrong with that?" Reilly digs in her purse for a cigarette.

I hand the valet five dollars and climb into the Rover.

"You need to get back out there," Grace pipes in.

"That's really easy for you to say now that you have passed your first wedding anniversary with Mr. Normal, good job, happy, stable thirty-six-year-old. I just don't want to be the girl dating the 'old guy' because I *can't* find anyone my own age."

"You can't," Reilly says while expertly lining her lips. I hit the gas a little and the liner runs off her lip. She turns and gives me one of those "piss off" looks before continuing, "What I meant was, you don't want a guy like," she looks at Grace and they both say in a hushed tone, ". . . Reese."

I squint my eyes at her and grit my teeth. "You know you're not supposed to say that name!"

Reason #2: *If you're not over your ex, you're not ready, no matter how old you are.*

Grace continues, "Let me expand . . . Some jerk who doesn't appreciate you is all she meant. But you do need the excitement and you want the fun."

"You're right," I mumble.

"The good news is, maybe old guy . . . what's his name?" Reilly questions.

"Charlie," I say.

"Maybe Charlie is still cool enough and young enough to give you what you're looking for. He did give you the . . ." Reilly pantomimes quotation marks with her fingers ". . . . flutter, flutter."

Reason #3: *Compromise is compromise no matter what season of life you're in.*

My friends, as gentle and amusing as they can be . . . are telling me to go for it. I hear it. But I believe it is their silent fear that I may never try again after becoming a crash dummy and being dragged for fifty miles on open asphalt behind

Reese's Range Rover of faux love that is making them so encouraging. I hear their not-so-silent excuse for why I should just go ahead and try.

Date number one with Charlie, aka Magnum, sitting on the beach, under my umbrella, slathered in sunscreen. We are in Maui, yes, Maui. I sip a rum-and-pineapple drink with a colorful umbrella in it, as I watch him snorkel in the clear blue water. It's funny that our first date would be a weekend in Maui at his house on a private cove at the north end of the island. I just couldn't resist. Why say no? How many chances does a woman get to be dropped off on a tropical island for her first date. I have my own room. Own life. Ability to fly home. What is the worst that can happen? Nothing. I will drink enough champagne and eat enough caviar to make even Robin Leach jealous.

Okay, reasons I told Dr. D. I was going: (1) I have never flown on a private corporate jet. Very cool. (2) I have never stayed in a house with servants. (3) I have never had anyone be this nice and generous. (4) I certainly haven't had the full treatment. (5) He is old enough not to reopen my wounds. Am I a bad person for soooo loving this pampering? Don't we all really deserve it—all of us? As my Magnum gets out of the blue water and walks toward me I notice something strange on his body . . . skin, weird skin that appears to be loose.

Look away. Now it's not fat, because he's in shape, it's just the skin isn't staying where it should—above his knees and a little on the under part of his arms. He has a body that looks like Clint Eastwood now . . . not Clint Eastwood in *Dirty Harry.* Oh, shit. I am so judgmental. Stop. Stop judging. Start enjoying. Keep drinking.

I pour the entire rum drink down my throat in one gulp. He sits next to me on a lounge chair and readjusts the umbrella a little to cover his face. Hey! I need that protection myself. "How ya doin', beautiful?" he asks with that yummy accent as he looks at me, all the while toweling off his big muscles and old skin.

Ah, beautiful, I like that. I like a man who thinks I am beautiful, tells me I am beautiful. "It's hard not to be good in paradise."

"I'm happy you came with me. Hope you don't feel too awkward. Did you get settled into your room okay?"

He pulls out a vial of ginseng and downs it with a champagne chaser.

"Yeah, it's really lovely and I appreciate that you let me stay in my own, well, room and all." I look away.

"What did you think, that I was going to take you to my place in Hawaii and lavish luxury upon luxury on you just so you'd shag me?" he laughs.

I shrug. Funny. He's amusing. I love that. I don't mind the skin. A servant brings me a fresh cocktail.

"I brought you here because it's beautiful and I like to share it. I brought you here because you're smart and gorgeous and it's away from the crowds and bars of L.A. It's the right place to get to know someone, and if you have the money, why not do it?"

He did have a point. A good point. But how was I supposed to be rational when his personal masseur was coming to give me an hour-and-a-half deep-tissue rub before dinner?

He holds up his ginseng vial and taps my glass, "Cheers."

Reason #4: *If you like his life more than you like him, it makes it hard to be objective.*

Three days in Hawaii.

What I have learned: Magnum is a passionate, sweet kisser. He likes candlelight, beach bonfires, and the warm ocean water. He likes excellent champagne, old rock and roll, ginseng, and making me feel good. No sex. Not that after the third day in the Garden of Eden I don't want to. I am just taking it slow. Dr. D. would be proud.

Back in L.A. and back on the couch, I tell Dr. D. about my new Magnum. "He owns a record label," I say as I play with the new Palm IV that Magnum gave me.

"And you own a PR company. How's that going? Must be hard holding down the fort when you're running off to Hawaii." Dr. D. studies me, knowing I have NO intention of looking him in the face.

Reason #5: *When your therapist knows, you know . . . he's probably the wrong guy.*

He did have a point. I was neglecting my work, but living my life. The MTV clients were happy. ESPN was happy. I had been asked to speak on a communications panel at the NCTA cable convention. JJ was handling the business nicely in L.A. When I was traveling I had the Blackberry, e-mail, and cell phone. Jesus, Magnum's jet even had video conferencing!

Three weeks. Three trips. I could get used to this. Although I didn't feel the way I felt about Reese. I felt good, though. I felt, I don't know, safe. Somewhat taken care of, which was something new, and it didn't feel bad.

My entire life I may have just needed an older man. But was that man Magnum or my Dad?

Reason #6: *There is no substitute for the real thing.*

At Two Bunch Palms, a health spa in the heart of Palm Springs, it is eighty-five degrees and sunny. Sting's new CD echoes from our private bungalow and I float in our private pool topless. Magnum strolls out, holding a glass of Crystal Rose champagne. I paddle over to him, never getting off the raft. He sits on the edge of the pool and hands me my champagne flute. It's kind of pink and tastes a little smoky. It's heavenly. This life is heavenly. Magnum pulls a little joint from his platinum forties cigarette case and sparks it. He sits there in swim trunks and a Lenny Kravitz T-shirt wearing shades and a ball cap, smoking a joint and sipping champagne, and I wonder—Is this what my life is destined to be?

He may be old, but he is 100 percent the coolest person I have ever met. And to top it all off, the sex was brilliant! He did everything I wanted, and as a bonus, he could go for hours. I mean hours! Two hours! It was wild!

"Want to go sit in some mud?" he says while trying to hold the smoke in.

"What kind of mud?" I take a hit off his joint, which makes me a little lightheaded. My exhale is followed by extreme coughing, eye-watering, and falling off the raft into the pool. Should have known better.

"Special mud imported from India, meant to rid your body of toxins."

Maybe that is why this guy looks forty-five instead of fifty-seven—except for that skin thing, which, I might add, gives "beauty is only skin deep" a whole new meaning.

I stand, looking at two huge tubs filled with mud on the balcony of the spa.

"Did I mention that I am allergic to many strange elements when they are applied to my naked body? I get . . . I'd rather not get into it, trust me, it isn't pretty." I look from him to the tub of mud. Okay, this stuff seriously smells like poop. Crap, shit. Like someone took a huge dumparooney in that tub and now I am supposed to get in. Maybe this is cool to people with lots of money, but to me it is simply gross, and somewhat scary.

I take a step backward. The only smell that is worse was when I was a kid and my older brother, Ben, polluted our bathroom every morning. And this runs a close second. What's worse? It's steaming. A hot, steaming tub of turds.

I scrunch my face and clinch my hands. "I can't."

"You can. Just take a chance. It's good for you."

"No. Really, last time someone put mush on me, I had some sort of itching thing."

"Yes."

"No." I back away.

"Yes," he reaches for my hand. "You can do it."

Okay, his tone just changed. It went from sexy, British, Magnum guy to fatherly and authoritative.

Reason #7: *You're not my dad, so don't tell me what to do.*

If I don't want to sit from head to toe, naked, in a hot, steamy tub of crap, I shouldn't have to. Wow, I just felt like I was about to have a tantrum. But maybe he was right. He had been right about everything else. I mean, the guy is Mr. Cool, Mr. Jet, Mr. Success. Maybe he did know more than me. I reluctantly climb into the tub, thinking that he must know something I don't. He wouldn't do anything to hurt me. Just do it.

Gag. I am physically gagging.

"You're being immature," he says, almost disapproving.

I try to breathe through my mouth, but now I am eating what tastes like Sam's gas after a steak bone. Ahhhh, I miss Sam.

But not enough to stay in this!

"How can you possibly enjoy this?" I say in one breath.

"It's an acquired taste," he says as the lady places cucumbers over his eyes.

But this isn't getting any better for me. I look around at my naked body covered in dark brown, stinking goop, twigs, and small things that appear to either be rocks or . . . oh God, I am starting to itch. I am having a flashback to the spa with the dirty scrubs. Really itch! The more I dig at my leg, arm, and boobs, the more nauseous I feel. The more dirt and ooze that slips under my nails, the more lightheaded I feel. Itching, scratching, barely breathing, my stomach begins to turn and I reach for the side of the tub, getting up, but I slip, fall, and go under. My face and head in the crap . . . I struggle to get out, scramble for the side, my hands, arms slippery, itchy, I try to get up but before I can get out, I lean over the side of the tub with only the whites of my eyes showing and throw up all over the Indonesian rug.

Reason #8: *No matter how old someone is, no one knows you better than you know yourself.*

"How was I to know that you were allergic to it?" Magnum says as some spa guy hoses me off.

"BECAUSE I TRIED TO TELL YOU! I KNEW!" I stand clawing at my calves, sides, and back. "Where's the cool dip?" I stomp off like an allergy veteran and walk down into the small, cool dip pool of ice cubes. "Holy shit!" I gasp as mud dissolves into the cold dip.

"The water will stop the itching and reduce the swelling of the hives," Magnum responds.

"Thanks, I know, 'cause it's going to kill me from fucking hypothermia." I bounce from one foot to the other.

We drove home that night from Two Bunch and I felt like a scolded child.

I call Dr. D. on my cell while Magnum fills up the car with gas and Dr. D. tells me what I've known the whole time. "This is not healthy. Isn't it more fun to experience something with a man for the first time than having someone show you something they've already experienced?"

I look back at Magnum in his cute Lucky Jeans and sweater. "I guess, but . . ."

Dr. D. cuts me off. "Did you say 'but'? You're not done with him. Call me when you break up. No bill for this one."

Two nights later, I look at the new black Armani dress that was hand-delivered from Saks in a large white box with an oversized red bow: a surprise from Magnum as an apology for the whole mud thing. He wants me to wear it to a black-tie fund-raiser on Saturday night. After spending the last three days covered in calamine lotion, I want nothing more than to put on that dress and feel beautiful, so I agreed, and somehow, for the first time, realized how Lance must have felt when I took him shopping.

Ok, good, bad, right, wrong, presents, gifts, champagne, wrinkly skin, hives, I am seeing the reasons on my list. But they are written on Tiffany letterhead and they don't seem so bad.

Saturday night, 8:15 P.M. I am standing next to Magnum. He is showing me off to his record industry friends. My dress is a little too tight, and my boobs are a little too pushed up and smooched at the top. I stand there in a group of fiftyish guys with their eyes darting from my boobs to my hand, which is wrapped in Magnum's.

We walk away, and one guy says, "Nice meeting you, Amy." I open my mouth to correct him and notice the smirking and looking at each other . . . like who cares anyway. I realize that it really doesn't matter what my name is.

I was fucking arm candy! I thought at thirty-two you couldn't be arm candy anymore! I own a home. I have my own money. I have clients and a company. I thought that at a certain age you just outgrew the bimbo status. But as it turns out, you don't.

Reason #9: *Don't be a float at the old folks' parade.*

As the night went on I realized no one really even cared that I was a fairly successful, somewhat witty woman! And even if I had worn a pantsuit it would never have made the point. Don't date a man twenty-five years your senior or you will most definitely be his . . . booby prize. I woke up in Magnum's oversized king bed with down pillows and the comforter wrapped gently around my naked body.

Ow, my head, what is that pounding? Wow, that's my breathing. I roll over and look at the nightstand where Magnum has left me two Advil and a large glass of orange juice. Ah, he knows. See, this is something older men do. But he is nowhere to be found. I get up to open the long, heavy tapestry drapes and the sunlight pierces my skull like pins in a voodoo doll. Maybe a shower will help.

Standing in the middle of the marble shower with two huge showerheads pouring down on me, I start to remember the Citron martinis, the dancing, the champagne, maybe the karaoke. I can't remember exactly when I accepted my bimbo status and just went with it . . . I remember more Citron martinis and then . . . being dragged home as if I was a naughty schoolgirl after getting caught drinking beer and making out with my boyfriend sophomore year in high school.

After toweling off and slipping into his fluffy robe from the Four Seasons, I look for lotion, any lotion, to apply to my very dehydrated skin. I open the medicine cabinet and there, staring me in the face, is the bottle! And not of lotion.

Okay, it's a medical revolution. It's a damn miracle in some cases, but . . . I reach for the phone on the bathroom wall and dial.

"Hi, it's me," I say in a whisper as I climb back into the shower with his robe on, clutching the bottle. "Are you up?"

"Of course I am. It's noon," shouts Reilly. "What's wrong? You sound like you're standing in the toilet."

"I am. Sorta. Look, I found something in his medicine cabinet," I whisper, eyeing the bottle.

"Oh, shit, what? Antidepressants. That's okay, he's balancing," she laughs.

"Worse," I say.

"Barbiturates? Crack? Coke? Herpes medicine?"

"Worse. I could live with all that," I say, ducking further into the corner of the shower. I sit, climbing up on the little bench, crouched.

"C'mon! What? What's worse than crack?" Reilly starts to match my whisper.

Silence hovers between us for a good five, six seconds. "Viagra," I say.

"Well, no shit, Em. What did you think a guy who can 'do it' for two hours is using? It doesn't even matter how old he is . . ."

The shower door opens and Magnum is standing there looking at me, bewildered.

"Whoaaa!" I fall off the shower seat, dropping the phone and spilling the little blue pills all over the marble and down the drain.

Magnum had come to tell me that a friend at his company had passed away last night. A heart attack. A young music executive who was really talented. A husband, a father of young twin boys, and, more important, a friend.

Lower than a bottom feeder. I feel lower than a bottom feeder.

How could I break up with this man who was standing in front of me—not mad that I got wickedly drunk last night, probably embarrassed him at some point, fell asleep minus any Viagra-induced sexual activity, who had bought me nothing but beautiful, thoughtful gifts, spoiled me rotten, told me I was "beautiful," who now needs me to stand next to him at his friend's funeral. I can't. I simply can't break up with him no matter how many reasons I have.

Two days have passed since the Viagra incident. We are on our way to Forest Lawn Cemetery. I hate funerals. Did I mention that? The whole death, gone forever . . . scares the shit out of me. I mean, I have abandonment issues. Isn't death the ultimate abandonment?

But here I go. Bravely holding my man's hand as we sit across the casket from the widow and two of the most beautiful, curly-haired three-year-old twins I have ever seen.

The priest goes on about loss, the afterlife, and returning to the earth. I can't help but stare at the widow. Her blonde hair, blue eyes; tired, almost scared face. My heart sinks for her. I think of the many nights alone she is going to have to brave in a king-size bed with his pillow empty. Her soul mate, her husband, her friend taken in the prime of their lives. I think about the struggles she will face raising those two little boys alone. I wonder what he must have been like? Handsome and young and a good father. I can imagine him playing touch football with his boys as they grow up. It's all so upsetting. I lean over and whisper in Magnum's ear, "It's very sad, I mean the wife, alone, with those babies. It's such a shock."

He nods his head in agreement.

I keep staring at the widow, wondering, feeling, identifying.

"My God, it's seriously such a tragedy," I whisper again.

Magnum whispers, "Yes it is."

Listening to the priest continue on about "ashes to ashes, dust to dust," I look again at the widow before whispering to Magnum, "How old was he?"

Magnum leans over and whispers in my ear, "My age."

But it seemed louder than an AC/DC concert. "MY AGE . . . MY AGE . . . MY AGE!"

I almost fall off my chair.

There it was . . . the motherlode, the biggest REASON of them all.

Reason #10: *If he's going to die of old age before your children are in junior high, he's too old for you!!!*

She was me, an image of tomorrow, a ghost from Christmas future. Me alone. Abandoned at thirty-six with two small children under the age of five. Nope! Not gonna happen. I start to get up and the priest eyes me.

Everyone eyes me.

I cover my face as if to be crying, which at this point isn't far from the truth, and I walk away. Magnum looks from me to the group.

"It's very upsetting to her," he says and they all nod in sympathy, understanding. As if I was that widow—they know. He looks back at me. This time I have broken from a fast-paced walk to a full-blown sprint.

Up the hill, past a hundred graves, up another hill, past a hundred more . . . Jesus, how big is this place? Surrounded by tombstones, I sit resting as the sun starts to set toward the ocean.

I watch cars leaving. I can breathe again. Magnum finally finds me, sitting against the headstone of a woman named Irma Banks. Apparently she was a devoted wife and mother. We drive home in silence, like I'm doomed to be grounded, a bad high schooler, and he's a disappointed parent.

He drops me at the front of my house and doesn't get out.
I turn around to apologize but he just drives off in his black
850 BMW. Not that I expect him to come in or anything.
He is old enough to know better.

Reason #10: *If he's going to die of old age before your children are in junior high, he's too old for you!!!*

Reason #9: *Don't be a float at the old folks' parade.*

Reason #8: *No matter how old someone is, no one knows you better than you know yourself.*

Reason #7: *You're not my dad, so don't tell me what to do.*

Reason #6: *There is no substitute for the real thing.*

Reason #5: *When your therapist knows, you know . . . he's probably the wrong guy.*

Reason #4: *If you like his life more than you like him, it makes it hard to be objective.*

Reason #3: *Compromise is compromise no matter what season of life you're in.*

Reason #2: *If you're not over your ex, you're not ready, no matter how old you are.*

Reason #1: *If his age is old enough to notice, it's old enough to matter.*

chapter ten

Smooth Sailing

Friday evening. Walking on the strand, I see dolphins just past the shore break. It warms me inside. I look at the sun setting and I get an overwhelming sense of "okay." Maybe it is my thirties or maybe it is just that I am finally at a point where I am happy being Emily. Magnum had done one thing. He had helped me over the hurdle of Reese. I wasn't mad at Reese anymore, or for that matter, any of them. I wasn't unhappy. I was just me. Still single and somewhat normal and now drama-free. I have resolved that my life isn't supposed to be the cookie-cutter life that everyone else has. Or pretends to have.

I sit down on the beach and dial Dr. D.

"I want to see you," I say into the phone.

"Why? Are you breaking up?" he says in a way that might be categorized as humor.

"No, it's just . . . I feel a little strange. Like I am standing on one foot but I have learned to balance on it and I don't know if that is, well, just how life is or if I have just come to accept that my life will never be fixed and will always be an evolving 'work in progress, please excuse the mess.'"

He lets out a long breath. "Okay, come into the office tomorrow, Saturday, at ten in the morning before I launch my boat for the first time."

As Dr. D. walks into the waiting room of his outer office he stands there a good long minute looking at me, then smiles. I am happy that he slipped me in on short notice and even happier he has given up part of his Saturday for my mental well-being. He turns and I follow him back into his office. We both sit. I catch a glimpse of myself in his mirror and wonder who that girl staring back at me is. She seems more peaceful.

"You've stopped with the lists, haven't you?" He begins what I know is going to be a speech.

I shrug.

"Good." I look up at his sort-of proud face. "I do care about you, Emily," he says softly. "I want you to be happy, and you may be past that work."

Dr. D. gets up, opens his arms.

I stand and he gives me a huge hug.

I push back and look in his eyes. "I know I can survive any man, mortgage payments, management issues, and carrying in the groceries, but it all makes me, I dunno, a little sad to be so damn self-sufficient."

"You've become your own prince and life is just a little scary, but it's good," he sighs.

"I know, and I am okay with it. You know, I never wanted someone to save me. I just wanted someone to love me. And somewhere along the way, I learned to love myself."

"I understand," he says, gently setting me down on that couch where I have spent a hundred hours.

"I think that maybe my picker or my 'flutter, flutter' for men is broken." I say matter-of-factly.

"Your picker is not broken," he says. "The good thing is, you kept your heart open, Emily. You are not one of the ones I worry about living 'the good life.' You already are. You have something magical in you that lights up even this room. You've been trying to prove you're successful and witty and sporty. That you're a good cook and that you'll make a perfect soccer mom and wife someday. Somehow trying to fit into some man's blueprint of *his* life." He looks me in the eye. "But you just have to be you," he sets down his yellow pad, "because you're amazing."

The light just caught the sparkle of Dr. D.'s white teeth as he smiled. He has a great smile. He's still talking, but I am caught in the sound of his smooth, sexy tone saying: ". . . with a big heart that gets you in so much trouble."

My eyes drift down as if I'm embarrassed and land on the brown hairs of his strong forearms, as if I have never seen them before.

"There is a guy out there who deserves you—and he's going to hold your hand when you cross the street." He takes a breath and continues, "He's going to dance with you in a movie theater when the credits are rolling. He's going to sweep you off your feet and make you feel like everything that you have gone through was to finally be with that one man." He lets out a little chuckle. "And he'll be your equal, which is no easy job. You will have that picket-fence life at the beach, because you already do, and now you just have to open your eyes to that person who is finally going to really, deeply love you."

Flutter. Flutter.

I am frozen, gazing in his big brown eyes with the promise of a happy tomorrow.

"Time's up," he says, standing.

I sit in my Rover, dumbfounded. I can't put the key in the engine. I can't move. I see Dr. D. roll past the parking structure in his Bronco towing his classic, cleaned-up, sparkling wooden boat with a huge mast and white sail ready to be pulled taunt. I eye the back of her, looking for her name, and it says . . . *Smooth Sailing.*

I can't help but laugh.

I want to follow him, to catch him, to tell him, because I can't think of one reason why not. I find myself wondering . . .

Would it be a bad thing to date your doctor?

Helpful Hints from Emily

INDEX OF REASONS

Keep It Out of the Office

Reason #10: *You get fired.*

Reason #9: *Crying at work is unacceptable.*

Reason #8: *People will talk about how well you perform in bed verses how well you perform your job.*

Reason #7: *If your friends, mentors, and co-workers think your boyfriend has ulterior motives, he probably does.*

Reason #6: *If what you're doing for your boyfriend can get you fired, stop doing him.*

Reason #5: *If you have to hide your relationship, it isn't worth hiding.*

Reason #4: *If helping your boyfriend makes you lie to your friends, boss, and mentor, don't help him.*

Reason #3: *That which is considered scandal in a relationship is bad, really, really, bad.*

Reason #2: *If there are kitschy little sayings about the guy you're dating, there is probably a universal reason why it is a bad idea.*

Reason #1: *If your boss is bigger than life in your company, that doesn't necessarily mean he is bigger than life in real life.*

Leave it in St. Croix

Reason #10: *Face it, we're all different on vacation.*

Reason #9: *You will spend two months trying to get back to those few perfect days in paradise.*

Reason #8: *If you are rooted, choose carefully where, when, and with whom to replant.*

Reason #7: *It was the best it's going to be on vacation.*

Reason #6: *He should have offered.*

Reason #5: *Your phone bills could buy you a new pair of Gucci loafers every month.*

Reason #4: *Beware of the love bug on vacation.*

Reason #3: *He's not who you think he is.*

Reason #2: *When you don't want the answer, it's probably bad.*

Reason #1: *Beware of promises made in paradise. Men talk about the possibility of a future with you on a romantic island when you are tan and easy-breezy, but it never makes the flight home.*

Don't Go Pro

Reason #10: *If your man seems too good to be true, he probably is.*

Reason #9: *Wondering if I was the only one or a priority at all.*

Reason #8: *Waiting, knowing the game will soon be over.*

Reason #7: *Too much competition makes me batty.*

Reason #6: *He doesn't read, except for the sports page and the highlights on ESPN at the bottom of the TV screen.*

Reason #5: *He lives in two different cities.*

Reason #4: *By design, he is going to be constantly leaving me.*

Reason #3: *He owns more than one cell phone.*

Reason #2: *He will be sleeping in eighty-one different hotel beds in six months . . . possibly with eighty-one different women.*

Reason #1: *He "plays" for a living.*

Gay/Straight

Reasons #7, 8, 9, and 10: *No sex.*

Reason #6: *You don't need any more reasons when they won't have sex with you.*

Reason #5: *Rejection from your partner is unacceptable.*

Reason #4: *Tests of any kind set your partner up to fail.*

Reason #3: *Animal haters need not apply.*

Reason #2: *A man/woman relationship without sex is called . . . "just friends."*

Reason #1: *You should never have to wonder why a man doesn't want to have sex with you. Because no matter what the answer is . . . it isn't good.*

Arm Candy

Reason #10: *When you're not sad he is not the one, maybe it isn't a bad thing.*

Reason #9½: *Your boyfriend shouldn't have to ask permission.*

Reason #9: *You'll always pay as he hasn't had an adult job . . . as he isn't an adult.*

Reason #8: *Too much paying will end a relationship.*

Reason #7: *Leaving lunch money for your boyfriend is a no-no.*

Reason #6: *I don't want to be the boss at home.*

Reason #5: *If you want to dress up your boyfriend, buy a Ken doll.*

Reason #4: *He lives with his parents.*

Reason #3: *When your therapist flat-out tells you that the guy you're dating is wrong for you, he probably is.*

Reason #2: *Male or female, dating someone in college is too young if you're in your thirties.*

Reason #1: *Monetary gaps in the bridge over the river of a relationship are unsteady.*

Never, Never, Never . . . Go Back

Reason #10: *It doesn't matter what is happening, it only matters how you feel.*

Reason #9: *When they ask you to hang on, it'll feel like you're hanging from your neck.*

Reason #8: *They absolutely must be willing to fight for you because if you're fighting every battle yourself, then you're still alone.*

Reason #7: *Hold on to reality or you're choosing insanity.*

Reason #6: *When things go bad you see the real man.*

Reason #5: *If he's always leaving, he has to go.*

Reason #4: *Never listen to a man who says he "knows you" when he doesn't. He knows what he wants to know.*

Reason #3: *If and when a guy who completely wrecked you shows up again and wants back in, he must be willing to work extra hard to get you back. He can't just slip away like a shadow at dusk. He must be tenacious, must prove that he will never, never, never do whatever he did again and that this time it will be different.*

Reason #2: *If there was a reason you left, remember what it was. At some point, if you take them back, they will* *leave you or you'll leave them AGAIN and probably for the same reasons you left in the first place.*

Reason #1: *If it feels like a test, it probably will be.*

Don't Date Your Dad

Reason #10: *If he's going to die of old age before your children are in junior high, he's too old for you!!!*

Reason #9: *Don't be a float at the old folks' parade.*

Reason #8: *No matter how old someone is, no one knows you better than you know yourself.*

Reason #7: *You're not my dad, so don't tell me what to do.*

Reason #6: *There is no substitute for the real thing.*

Reason #5: *When your therapist knows, you know . . . he's probably the wrong guy.*

Reason #4: *If you like his life more than you like him, it makes it hard to be objective.*

Reason #3: *Compromise is compromise no matter what season of life you're in.*

Reason #2: *If you're not over your ex, you're not ready, no matter how old you are.*

Reason #1: *If his age is old enough to notice, it's old enough to matter.*

Acknowledgments

There are many people to thank and acknowledge for this book. I know I'll forget more than one and kick myself later. But here it goes . . . let's start at the beginning.

First I need to thank God for helping me along the way. For *not* answering many of my prayers but instead for answering the ones that led me to the life I am now living.

To my mom, Sandy, who without a lot of money raised two kids but had enough love, hugs, Barry Manilow, and Barbra Streisand to sustain us for a lifetime. She made me who I am, a fighter and a dreamer with a heart as big as her own. Mainly she taught me to believe in myself and never give up. She is my constant source of unconditional love. To my gram, Deed, for making Sunday dinners at 5:00 P.M. a ritual, for our hikes in the mountains, teaching me to bait a hook, counting chocolate chip cookies, listening to my dreams, cuddling, praying, and being the glue of our family—our angel. My big brother and friend, Jeff, who I am so proud of. Thank you for still watching over me, sharing my life, making me laugh and feel like I belong in this lifetime. My sister-in-law, Laurie, for still loving my brother after ten years, but more than that, for showing me what I really want in life, and bringing Reilly and Brookie into the world. To my Dad, my weekend warrior, my friend, my handyman, my humor. You're the father I always dreamed of having and more. You'll never know what it means to me to have my daughter-dad time.

To Kristy, for understanding and not judging our entire lives! For loving and laughing. You're the best friend any girl could ever want! You're my ticket to heaven. To my wing man Holly, the talented and loving Mim, and my JJ, who takes care of me day-in and day-out. To Kath K. and Robin, who are just a short drive away. These ladies keep me sane and surround me with women who are smart, sexy, and sassy. And let's not forget Andrew, who is so much more than a backup donor. My friends' belief in me is boundless, and their support and shoulders to lean on are only a phone call away.

To my team: Jennifer Johnson (JJ), for finding the balance and holding the business together on many levels; Grady, for being the hot guy in the office who lets me win at ping-pong; Braunstein, the be$t guy around, friend, and believer; Abby, for putting up with me and getting Visa paid on time; my handsome, talented agent and manager and ruler of the book universe, Alan Nevins, and his lovely colleague Mindy at The Firm, for championing this book on so many levels and validating me as a writer; my publisher, HarperCollins, the marketing and PR teams, Lindsey Moore—but most important, my stellar editor, Maureen O'Brien, for your patience, finding my book a home, and giving me the ability to let my wings soar; and Dr. Liu and his team for always "calling something in" when I really, really, need it!

To Anachel's clients: You're a chosen group—for your brand, your talent and product, but mainly your great teams that we work with every day. Thank you for making us truly a part of your companies and families. To the many journalists and editors who make the butter on our bread possible. As you all knew, I am a closet writer!

To the many dates, tears, nights alone, and men who made me wonder "Why?" Now I know . . . you make good chapters.

And lastly, but certainly not least, to the love of my life, my husband, # 26, Chuck Cecil. For finding me and rescuing me from a life without knowing what real love from a man and partner felt like. For being on your white horse with your tarnished armor and showing up for this life that we've made together, which is more than I thought possible. You marvel me daily with your growth as a kind and powerful man and giving husband. Your pure dedication to everything that you touch is a blueprint of the person you are—from a kid with big dreams to a walk-on at the University of Arizona to Pro Bowl, *Sports Illustrated* cover boy, and someday being the head coach of a Super Bowl team, I believe! Thank you for supporting my dreams and letting me shine in the spotlight when you're such a star on your own. For being the peas to my carrots. For being my Forrest. For being patient and understanding when it's cloudy. For making me feel sexy, wanted, and deserving of the best. You're my best friend. You're my beginning and end. Thank you for loving me the way only *you* can. I'll always be your girl.

Writing this acknowledgment makes realize how lucky and blessed I truly am. The people who stand beside me and oftentimes hold me up are the true testament of the woman I am, and the woman I strive to become.

We all really do deserve to be happy, and I hope that whoever reads this novel laughs a little, relates a little, and feels a little. Thanks for reading it. I'll leave you with this one closing thought . . . Never give up your dreams; I am proof that they come true.

—Carrie